Dark Refuge

Works by Kate Douglas

Paranormal Romances

DemonFire
HellFire
"Crystal Dreams" in *Nocturnal*
StarFire
CrystalFire

Erotic Romances

Wolf Tales
"Chanku Rising" in *Sexy Beast*
and as the ebook
Wolf Tales 1.5—Chanku Rising
Wolf Tales II
"Camille's Dawn" in *Wild Nights*
and as the ebook
Wolf Tales 2.5—Chanku Dawn
Wolf Tales III
"Chanku Fallen" in *Sexy Beast II*
and as the ebook
Wolf Tales 3.5—Chanku Fallen
Wolf Tales IV
"Chanku Journey" in *Sexy Beast III*
and as the ebook
Wolf Tales 4.5—Chanku Journey
Wolf Tales V
"Chanku Destiny" in *Sexy Beast IV*
and as the ebook
Wolf Tales 5.5—Chanku Destiny
Wolf Tales VI
"Chanku Wild" in *Sexy Beast V*
and as the ebook
Wolf Tales 6.5—Chanku Wild
Wolf Tales VII
"Chanku Honor" in *Sexy Beast VI*
and as the ebook

Wolf Tales 7.5—Chanku Honor
Wolf Tales VIII
"Chanku Challenge" in *Sexy Beast VII*
and as the ebook
Wolf Tales 8.5—Chanku Challenge
Wolf Tales 9
"Chanku Spirit" in *Sexy Beast VIII*
and as the ebook
Wolf Tales 9.5—Chanku Spirit
Wolf Tales 10
Wolf Tales 11
Wolf Tales 12

The Dream Catchers Series

"Dream Catcher" in *Nightshift*
Dream Bound
Dream Unchained

The Spirit Wild Series

Dark Wolf
Dark Spirit
Dark Moon
Dark Refuge

Contemporary Romance and Romantic Suspense

68 & Climbing
Cowboy in My Pocket
Lethal Deception
Lethal Obsession
Carved in Stone

For a full list of all of Kate's books,
visit her website at www.katedouglas.com

Dark Refuge

Spirit Wild Series

KATE DOUGLAS

BEYOND THE PAGE
publishing

Beyond the Page Books
are published by
Beyond the Page Publishing
www.beyondthepagepub.com

Copyright © 2014 by Kate Douglas
Cover design by Dar Albert, Wicked Smart Designs

ISBN: 978-1-940846-17-0

Acknowledgments

My sincere thanks and appreciation to my terrific beta readers: Ann Jacobs, Jan Takane, Rose Toubbeh, Angela Knight, Lynne Thomas, Kerry Parker, and Karen Woods. Thank you, ladies. I hope you realize how much your support, your terrific ideas, and your friendship mean to me.

To Bill Harris—the perfect editor—not only do you know what a story needs to make it better, you get your points across while maintaining a truly warped sense of humor (an extremely valuable asset in this business).

And to my agent, Jessica Faust—thank you for being so damned smart, and always proactive in the ever-changing publishing landscape.

1

December 1, 2039

Goddess but it felt good to be back in the United States, specifically San Francisco, with the clean smell of the ocean mingling with the spicy scent of tacos and salsa on one side, fiery Thai on the other. After almost two years of working and living all over Asia, the comforting mixed bouquet of Americanized ethnic cooking had Emeline practically salivating.

Water rushed down the street gutters and dripped from the tall buildings. The storm had been short but wet and windy, cleansing the air, washing trash off the sidewalk, leaving a clear trail between her office at Chanku Global Industries and the Platinum Duck, her favorite Chinese restaurant.

She flat out refused to let sixteen hours of travel and a lost bag at San Francisco International get in the way of the meal she'd been thinking of since she'd boarded the jet in Beijing.

Oh, God. Can't someone help me?

Now that definitely caught her attention. The voice in her head, feminine, laced with terror and coming from somewhere very close by, stopped Emeline mid-step. Pausing as if to check her phone for a call, she scanned the crowded sidewalk. It was a little after seven, well into the dinner hour.

Nothing seemed out of place—except for that perfectly clear telepathic plea for help. *Where are you? How can I help you?*

You can hear me? No one ever hears me! Where are you?

1

Em glanced at the building behind her. *I'm on Powell, south of Washington. In front of the coffee shop. The one with the Chinese dragon wearing a Santa hat in the window.*

I'm north of there. On the corner. Short black skirt, red thigh-high boots. Black sweater.

I see you. Holding her mobile phone to her ear, she walked toward the tall, slender woman standing on the corner. *How can I help?*

My pimp is too close. You can't do anything. Damn. No one has ever answered me before.

I'm going to bump into you and slip my card into your hand. Be ready. I'm wearing a red coat, black wool cap and a white scarf around my neck. My name is Emeline. Emeline Cheval.

I'm Sissy Long. I see you.

Good. At that moment, a heavyset man walked by. Emeline stepped into his path, jostling him and managing to get herself turned around. "I'm so sorry." She backed out of his way and nudged the woman behind her, turned, laughing as if to brush her shoulder where she'd connected and slipped her card into the woman's hand. *Call me as soon as you can. I can help.*

Thank you.

At that moment, a large, silent car pulled up; the back window slowly lowered and the driver leaned over. He nodded at the woman and jabbed his thumb in the direction of the backseat. She opened the door and, without a backward glance, climbed into the car and closed the door. Em forced herself not to watch as the vehicle slid back into the stream of traffic, but her last glimpse was of the blonde facing forward, looking neither right nor left.

Emeline continued on to the Platinum Duck, but her sense of pleasure, of homecoming, was gone. Now, instead of enjoying the frenetic pace of the city, she wished she were home in Montana. Home with the rest of her pack, running through the forest, surrounded by her own kind.

She'd been away much too long.

• • •

Sissy buckled herself into the backseat of the limo and kept her eyes forward, though she couldn't have said what she actually saw. That woman had heard her! For the first time since this nightmare began, someone actually heard her silent cries for help. She'd always felt as if she were actually speaking—at least on a level that someone should be able to understand—but no one had ever heard her before. That woman, that Emeline Cheval, actually answered her! But how? And who was she?

Her name didn't mean anything to Sissy, but she'd been out of touch with the world around her for so long she didn't even know how old she was. How long it had been since she'd first been kidnapped. First sold to a strange man for the night. All she knew was the date. The day her life ended.

Sissy fingered the business card in her hand. It was warm to the touch, and she wondered what it said, but she couldn't look at it here. Not where the chauffeur could see and report back to Russo what he'd seen. That woman said to call her. If only . . . Sissy was never allowed near a phone. None of the girls were.

But that woman had heard her. Maybe she'd come back when Sissy didn't call. Russo used that corner a lot when he had appointments for her to keep. Maybe Emeline Cheval would come back.

• • •

It had been so long since he'd run with anyone but a few of his pack-mates that Gabe Cheval had actually forgotten how much he loved running in a big pack. With so many wolves racing through the night together, it was all about the harsh rush of breath from more than a dozen sets of wolven lungs and steam trailing behind like silvery snowflakes in the frozen air of a Montana winter's night. Snow crunched, hard and brittle beneath broad paws as they flew across the ice, so intent on the joy of running they passed by startled elk and even a moose without turning away to hunt.

Gabe followed close behind Jace Wolf and his mate, Romy, and Romy's constant companion, Wolf. The wild wolf had adopted them late last summer and remained as Romy's shadow. Others raced beside and behind Gabe—his sister Lily and her mate, Sebastian, had come from their home on the other side of the mountain ridge to join tonight's run. They ran as if they'd run this way forever, though Gabe thought this might be a first for Sebastian, to run with so many wolves. He was new to his Chanku roots, still learning the ways of the pack.

It didn't happen often enough, so many of them racing together through the night. They all had busy lives, and many in the pack had jobs that took them away from Montana and their Chanku home, but this night the moon was full and Anton had called everyone who was able, inviting them to take a few hours to return to their feral roots. It was a chance for the pack to bond, to tighten that sense of family that forever held them close.

Even Sunny Daye and her new man, the forest ranger Fenris Ahlberg, were running, and Igmutaka, once a spirit guide, raced through the moonlit night as a wolf rather than his usual puma. He ran full out, staying ahead of Gabe, hard on his mate Star's heels. And damn, but the two men were huge wolves. Gabe was large, but he felt like a pup next to either Fen or Ig.

Both of them were Berserkers, another species of Chanku bred eons ago as the race's warrior class. Instead of human mothers, they'd been born as wolf cub and puma kit respectively, yet they were able to shift to human form as easily as they could become any predator. They were huge, almost twice as big as the average Chanku wolf, but their size wasn't all that set them apart—their mating had been unusual, too. Ig and Fen as well as Star and Sunny had mated in a four-way bond, and wasn't that a new twist for the pack? Yet when the men—both already mated to their women—had also experienced the mating bond with one another, not only the goddess but the Mother Herself had blessed their union.

Gabe had never actually considered his unmated status, yet now, when all those he felt closest to suddenly had someone even closer to them, he was all too aware of his lone wolf state.

Times were definitely changing and Gabe was still coming to terms with all of it, but tonight it wasn't about him. It was about the pack. About bonding with those he loved, including his parents, who had called all of them together to run tonight. His dad, the pack's alpha, held back a bit, his nose close by his mate's flank. Gabe had a feeling Anton and Keisha would be slipping off into the woods before long, going in search of time alone, away from the rest of them.

He wondered if he'd ever have anyone to slip away with. Anyone who loved him the way his mom loved his dad, the way Romy loved Jace or Lily loved Sebastian. Everyone here was paired up. Everyone except Gabe. Well, Gabe and his buddy Aaron.

Aaron Cheval, son of Oliver and Mei, shared a last name with Gabe but was not related, thank the Goddess, because no matter how powerful the Chanku libido, incest was never acceptable.

Maybe he and Aaron needed to get together tonight and have a good, rousing drunk and fuck like there was no tomorrow. Just the two of them. He sent the thought to Aaron, who nipped his flank in agreement.

Then Aaron slipped back to run beside his parents, Oliver and Mei. Gabe glanced around and realized EmyIzzy wasn't with them. He hadn't seen Aaron's baby sister, Emeline Isobelle, in years now. Last he'd heard, she was working in Asia. Hard to imagine her in a job halfway around the world. She'd always be little EmyIzzy to him, and how she loathed the nickname Gabe and Aaron had bestowed on her almost from birth.

Which, of course, was all the reason the guys needed to continue using it. Emeline had not been happy, but he wished she were here tonight. She was always fun to tease.

The pack circled a large pond, one grown even bigger this past year with the addition of a pair of industrious beavers. They'd dammed one of the smaller creeks and the shallow pond had become a prime hunting site. Deer and elk and even the occasional moose stayed near the water, breaking through the ice in winter, nibbling on green shoots in spring.

Moonlight cast everything in dark shadows and silver reflections. Gabe was so intent on the beauty around him, he almost ran into Jace's butt when the pack stopped quickly. All of the wolves went still, noses to the air. The scent of game was strong, and by now they'd run far enough and fast enough that hunger had become a living entity, racing alongside them through the snow-covered night. The full moon leant a ghostly silver glow to snow and trees alike, but it was the scent that held them still.

Elk, nearby if his nose was any indicator. Gabe was known for his ability to scent game—and whatever else he looked for. He nudged Aaron and the two gazed at Wolf. The feral beast stood beside Romy, but his ears were laid back, his tail low to the ground. He growled, a low, chest-rattling rumble. Romy glanced at him and then her voice filled Gabe's mind and the mind of every other wolf in the pack.

Wolf says man is near, on the far side of the pond. Hiding near the beaver dam.

Thank our brother for us, Romy. Anton trotted ahead to stand beside the newest members of the pack. *Does he have any idea how many?*

She stared at the wolf a moment. *Not as many as we are, but he can't tell me. Specific numbers aren't within his ability to communicate.*

Anton turned and gazed toward the back of the pack. *Gabe, what are you picking up?*

He took a deep breath, moved forward ahead of the pack and past the smell of wolves, raised his nose into the icy air and drew a deep breath, taking a moment to separate the various scents, allowing his wolven brain time to identify what his nose was collecting. *At least two men. They've been smoking pot and they're armed. I can smell gunpowder, the faint scent of blood. Goose, I think. They probably shot at least one earlier.*

What say we give them a good scare? Anton swept his gaze over the pack, making eye contact with each of them. It wasn't quite a democracy, but he always appeared to welcome input from anyone with ideas. This time the pack merely listened.

He dipped his head, easily reaffirming his role as their alpha. *We can all use the practice. We're going to sneak up on them, carefully. No one is allowed to get shot.*

The laughter was silent but impossible to ignore. Anton managed to lift an eyebrow, something that never ceased to amaze Gabe, how his dad could still be so human even when standing on four legs.

That was not said in jest. Our healers are out for an enjoyable run tonight, not to fix anyone, so don't do anything stupid. Whoever gets in behind these idiots first might as well go ahead and shift and remind them they're trespassing, but not until you scare the crap out of them. Got it? Gabe, take this side of the pond. We'll go around the other side and come across the dam.

Without a sound, Anton and more than half the pack were gone, slipping like wraiths through the moonlight, gliding silently through the shadows to circle around the south end of the beaver pond. Gabe and Aaron veered north around the upper side with Romy and Jace and a few of the others, including Aaron's parents. Anton had Adam and Liana and half a dozen more.

They moved quickly, dark phantoms slipping silently through even darker shadows. Gabe loved the hunt when their prey was sentient, when he hunted something that could just as easily hunt him. The challenge had his heart pounding and his blood racing, and he moved almost soundlessly, slower now as he sensed and scented humans nearby.

He heard them whispering, at least two men. The pond was in a natural bowl, an amphitheater with hills on three sides that magnified and distorted sound, but they had to be close by. The leaf-burning, skunky smell of marijuana irritated his sensitive nostrils. Gabe searched for visual clues until he saw movement, much closer than he'd originally expected. He stopped, breathing slowly, steadily. The others paused around him, crouching low behind frozen tules and cattails at the water's edge.

There, he said. *Between those two big aspens.* He cast his thoughts out, connecting with Anton on the far side of the pond. *Dad, I've got a visual. Looks like two men in hunting gear. They're about twenty feet ahead of us, hunkered down between those big aspens this side of the beaver dam.*

I see them. They're all yours. Be careful, son.

You got it. He glanced over his shoulder. *Romy and Jace, take Wolf and block the trail above us. That's their most obvious means of escape. It looks like they came in on at least one ATV. Dad and his group are waiting across the beaver dam. The rest of you, block exits and watch for any possible escape, but stay hidden. I think there are only two, but I don't want to take any chances. We know they're armed. Aaron, let's you and me go play big bad wolf.*

They took their time, working their way closer, moving in from above until they had a clear line of sight to the two men. Both appeared fairly young, late twenties, maybe. The ground around them was littered with beer cans, the air thick with the stench of the dope they'd been smoking.

A couple of dead geese lay in the snow beside them.

Hunters were bad enough, but slobs were even more irritating. He wouldn't bite them, but that didn't mean he couldn't scare them enough to keep them from coming back. Gabe shot a quick look around, saw that everyone was out of sight of the hunters. *I want everyone to howl, loud and long. If they try and run, block their way. Now!*

The night exploded from absolute silence to a wild cacophony of howling wolves in little more than a heartbeat. Gabe noticed a few snarls and barks added for effect as he and Aaron slipped into the open space beside the hunters' ATV.

Cursing, the crunch of branches snapping and loose snow falling from the aspen branches preceded the two hunters. They burst out of the brush heading for their vehicle, almost colliding with Aaron. Standing a full three feet tall at the shoulder, he was huge and deadly, and when he snarled, baring long canines, both men stopped dead in their tracks.

Other wolves drifted in from the shadows, and Anton led his group across the beaver dam to join the rest of the pack. Taking positions that ringed the two in a tight circle of dozens of snarling wolves, they waited while the two men clung to each other, babbling unintelligible, panicked gibberish.

Gabe shifted. At six three and two hundred pounds he wasn't the largest of the men, but he had the presence of his father and the confidence in knowing the entire pack was behind him. It didn't hurt that he was bare-assed naked. He'd discovered long ago that humans were notoriously nonplussed by a large, naked man, especially one who was totally unconcerned with his lack of clothing. "You are trespassing on Chanku land." He held out his hand. "Put your weapons down and show me your IDs, please."

• • •

"Why was I not surprised those idiots were from California?" Gabe tipped his beer and took a swallow. Freshly showered and dressed, his body sated after a hard and fast fuck with Aaron following their run, he hooked his bare feet in the rungs of the bar stool in his father's den and stretched his arms high over his head, twisting to loosen up the kinks.

Sitting on the big leather couch with Mei sleeping beside him in her snow-leopard form, Oliver Cheval swirled the dark cognac in his glass and shook his head. "What bothers me is that they seriously believed those stupid ID cards they'd bought—for one hell of a lot of money, I might add—gave them access to our property. In that respect, they didn't think they were breaking the law. I'll give them that, but their maps were too damned good for my peace of mind."

Aaron walked into the den with his digital notepad. He scrolled through a few pages and highlighted a website. "It's a good thing we caught them. I watch for this sort of crap all the time, but this is a new website, and one I've missed. This group is selling private hunting privileges on Chanku land. They have a very authentic—though false, I checked—U.S. Forest Service certificate of approval. The only restriction is that you can't shoot wolves or other predators, but any other game is fine."

Anton leaned on the bar, his favorite spot when they met in here for drinks and conversation. "That caveat will keep them from an attempted murder or even murder-for-hire charge, but Aaron, you didn't get that law degree for nothing. I want to hit the owners of that website with a lawsuit that's big enough to get their attention. Have you got screen shots of everything?"

"I do, along with the taped confessions of our two erstwhile hunters. I believe they were honestly apologetic." He laughed. "They also cleaned up all their trash, so Gabe let them keep the dead geese. But yes, I'll get right on it."

Oliver's mobile phone chirped. He stepped away from the group and answered the call. "Emeline. I didn't realize you were back in the states, sweetie. How are you? What? Tell me more." His voice faded as he left the room.

It was a full five minutes before he returned, still talking. "Honey, Aaron's busy. Anton gave him an important project. Just a minute." He covered the phone, glanced at Anton. "Who can make a quick trip to San Francisco? Em's got a situation. It's not one I want her to handle alone."

Anton glanced around the room until his gaze settled on Gabe. "Gabe? Can you do it? I know you wanted to be here for the winter solstice celebration, but . . ." He shrugged.

Gabe shot him a grin. "Sure. I can go. I haven't seen EmyIzzy in years. Whatever it is can't take three weeks, so there should be time." He glanced at Oliver. "When, and what do I need to take? Let me talk to her." He held his hand out for the phone.

Em's father shot Anton a look that was impossible to interpret. Then he turned to Gabe. "No. I'll get the particulars. You go pack. She needs someone there as soon as possible, preferably tonight." He lifted the phone, covered it again and then shot another look at Gabe. "I'd suggest you drop the EmyIzzy tag for the duration, okay?"

Laughing, Gabe stood. "Suggestion noted." He saluted Oliver and headed for his cottage, well aware his mood was vastly improved.

2

Emeline arrived at San Francisco International and waited in the Chanku Global Industries hangar. The company maintained a fleet of jets and helicopters, which allowed her to bypass the general airport entrance and all the security hassles. After the frustrating couple of days she'd had, Em really didn't want to deal with all that.

She watched as the company jet with the bold CGI logo and its proud pack of wolves racing across the fuselage touched down, circled back on the runway and rolled smoothly across the tarmac. Too bad she didn't rank a corporate jet for her trips to Asia. No lost luggage that way.

She wondered who was on it, what packmate her father had found to help her. She was sorry it wasn't Aaron. She actually missed her big brother, but her dad had only said he'd make certain someone was here by midnight. She hoped so. She was still haunted by that poor woman's unspoken plea for help.

She'd not heard from her since. It had been Thursday evening when Em gave her the business card. She'd waited all day Friday, but no word. She hadn't planned to call her dad, but until she got this settled, Em didn't think she'd be able to quit worrying. The woman, Sissy was her name, had to be Chanku. Em had gotten a glimpse of dark amber eyes, a dead giveaway when combined with the strong telepathic voice.

Mindspeaking was not broadly known as a Chanku trait, but as far as Emeline knew, no other sentient species had the ability. Sissy had contacted her as clearly as if they'd been speaking aloud, face-to-face.

The door on the side of the small jet opened and a staircase lowered. Em stepped out of the shadows as a large figure filled the doorway, so it definitely wasn't Aaron, and not one of the women, either.

She heard male laughter and then a man swung into view and came quickly down the steps. Her heart stuttered in her chest and shivers raced along her spine. It couldn't be.

She glanced behind her and fought the compulsion to run back inside, into the shadows where he wouldn't see her. How could her father do this? Didn't the man have any compassion at all?

"Hey, Em. Goddess, girl, it's good to see you."

And he was there, dropping his bags, wrapping his arms around her in a big brotherly hug, swinging her around as he'd done when she was three. When she was five, when she was fifteen. Even now, when she was twenty-six years old, a fully grown woman in charge of an entire division of the same company he worked for.

"Put me down, you oaf." She hated the fact she was laughing, but she shoved against his chest, and as always it was like pushing against a brick wall. At least he hadn't called her by that horrible nickname he and Aaron had tagged her with.

He set her lightly on the ground. "EmyIzzy, you never change, except to get more beautiful. How come you haven't found a man?"

She brushed her hair out of her eyes. Then she carefully smoothed her skirt over her hips and glared at him. "Please don't call me that. I've hated that name ever since you and Aaron cooked it up." Before he could answer, she spun about and headed back to her car. "It's late, but I'm hoping we can go look for her."

"Her who?" Gabe slung his pack over his shoulder and followed her. "Emeline," he said, and she couldn't help but notice his emphasis on her name, "I have no idea why I'm here. Oliver said that you were involved in a situation, but not what the situation is."

Em opened the trunk on the little SUV and Gabe tossed his bag in the back. She got behind the wheel, and once he was settled, she turned and glanced his way. "A woman contacted me telepathically. She's a prostitute, working in Chinatown, and she's terrified. I gave her my card, told her to call me, but she said her pimp was close by, and I could tell she's afraid of him. Then her client showed up and she got in his car and left. I haven't seen her since, but I'm sure she's still out there." She backed out and headed for the freeway. "If she's still alive. That was Thursday evening, and she was very afraid."

Gabe sat silently beside her. Finally he turned, and she felt his heavy gaze. "I'm sorry. I don't know what to say. I certainly didn't expect anything like this. But you're right. We need to find her. Whatever I can do, Emeline."

She noticed that he said her name in a much kinder tone this time. Without the snark. Then he softly added, "You know you can count on me."

• • •

Em drove back to her apartment in the Sunset District so unnaturally *aware* of Gabe, who was sitting so close beside her in the small vehicle that it felt as if he took up all the air. They didn't talk, beyond a few questions from him about her latest travels, and she was so relieved. She still wasn't sure how to act around Gabe, almost as if she didn't know how to be an adult around him.

Their entire relationship had been more of a big brother–little sister sort of thing, and that wasn't at all how she wanted him to think of her. She'd quit thinking of Gabe as her big brother by the time she was into her early teens. The fact he still treated her like a kid had made her crazy, but then he went away to college, and that was so much better, because she didn't have to think about him at all.

Except she did.

Goddess help her, she hadn't been able to put him out of her mind. She'd gone away to college herself and then straight into work at CGI, the same place where Gabe worked, except it was a huge company and she traveled a lot. They hadn't run into each other since she'd started her job at CGI as an intern almost six years ago.

She had been so certain she'd find peace when her job took her out of the country.

So much for that idea, though maybe it was a good thing he was here. Maybe it was a chance to see if there ever could be anything between them, though she'd noticed his interest when she'd described the woman. She'd had him at tall and blonde, exactly what she wasn't, but he was never going to notice her, not while he still saw her as "cute little Emylzzy."

She turned off the 280 for Highway 1 and headed west to the Sunset District and the old refurbished mansion where she lived. It was the same building where the first members of Pack Dynamics had stayed before they moved headquarters to Montana. The building had been converted to separate apartments, and now it provided temporary housing for Chanku who worked for CGI or its subsidiaries here in San Francisco.

Gabe stared with open curiosity at the three-story building as Em pulled into the underground garage. She shot him a quick glance after she parked. "Haven't you ever been here before?"

He shook his head. "No. I've heard about it. It was being renovated when I was looking for a place to stay, but that was years ago. I ended up sharing an apartment with Alex Aragat over in North Beach, but we gave that up last summer. He was hardly ever in the city after Anton put him to work as pack liaison with the Flathead County sheriff's department, and I knew I'd be gone all summer with Jace Wolf on our annual survey of the wild wolf populations. Since we got back, I've been handling some of Alex's work with the sheriff's department and telecommuting. It's good to get back to San Francisco, though. I've actually considered moving in here. Now that Alex and Annie are here and he's taken over Lily's work at Cheval International, they're living in Lily's house on Marina. Annie's still programming for CGI, and Lily's moved in with Sebastian in his house in Montana."

Em grinned at him. "That's a lot to keep track of." Then she laughed, finally beginning to feel a bit more comfortable with this overwhelmingly adult version of Gabe Cheval. He'd always been such a cutup, it was sort of nice to carry on an adult conversation with him. "I can't believe all the matings that have taken place in the past few months. The party crowd is growing up."

Gabe smiled at her. "Happens to the best of 'em. Annie's dad, Tinker, said they had some wild parties here before they all settled down."

"I can believe it." But it wasn't home and it wasn't pack. She glanced at Gabe as she checked to make sure everything was turned off. He looked pensive. She wondered what he was thinking.

What he thought of her.

She scrubbed that thought out of her mind immediately. He still thought she was just a little kid. She was the same age as his little sister, Lucia, and he still talked about Luci like she was a baby. Damn. That was never going to change, no matter what she wanted or what she did. Scowling, Emeline grabbed her purse. Gabe got his bag out of the trunk and then followed her up the steps to the first floor.

"This is nice." He paused in the foyer and gazed at the beautiful entry, all polished walnut and old brass. "How many of you guys live here?"

"I'm it for now." She set her bag on an antique hall tree. "Most of the younger employees live closer to the financial district. There's a lot more going on there, more nightlife. I travel so much with my job that I like the quiet when I'm home."

"You think of this as home?" He had a disconcerting way of looking at her, as if he saw inside, knew what she was thinking. She reinforced her shields when he said, "What about Montana?"

She shrugged. "In Montana, I'm Daddy's little girl, obviously one without a mind of her own. Mom babies me, questions everything I do, every move I make. It's suffocating. I miss the pack, but I need my freedom more."

"I'm sorry to hear that."

The honest sympathy in his voice stopped her. She turned and gazed at him, really seeing him for the first time. Not as the guy who loved to tease and joke around, but as a serious and thoughtful adult. It wasn't nearly the stretch she'd expected.

"I always wondered why you stayed away," he said, "but that makes sense. Luci has the same complaint. I heard her arguing with Dad last week. She wants to move down here instead of telecommuting. He's not real pleased with the idea, especially since Lily's not in the city anymore."

"I'd love it if she moved here. Luci's so much fun. And Lily came to San Francisco by herself." Em headed toward the stairs.

"Yeah, but Lily's best friend is a goddess, and Dad had Eve's promise to keep an eye on her."

Em tried not to laugh. Really. "Well, there is that. I didn't ask. I hardly ever went home after I went away to college. I think I was nineteen the last time. What's weird is that my parents have never insisted I come back. They always seem uncomfortable around me. And no, I have no idea why, and I don't get it. C'mon. Let me show you your room. You can get settled and I'm going to change clothes. I'm thinking jeans and a warm sweater. The last thing I want to do is attract any attention, but I'm hoping we can track her down. I know her name is Sissy, and that she's tall and beautiful, with long blonde hair and dark amber eyes. And she can mindspeak as well as anyone in the pack."

. . .

Tall and beautiful with long blonde hair? This trip to San Francisco was looking better all the time, and once he got over the shock of seeing EmyIzzy again . . . Crap. Emeline . . . He actually sighed. Sighed! What the hell was that all about? Em always had been just one more little sister, attached at the hip to his baby sister Lucia, and Gabe had figured she'd still be much the same—sort of like Luci. Cute and silly and someone he could tease and relax with. He hadn't seen her in . . . Goddess. He hadn't seen her in at least six or seven years.

It appeared a lot could happen to a woman in six or seven years, and looking at Emeline now wasn't the least bit relaxing. She'd been short and cute, and a little on the pudgy side, but somehow that baby fat had managed to rearrange itself in absolutely stunning fashion. She'd seemed shocked to see him, though, and that was weird. Why hadn't Oliver told her he was the one coming to help? No matter. It was after midnight, and they still needed to go look for the missing woman.

Gabe tossed his bag on the bed and went in to use the bathroom and brush his teeth. He'd had more beer than he should have this evening, including a couple on the plane down from Montana, and sleep sounded way too inviting. This had all the makings of a very long night, and he'd already been on a long run, helped catch some bad guys, topped Aaron and gone through the complete dissection of the evening's activities with Anton and the rest of the pack who'd been hanging out in Anton's den.

Splashing water on his face helped perk him up. His mobile phone chimed as he rinsed his toothbrush and stuck it back in his overnight kit. He answered the call, and Alex Aragat's face filled the small screen. "Hey, Alex. What's up?"

"Dad said you were in town for a couple of days. Wanted to make sure you saved time for Annie and me."

"Will do. Can't talk now, though. Emeline Cheval thinks she's got a lead on a Chanku woman, a prostitute she met a couple of nights ago. We're headed out to look for her. I'll call you tomorrow."

"Sounds good. Didn't know Em was back. She's gone most of the time."

"Yeah. I'm finding that out. I'll give you a call tomorrow. I imagine it'll be a late night."

He signed off and left his apartment. Em waited in the entry by the door to the garage. She was tinier than a lot of the young women in the pack, with her father's slight build, but she had all her mom's sex appeal.

Except he didn't want to see Em that way. It wasn't easy, though, ignoring the subtle, sexy sway of her hips as he followed her down the steps to the garage. She'd put on tight black jeans with high black leather boots that almost reached her knees, and a dark blue sweater that showed off more of Emeline Cheval than Gabe ever imagined she'd have to show.

It was a struggle, reminding himself she was EmyIzzy, for Goddess's sake. Not a fuck buddy. Besides, he'd just had excellent after-run sex with Aaron. There was no way he was going to screw with Em after what he'd been doing with her brother a few hours ago. Nope. Wasn't going there.

"I thought we'd park at CGI. Last time I saw her, it was only a couple of blocks from the office."

"Okay." He buckled himself into his seat and willed his fascination with the shape of her lips into the darker compartments of his mind. "You're in charge." He flashed her a grin, expecting a snarky response, or at least hoping for one, but she didn't look his way. Sighing, he settled back in his seat. At least her response—or lack of one—cooled his libido.

After a couple of minutes when Em hadn't said a word, the quiet was beginning to make him twitch. "Alex called while I was cleaning up," he said. "He's hoping we can get together while I'm in town."

She shot him a quick glance. "That would be nice for you to see each other. How long's it been?"

"A few months. You know he and Annie McClintock are mated, don't you?"

She nodded. "Mom told me. I've always liked Annie."

Chatty little thing, wasn't she. "How long did you say it's been since you've made it back to Montana?"

"A long time. Seven years."

Seven years? "Crap, Emy . . . Em. Sorry . . ." He chuckled softly. "Old habits are hard to break. How do you stand it? Don't you miss the pack? Your family?" This time he turned in his seat so he could see her.

She focused on the street ahead. After a few seconds, she shrugged. "Yeah. I guess, but it's not worth the hassles when I go home." She sighed, and softly added, "You just don't get it, Gabe."

"You're right. I don't. I can't imagine being away from everyone. Not running with the pack, not spending time in the mountains. I work here most of the time, but Montana will always be home to me."

She shrugged. More silence. Finally, she started talking again. "I imagine your parents treat you like an adult," she said, glancing his way before focusing on the road. "I go home, I might as well be four years old. I'm twenty-six, Gabe. I'm a grown woman with a lot of responsibility. I work most of the time in Asia, where both I and my work are respected. I'm fluent in Mandarin and Cantonese and can get along in most of the dialects. I also speak Russian and Japanese, and I'm in charge of employee safety in literally hundreds of shops across Asia and Tibet. The last time I was back in Montana, when I was nineteen, every move I made was questioned, every decision ignored or even countermanded without my consent, and I came away feeling worthless. It's not a healthy environment for me, so I choose to stay away."

The bitterness poured off her in waves. Stunned by the vehemence in her tone, Gabe reached out, wrapped his fingers around her right arm above her elbow, and gave her a gentle squeeze. "I'm sorry. I had no idea. Aaron has never said anything about problems like that. I never noticed it when you were younger."

"That's because they're totally different with Aaron. They were with me, too. When I was little, they were wonderful parents. All I know is that something happened when I was around fourteen or fifteen, but I don't know what. They won't tell me why, but they changed, suddenly became so overprotective that it was suffocating. I couldn't wait to get away from them." She glanced quickly in his direction, her eyes sparkling with unshed tears. He didn't remember her eyes being so green. Just like her mom's. Cat's eyes.

"I'd love to go home, Gabe. I'm tired of traveling all over the world. I miss the forest and the pack. I miss my friends and I miss Aaron. I even miss Mom and Dad, but I can't have my own life if they're nearby. Not if they won't let me be myself. Think for myself."

Her cheeks were flushed when she looked away and carefully pulled into the underground parking garage. Gabe had a feeling she was embarrassed after being so open about the problems with her folks, but he was glad she'd said something.

It changed his perception of her, showed him that she wasn't a kid anymore, but a sharp, beautiful woman with a mind of her own. There was nothing childish about the Emeline Cheval sitting beside him. He was finding her a lot more fascinating than he'd expected.

The underground garage was spacious and well-lit beneath the huge building that housed Chanku Global Industries and many of its subsidiary companies, including Cheval International, where Lily had worked and Alex now worked. The security guard recognized both of them, greeting Em and Gabe by name as he raised the gate and let them enter, but Gabe hardly noticed. The pain in Em's voice wouldn't leave him alone, but he had no idea what was wrong. Why Oliver and Mei would be so overprotective with their daughter—a daughter they obviously loved. There was no denying the sound of pride in Oliver's voice when he'd talked to her earlier this evening. It made no sense.

They left the car and Gabe followed Em out into the night, the two of them walking swiftly toward the area where she'd seen the woman she thought might be Chanku, but he wasn't thinking about rescuing a stranger in trouble. No, he was thinking about Emeline. Wondering what he could do to help.

Wondering how so much could have changed in just a few years.

Little EmyIzzy was all grown up, but she was hurting. Hurting and alone, cut off from the pack for some unknown reason. He caught up to her and then grabbed her hand, and when she turned startled eyes on his, he shrugged and pulled her closer. "If we look like a couple, it'll be easier to go undetected. When you're walking so fast, with an obvious destination in mind, it makes you stand out."

"Okay, though I can't see why I'd stand out that much." She glanced at their linked hands and then focused on the sidewalk ahead.

"You realize, of course, that there's no way in hell people aren't going to notice you."

She stopped dead in her tracks. He had to bite back laughter. "Why? What's wrong with me?"

"You're gorgeous, Em. Absolutely beautiful. Men watch you walk by. Women even turn to see. I can't imagine you going anywhere and not being noticed."

She frowned and then looked away. Very softly she said, "Why do you do that, Gabe?"

"Do what?" He tugged and they started walking, but her steps were stiff, almost awkward, as if she didn't want to be close to him. What the hell was bugging her now?

"Make fun of me. You've always made fun of me."

"Telling you you're beautiful is making fun of you? I don't get it, Em." This time he was the one coming to a stop. Even as late as it was, people passed by, going around them the way water broke around stone. "Why would you think I'm making fun of you?"

"Aren't you?" This time she looked at him. "Aren't you saying nice things so you can pull the proverbial rug out from under my feet later? That's what you and Aaron used to do. Act all nice and friendly and then laugh when I believed you."

"I don't believe we're having this conversation." He shook his head, not in denial but to clear his thoughts. This definitely wasn't the Emeline he remembered. He tried to think of the last time he saw her and realized it was a lot longer than he'd thought. Closer to ten years since he'd gone off to college, and when he was home the last person he'd wanted to hang out with was Aaron's kid sister.

"Look," he said, so frustrated he didn't know quite what to say. "Let's do what we're here to do, but when we get back to your place, you and I are going to talk. Okay?"

He realized he was holding her still, his big hands wrapped around her upper arms, and her eyes had gone wide. He turned her loose and stepped back. "Goddess, Em. I'm sorry. I wasn't trying to frighten you. Honest. I'm just . . ." He turned away, stared at the tall buildings across the street and called himself all kinds of fool, but that wasn't going to solve whatever was going on.

Talking would help. Searching for the reasons behind her strange reaction to everything he said. The way she read things into every word, every action. Things he didn't mean, hadn't said. It sounded as if her memories of what he and Aaron considered typical "big brother teasing little sister stuff" had been bullying in Em's eyes. If that was the case, he had a lot of apologizing to do. Both he and Aaron did.

"Gabe! I see her." She grabbed his arm and hauled him down the sidewalk. "There. Do you see the tall blonde? The one with all the long braids?"

"Yeah. I do. Stay behind me. I'm going to act like a customer. See if I can pick her up."

"Okay. But be careful, Gabe. I don't want you hurt."

He gave her a quick grin and walked on ahead, but he almost laughed. She didn't want him hurt, but he had a feeling she really wanted him gone. Not yet. Not until he figured out what was going on with Ms. EmyIzzy.

17

But for now, his focus was on the tall blonde. She was absolutely beautiful, and her long, lean frame fit the look of the typical Chanku female, if you could call any body type typical. Many of the women in the pack had the same look of sleek strength, and they carried themselves as if they possessed more than average power.

Which, of course, they did. The woman had turned to watch him. He thought of mindspeaking, but decided against it. Not here where she might startle or otherwise give away the fact she was communicating with him.

He paused a few feet away. She watched him with a practiced look and smiled, as if she liked what she saw. "Hi."

"Hi to you, too." He glanced at the light pole she leaned against. "Looks like you're working hard, holding up that pole."

"It's a job." She slowly looked him up and down, pausing her gaze at the front of his jeans. "I'm quite good at keeping poles vertical." She glanced up at the pole behind her back before turning her attention to Gabe once again. "I imagine I could do wonders for yours."

"I don't doubt that at all, but I'm guessing pole work is expensive."

She shrugged and named a figure much higher than Gabe expected, but he merely nodded. "Damned expensive. You say you're good. I guess I'll have to take you at your word. Will you come with me?"

She laughed. "Depends on how fast you are. I prefer to take my time, but yes. If you've got a place nearby, I can go there. How far?"

"Over on Kearny." He glanced at her boots with their high, spike heels. "You okay walking in those?"

"I am." He noticed as she glanced over his shoulder at someone behind him. Gabe turned and saw a large man standing in the shadows. "He your guy?"

She nodded. Gabe turned and faced the man. "I'll have her back in a couple of hours."

"Damn right you will."

Smiling, Gabe held out his arm. "Let's go."

3

Whoever this guy was, he was drop-dead gorgeous. Sissy sensed absolutely no anger in him at all. For whatever reason, he made her feel comfortable, as if she was safe with him, but she knew better than to trust any instincts that made her think she was safe. She'd never be safe again. She fingered the card in her coat pocket. That young woman had made her feel safe, too. Just by caring. She couldn't know that Sissy didn't have a phone, that there was absolutely no way she'd get a chance to call, unless maybe this guy was taking her somewhere that she could find a phone, could call this Emeline person.

The man glanced at Sissy and smiled. "I'm going to talk to you, okay. Without sound. Don't act surprised, please?" *My name is Gabe. I want to help you. There's a woman waiting up ahead. She's the one who mind-spoke with you the other night. Your man is following behind us, so we're going to walk all the way to the place where we work and go inside. The woman is going to come after us, so he can't connect you to her. Your pimp can't follow us once we go into the building, but once we're in there, we'll be able to tell you more about us. About you.*

"Okay," she said, smiling as if Gabe had said something funny. Then she looked straight ahead as they walked past the woman who'd given her the business card a couple of nights ago. She was looking at her mobile phone and didn't raise her head. Sissy and Gabe kept going. *That works for me. I couldn't call you when you gave me your card, Emeline. I don't have a phone, and we're not allowed near them. I'm not alone. There are five other women, and one of us is always kept prisoner so the others will return. These people holding us are horrible.*

I didn't even think of you not having a phone. I'm sorry. Your pimp just walked past me. I'm going to follow him after he gets far enough ahead. Gabe will keep you safe.

I've forgotten what safe feels like. And that bastard following us has held me against my will for so many years, I've lost count.

When were you taken? Gabe glanced at her and smiled. She clung to his arm.

I remember it was in the spring and I had just turned twenty-three. I was born April 4, 2011, and captured early in May, 2034. They've kept me ever since. I don't even know what year it is.

It's December, 2039. Those bastards have had you for over five and a half years.

She stumbled and Gabe caught her. *Oh, God,* she said. *I knew it was a long time, but I had no idea . . .*

We're almost to my office. We'll get you free, Sissy. Trust us. And we'll get the others out as well. But first, we need to find out everything we can about you and where you're being held.

• • •

As planned, Emeline went in through the garage and notified the security guard of the man following them. Sissy's pimp was big and mean-looking, taller and heavier than Gabe, dressed all in black leather. She told the guard he might want backup, just in case. The man was calling for extra guards as she slipped through the doorway into the elevator that would take her to Gabe's office.

They met in the hallway on the sixth floor, Gabe unlocked his office and the three of them went inside. The girl looked badly shaken. Em took her hands in both of hers and squeezed. "Are you okay? We're not going to hurt you. We just want to find out how we can help."

"It's been over five years," she said. Her voice trembled.

Em glanced at Gabe, but he shook his head.

"Sissy had no idea how long she's been held by those bastards. Over five years, Emy. Five fucking years."

"Crap. I'm so sorry." She wrapped her arms around Sissy and hugged her. "We'll do whatever we can. Then she glanced at Gabe. He was pouring a drink for her, one that made Em smile in spite of the situation. "How'd you get Anton's cognac? I thought he owned every bottle of Hennessy around."

"Close. This was a gift on my twenty-first birthday."

"Gabe, you're thirty. I thought you were a party boy. This bottle's still full."

He handed the glass to Sissy and poured two more, one for himself and one for Em. "I always said I wanted to save it for a special occasion." He raised his glass. Sissy still looked a bit stunned. She held the glass with both hands and stared at the amber liquid, but Em raised hers.

"It doesn't get more special than this, Sissy. Emeline and I are Chanku shapeshifters. We believe you are, too. Somehow, we have to get you and the other women free of the bastard holding you prisoner, and then I hope you'll come with us to meet the pack in Montana."

He took a sip and winked at Em. She turned and smiled at Sissy, and that's when she saw the tears rolling slowly down the woman's face. Carefully Em took the glass from her hand. Sissy hadn't even tasted it, but this whole evening had to be overwhelming for her.

Em wrapped her arms around Sissy once more, but this time she hugged her close. After a moment, Sissy hugged her back, sobbing against Em's shoulder. Her thoughts spilled out, scattered and so jumbled it was hard to interpret what she was saying. It took her a few minutes, but finally she got herself under control. Gabe hadn't said a word, but he must have made a quick trip into the executive washroom because he handed her a damp washcloth. Sissy wiped her face, and then held it against her eyes for a moment, almost as if she hid herself from the two of them.

"That explains so much." Her words tumbled out as she scrubbed more tears away. "I have dreams of running through the forest. I can smell trees and fresh clean grass and feel pine needles beneath my paws. Those dreams are all that keep me sane. I know what Chanku are, and I took the pills before, because I was so sure, but I never shifted."

"How long did you take them?" Gabe sat on the edge of his desk, while Emeline and Sissy each took one of the big overstuffed office chairs in front of him.

"Only a few days. Then I was abducted. I was hiking on Mount Tam, it was early evening and I think they darted me. I remember a sting in my leg, and the next thing I knew I was waking up in a cage somewhere in the city."

Em took her hand. "Do you have family? Anyone who would be looking for you?"

Sissy shook her head. "No. I was a foster kid. My mom was a drug addict and a whore. She died when I was ten. I don't know who my father was. One of the johns, I guess."

Gabe went around to the back of the desk and pulled a bottle of pills out of a drawer. "Here are enough nutrients to get you all the way to changing. Is there a way you can hide them when you go back?"

"Go back?" Em looked at Sissy and then Gabe. "She can't go back."

"She has to, Em. I don't like it either, but there are six women being held captive. One of them is kept at all times to insure the others return. If

Sissy doesn't go back, whoever is being held as collateral will die."

Sissy took a sip of the cognac and smiled at Em. "Gabe's right. I have to go back, but somehow we need to figure out how you can get all of us out."

"Where are you kept?"

"I don't know. There's always a handler with us, and we're taken out blindfolded. Russo's mine tonight. He's so mean." She swallowed, and the tension radiated off her in waves. "How long have we been here?"

"Only half an hour or so." Gabe laughed. "You're pretty high-priced, Sissy. You can tell Russo that I wanted my money's worth. Here's what we're gonna do." He walked across the room to a small cabinet, spun the combination lock, removed an envelope and took out what looked like a clear bandage.

He showed it to Emeline and Sissy. "Em, do you remember that espionage case Dad had me investigating, the contract employee we suspected was stealing company secrets? This is how we got him."

"What is it?" Em took the item from Gabe and showed it to Sissy. "A plastic bandage?"

"It's a location device with a built-in GPS. I have a pretty sophisticated tracking system built into my mobile that can lock on to the signal this thing throws out once it's activated. It's linked specifically to my equipment, but I can add the app to yours, Em. We'll be able to track Sissy and find where they're keeping her."

"I actually have a bandage over a scrape on my thigh. Can we stick it there? No one should think anything of it, in case they notice it."

Gabe knelt beside Sissy as she pulled up her skirt, exposing what looked, to Em anyway, like an inordinate amount of perfect creamy thigh. She felt like a troll next to this beautiful woman, but she watched, fascinated by Gabe's strong, dark fingers as he peeled the older, more traditional bandage off her thigh and replaced it with the GPS.

His phone rang, and Gabe answered as he stood. "Okay. Let him stay in the lobby. Tell him we'll be down in about ten minutes. Thank you."

"It appears Russo is growing impatient."

Sissy shuddered. "I hate him. He rarely lets me go with someone he doesn't recognize. He probably thought you must have a lot of money, and he's greedy."

Gabe nodded. "Gotcha. Emeline, I'll go down with Sissy. I want you to wait here. Use the tablet to familiarize yourself with the app. The tracking software's already loaded on it, too. In fact, go ahead and download the app to your phone while we're gone." He grabbed the computerized tablet and clicked it on, typed in a password, hit one of the icons and handed it to Emeline. A schematic of the CGI building came up on the screen with a yellow dot blinking right where it should be. She showed it to Sissy. "There you are. Just make sure you don't wash the bandage off."

"Not a problem," Gabe said. "It's got waterproof glue. That thing's not going anywhere without solvent." Then he grabbed the bottle of pills and dumped about a dozen into a small plastic bag and gave it to Sissy. He watched while she stuck them in her pocket. "Your mindspeech is already strong, Sissy, but if you can take more of those pills, at least two a day for the next few days, you should be able to project a couple of miles, at least. Are any of the other women Chanku?"

"I don't know. I can't talk to them without words, not the way I can with you two."

"When are you all there at the same time?"

"Generally during the day. We sleep then. Russo's anxious because he still expects me to go out and pick up another john tonight."

"Crap." Em grabbed her hands. "I'm so sorry."

"I'm okay." Sissy sighed. "I've been doing this now for way too many years. One more won't be a problem. Not when I know there's actually someone trying to help me."

"If anything happens, you're at Chanku Global Industries on Kearny. This is a safe place for you. You have my word. Your image is already in our security files, and I'll make sure our men know you're to be offered refuge at any time. If you have the other women with you, that's even better." Gabe stood. "Now, though, we need to head down to meet Russo." He went back to his desk and reached inside. When he shut the drawer, he was holding a stack of bills. "There's three thousand dollars here."

Sissy gasped. "But why?"

"Because you're very good at what you do." He laughed, but Sissy looked at him like he was nuts.

"I'm teasing. We're going to work with your bodyguard's greed. I'm going down there with you and I'm going to peel off two thousand and then tell Russo there's a tip in it for him if I can have you again tomorrow night. And only you. He'll get the other thousand then, and I imagine there won't be any problem arranging for your time. We'll move as fast as we can on this, but you might have to be patient for a day or two longer. I don't want to go in without backup, and not until I know you and either Em or me can communicate telepathically for a fairly good distance. That way we can let you know when we're coming and you can tell us what to expect, how many guards there are, that sort of thing. You okay with that? We'll only come after you when we can get all six of you out at the same time."

Em squeezed her hand. "Whatever you do, Sissy, don't tell the others. We can't risk one of them giving anything away, okay?"

"Okay. I understand. Thank you. I don't know what to say."

Em grabbed her glass of cognac and tapped the one she put in Sissy's hand. "I know what to say. Goddess be with us, and here's to springing you from those bastards ASAP." She tipped her glass, took a sip of the cognac, and memories flooded her mind. Memories of home. Of life with the pack.

Of her life before whatever happened that made everything change.

She raised her head and caught Gabe staring at her. His eyes were troubled, and she knew he must be horribly worried about Sissy. Still, she sent a silent message, directed only at Gabe. *She'll be okay. We will save her.*

The corner of Gabe's mouth twitched into a small bit of a smile. *I know we will, Emy. It's not Sissy I'm worried about. Whatever has put those shadows in your heart, I promise to help you find out what they're hiding. But you're right. We'll save Sissy and the other women first. Time to get going.*

Gabe upended his glass and finished the cognac. Em and Sissy did the same, and then both of them got the giggles when they started coughing. Em wiped her eyes, still giggling, and grinned at Gabe. "Well, that's certainly not the way Anton's precious cognac is meant to be enjoyed."

She gave Sissy another tight, fast hug. "Good luck, and remember, we're going to do everything we can, as soon as we can. And when you're free and we've got the time, I'm going to have Gabe tell you everything about his father. That's where the cognac comes from."

"Okay." Sissy looked confused, but she took a deep breath and turned to Gabe. "It's time, right?"

"It's time." He took her arm, leaned over and gave Em a quick kiss, and before she had time to react, he and Sissy were out the door.

Em grabbed the tablet and her phone, downloaded the app and watched the little blinking light move down the hall to the elevator. Sissy had guts. She was the bravest woman Emeline had ever met. And she hoped like hell that between Gabe and herself they'd be able to save everyone being held by Sissy's captors.

And Gabriel Cheval had kissed her.

• • •

Gabe sipped at his cup of coffee while he flipped through email. It was early, barely after five in the morning, but he was enjoying the quiet, and since his body was still on Mountain Time, it felt like his usual time to get up.

The fact he and Emeline hadn't gone off to their respective beds until around three this morning was going to catch up with him later. Of course, if he'd been in Em's bed, he'd probably still be there, but that wasn't going to happen. She obviously had some huge issues with him, issues she wasn't about to share, and if he was totally honest, he had issues of his own.

He still saw her as that adorable—and then as she got older and more mobile—irritating little sister, tagging along with little Luci and bugging the hell out of Aaron and Jace and him. But somehow, those visuals were becoming less important the more time he spent with her.

Physically, she didn't resemble the munchkin of his memories at all, and Goddess be damned, but he certainly wasn't thinking of her as a kid sister anymore. They weren't related at all, though they shared the last name, but when she was little and he was a cocky teenager, it had been easier to lump all the little girls who played with his sister Luci into the same mold—they were all bratty little sisters.

Not anymore. No, now she was funny and smart and so fucking hot. All that glorious long black hair waving around her shoulders clear to her waist, her silky skin the color of toffee. He'd fallen asleep early this morning with images of Em wearing nothing but waves of dark, shiny hair and a beautiful smile.

He glanced up as she shuffled into the kitchen, looking all sleep-rumpled and hugely approachable, but she went straight to the coffeepot and poured a cup before taking a seat across from him at the long trestle table. This place was designed to feed a crowd, but it somehow felt terribly intimate with just the two of them.

"Rough night?" he said, grinning at her.

She merely glared at him and took a sip of her coffee.

"Ah. Not a morning person, I see." He held up his mobile phone. "Sissy's still in the same spot."

"She'll probably get to sleep until noon. Shouldn't we go rescue them, while everyone's sleeping?" Scowling, Em took another sip.

"I don't think we should attempt the rescue today. I want to go out in a couple more hours. We go snooping around too early in the day it's going to look like we're snooping."

"Well, of course it is. Because that's what we'll be doing."

He couldn't believe how cute she was like this—grumpy and rumpled and not at all trying to put him off. He really liked her this way. "Exactly," he said, "but I don't want Russo and his buddies to know that. Today I only want to find out which floor they're on where they live, see if we can make mental contact with Sissy from outside the building. We've got the address because of the mapping feature with the bug. Tonight I'll wait for her on the corner, hire her for the evening, and that will give us time to go

25

over the layout of the place. Plus, we can figure out the best time to go in. I'm going to call Alex later this morning. I don't want us to go in on our own."

"Shouldn't we contact the local authorities?"

"Not with Chanku involved. We're not required to, and the more people we involve, the harder it will be to insure the women's safety. There have been too many bungled rescues of women in the past few months. I worry about a snitch inside the force."

"True. There's always a risk, the more you involve." She yawned and stretched her arms up over her head.

Gabe caught a glimpse of honey-colored belly between her gray knit yoga pants and white tee. He practically salivated, he wanted so badly to taste her. Instead, he glanced away. "You know, you didn't have to get up so early."

"I smelled coffee." She glared at the cup, took another sip.

"We could always go back to bed."

Her head shot up. She frowned again. "What did you say?"

He grinned and held his cup to his lips. "We could always go back to bed. You. Me. Warm, rumpled sheets. Warmer bodies." He dropped the leer and set his cup back on the table. "And no, Em. I'm not teasing and I'm not kidding. You really are beautiful, and looking like this, all tousled and sleepy, you're too damned hot for me to ignore. Besides, it's a big bed. I was lonely last night. I don't like to sleep alone."

She took another sip of her coffee and stared at him, and he wondered if he should apologize. But she was beautiful, and she was definitely sexy, and they were Chanku. They had sex with their packmates all the time, but for some reason, with Emeline it felt like a monumental step even to suggest it.

She set her cup down, brushed her tangled hair back from her face with one hand, and the knot between her eyebrows went even deeper. She was obviously thinking this through. Then she pushed her chair back and stood. "Okay. Your room or mine?"

Gabe had to consciously shut his mouth. "Okay? You're serious?"

She blinked. "Yeah. Weren't you?"

He stood and walked around the table, took both her hands in his—they were ice cold—and smiled down at her. She was such a tiny thing. "I'm dead serious, Em. I've never been more serious about anything in my life."

"C'mon, then. My room's on this level." She held on to his left hand and tugged him after her. Bemused, Gabe followed, but he made a point of leaving his mobile phone on the table. The last thing he wanted when he was finally buried deep inside Ms. Emeline was a phone call.

...

Okay. She could do this. Maybe. Who the hell was she kidding? Gabe's hand was so big, his fingers curled all the way around her hand, and while she knew that a Chanku bitch could take a very large man, Em hadn't. She'd had sex, but only with human men, and never with a man who was so, so . . . Goddess, there were no words to describe Gabriel Cheval, especially when he was wearing nothing but a worn pair of sweatpants. His chest was bare, dark toffee skin, all sleek and smooth and rippling with muscle, so beautiful she couldn't find the words.

Even though she'd been describing him in her dreams for years. Imagining just this scenario, leading Gabe to her bedroom, knowing they were going to have sex, that he would think she was really beautiful, that he'd profess his undying love for her.

Well, that wasn't going to happen. Yeah, he thought she was hot, but he was a guy. Anything with two legs and a crotch was hot to a Chanku male. She wanted Gabe to be special, but she had the terrible feeling she was getting herself in way too deep with a very nice guy who just wanted to fuck whatever woman was handy.

"That's not fair, Em. And it's not true." He tugged her hand, pulled her to a stop outside her bedroom door and then held her in place with both hands on her shoulders.

"Huh?"

"You're broadcasting. I don't think you want me to know what you're thinking, but I'm glad you gave up those thoughts. I don't want to fuck whoever or whatever's available. I really want to make love with you. You, Em. Not just anyone with two legs and a crotch."

"Oh, Goddess." She covered her face with both hands and didn't know whether to laugh or cry. Heat and cold shot through her; embarrassment heated her face while absolute horror chilled her from the inside out. "I am so sorry, Gabe. I didn't . . ."

"I know you didn't, but I'm glad you did." He choked off a bitter-sounding laugh. "I was thinking you were giving me a pity fuck."

"What? Good Goddess, Gabe. How could you possibly think that?" Flustered, she raised her head and glared at him.

"Em, you're gorgeous. You're smart. You travel all over the world with your job, speak way too many different languages, handle an important part of the company. You protect our workers all over the world through your oversight. I'm a marketing geek. I do most of my work from my office. I'm thirty years old and I've never had a serious relationship. I have no idea where my life is going. And then here you are. The little girl who used to drive me nuts is all grown up, and damn did she grow up

27

good. C'mon. If you'll still have me, I want to find out a little more about Emeline Isobelle."

Still flushed with embarrassment, she nodded, opened the door to her room and stepped inside. The bed was still rumpled and unmade, but at least she'd changed the sheets yesterday, and wasn't that a stupid thing to worry about. She turned her head to gaze over her shoulder, and Gabe was standing there, staring at her with a silly smile on his face.

"What's the matter?"

"I want to take those clothes off you, but I'm not sure where to start. Actually, I'm not sure how to start. I've never done this before."

She laughed so hard she snorted, and it took a minute to get herself under control. "You're trying to tell me you've never had sex?"

"Oh, Goddess, no!" He laughed and wrapped his arms around her. "I'm just saying I've never had sex with someone I've known as a little kid but not as an adult. You're a totally different person than that pesky little EmyIzzy, so it's not at all hard to think of you as Em or Emeline."

"You called me Emy yesterday." She liked the way his arms felt, holding her so comfortably. "I actually like that. It's that Izzy part that drives me nuts."

"I like Emy, too." He leaned close and kissed her, and then lifted his head. His eyes practically sparkled when he added, "I like Emy a hell of a lot." Then he kissed her again.

She wasn't expecting it, the soft flow of his lips over hers, the tentative exploration of his tongue against her mouth, tracing the seam between her lips. She opened for him, welcomed him in, tasting coffee and man, a taste that had to be all Gabe. He pulled her closer against him, so close she felt the heat from his chest and the steady thump of his heart. And something she couldn't ignore—the long, thick length of his erection trapped between them, pressing against her belly.

Something about that hot pressure against her midsection left her feeling like warm wax, all hot and soft and ready for him. She'd never had that overwhelming need for sex that everyone else in the pack seemed to experience. For her it had been the occasional itch she had to scratch, something easier dealt with at home with her favorite toys.

She'd never actually run with the pack. Not since she was a kid. It was difficult, staying away from home, but she'd had a few runs here when the Chanku working in the city had gathered at Mount Tam and run over the forested flanks of the big mountain. When the others had elected to head back to their rooms and screw themselves silly, she'd always avoided that. For whatever reason, it hadn't felt right.

But everything Gabe did felt more than right. It felt wonderful. His hands were under her top, caressing her back, her shoulders, the sides of her breasts. He slipped her T-shirt over her head and they were chest to chest, skin to skin, and her tightly beaded nipples rubbed over the broad expanse of his smooth, muscular chest.

Her breath caught in her throat and it was hard to breathe, hard to absorb all the impressions battering her senses—the sound of each breath rasping in her ear, the air rushing in and out of his lungs as his arousal increased, his heat radiating off his body and the pounding thunder of his heart, the smoothness of his chest and the coarse hair on his arms, the soft glide of his lips and the fierce thrust of his tongue, the sense that he couldn't get enough of her.

That she'd never get enough of him.

Still kissing him, her fingers fluttered over his chest, along the smooth lines of his ribs beneath taut muscle and sleek skin. She'd never explored a man's body before, never imagined that the first one she'd actually touch this intimately would be the man she'd fantasized about since she was a teen. She rasped her thumbs over his nipples, surprised when they beaded up beneath her touch. She was about to do it again when he dipped lower, his arms went under her back and her thighs and he lifted her, still kissing her, holding her against him briefly before carefully laying her on the bed atop the rumpled covers. She'd slept here alone, touching herself, thinking of Gabe. Wondering what it would be like to make love with him. To feel him deep inside, thrusting hard and fast, filling her. Loving her.

She wanted so much. To taste, to experience what every other young woman in the pack already knew—what it was like to make love with one of their own kind.

He wouldn't know he was her first. He couldn't know. It was too embarrassing, and she wasn't about to tell him. He already thought she was different. She could tell by the way he looked at her sometimes, that he just didn't understand why she said what she said, did what she did.

The last thing she wanted to do was give him more reasons to think she was weird, that she wasn't like other women, that . . .

"Okay, Em. What's going on in that pretty head of yours?"

Blinking, she frowned. "What do you mean?"

He grinned at her, or maybe he was just laughing at her. "I mean that all of a sudden, you're a million miles away. Everything was fine, and I thought you were having a good time, but then you sort of went away." He kissed her, but he was too quick for her to kiss him back. "We don't have to do this if you're not comfortable having sex with me. I don't want to push you. I'll never do that."

He brushed her hair back from her face and looked at her with nothing but understanding. How could he be so calm when he was hard as a rock against her thigh? When he'd practically been panting with need mere seconds ago. She'd felt his need, his desire, but now? Now he was all kindness and understanding. He should be more interested in getting inside her, not trying to figure out why she wasn't into whatever he was doing.

And why wasn't she? Goddess, this was so humiliating. She felt the tears filling her eyes, spilling over, and she turned her head away. She couldn't look at him. Didn't want him to see her like this. She was Chanku. They were all supposed to be running around, constantly aroused, always wanting sex, but she wasn't like that. For whatever reason, she'd never been like that. But why?

She'd never enjoyed sex with the human men she'd been with, but she'd always figured that was because they were human and she needed to be with her own kind, but none of the guys here ever interested her at all. None but Gabe, and she couldn't count the nights she'd brought herself off just thinking about him. Imagining him like this, in bed with her, making love to her.

Only, in her dreams he kept going. He wanted her and she wanted him. Without reservations, without any hesitation at all.

And now he was here, and she'd checked out. What the fuck was wrong with her?

4

Gabe eavesdropped on Em's private thoughts without any shame at all. Something was horribly wrong, and he didn't have a clue what it was. She wanted him, wanted to make love with him, and it sounded as if she'd at least had a crush on him for a long time, but he'd felt the shift in her arousal, picked up the change in her scent. When they'd gotten to her room, she'd been more than ready. When he picked her up, placed her on the bed, her mind had locked up for the briefest moment, and then her thoughts had gone off into another place altogether.

"Sweetheart?" He settled himself between her thighs and cupped her face in his hands. She wasn't afraid of him, but for whatever reason, her need, any hint of arousal, had totally disappeared. He sensed nothing from her beyond despair, but why? He nuzzled the soft skin beneath her ear, inhaled the citrusy scent of her shampoo. "I can feel your misery. It's practically radiating from your body, from your mind. Do you have any idea what's wrong? Why you feel this way?"

She shook her head. He knew she wasn't afraid of him, but her lips trembled and he really didn't want to make her cry. He didn't want to force himself on her, so he started to push himself away.

"No!" She wrapped her arms around his neck. "Please, Gabe. Don't give up on me. I don't know why I'm like this. It's never been this bad before, but I want to know what pleasure is. I want to feel what everyone else feels."

"Are you sure?" He kissed her. Just a feather kiss against closed lips, and he pulled away before she had a chance to open to him. "I don't want you to feel pressured into this."

"Well, I'm not going to beg, if that's what you want." She went to push him away, but he grabbed her and rolled to his back with Em astride him. She struggled for a moment, but he held her close and focused on her breasts.

"I will, if that's what it's going to take. Goddess, Em. I never dreamed that pudgy little twerp who used to drive me and the other guys crazy would grow up to be . . . oh, man. He raised his upper body and latched on to her left nipple, sucking and nipping at it, swirling his tongue around the tip.

Arching her back, she cried out. Gabe scooted up against the headboard with Em shivering in his arms, and managed to slip out of his loose sweatpants in the process. He shoved them the rest of the way down with one hand, holding on to Em with the other, his lips still wrapped around her nipple.

He gave it a final lick and went to work on her right breast, sucking, pressing with the flat of his tongue, scraping the sensitive tip with his teeth. Moaning, she thrust against his mouth and lifted up on her knees. He scooted her yoga pants down over her butt and she managed to lift first one leg and then the other out of the loose pants. Gabe tossed them aside.

She was slick and hot against the length of his erection and her fingers fluttered over his chest, but he wasn't ready yet. Not until he was absolutely sure Em wouldn't freak out when he entered her. He flipped her over on her back and knelt between her thighs, but he didn't turn loose of her breast.

She was whimpering now, finally displaying the signs of arousal he'd expected earlier, and there was no way she was faking. Moisture glistened in the dark thatch of hair between her thighs. Her eyes were tightly closed, her full lips curled in a rictus of pain that could only be pleasure. He licked her breast, teasing the nipple before releasing it, but she didn't have time to react before he changed his focus. Gently he stroked between her legs, running his middle finger between her engorged labia, lightly pressing circles against the slick walls of her vagina. She tightened around him, a reflexive action that had him thrusting deeper, a couple of times before dragging his finger free of her silken walls and then circling her clit, barely making contact with that taut little bundle of nerves, his fingertip gliding on a slick layer of her fluids.

He scooted down, kissing her belly, nuzzling the dark hair covering her pubic mound. So many women shaved, but he'd always preferred the more natural, womanly look. Just as he knew how appealing a truly strong woman could be. He sensed that strength in Emeline. For whatever reason, she dealt with ghosts that even she didn't understand, but she wasn't letting them stop her. They weren't stopping Gabe, either. Not if he could help it.

He parted her legs, gently spreading her knees apart, and planted soft kisses against the softer skin of her inner thighs. First the left, then the right. Then back to the left, only higher this time, and again on the right. She was shivering, trembling and clutching at the rumpled sheets when he finally reached his goal. He ran his tongue from her perineum to her vaginal opening, curling the tip against her soft inner walls. The slick tissues actually fluttered against his tongue, so responsive to his touch, rewarding him with more of the taste of her, an undeniable symbol of her arousal.

So far, he was keeping her with him. She'd not gone away this time. Her arousal had become a living, breathing entity, so powerful he felt it looping back at him. He wanted to link, to tie himself into her thoughts, her sensations, but not yet. Not until she was totally lost in the pure carnality of the two of them together. He wondered if she'd let him in, if she'd block his attempt to share what the two of them did together. If she'd not had sex with many guys, he could assume that was something she'd never done before. He didn't want to frighten her. He didn't want to assume too much, either.

Lying prone the full length of the bed, he slipped his hands beneath her buttocks and lifted her to his mouth. Licking and nipping, he lost himself in her exquisite flavors, in the scent and taste of her, the slickness against his tongue, and the clench and release of muscles on the edge of orgasm.

She bucked against his face, and the whimpers and soft little moans had become the background music to every move he made, to every response he wrenched from Emeline. She was so close and it was time. Opening his mind, he sought her out, but there was nothing but a swirling maelstrom of wordless need, as if he'd reached that primitive part of her brain that responded to sensation alone, without conscious thought, without any need to understand, but only to experience. The sense of her was addictive, this level of arousal so far beyond anything he'd expected, and he found himself falling into it.

Falling into Emeline. Her body undulated in his grasp and he flowed with her, holding her in his palms, controlling her with his mouth until he knew he had her, knew she'd reached that pinnacle and there was no going back. He wrapped his lips around her clit and used the tip of his tongue to chase her over the top. Screaming, she arched against him, her body shuddering, her thighs clasping the sides of his head as he continued to lick and taste until she finally relaxed enough to draw a great, shuddering breath.

Gabe didn't give her time to think. He moved forward over her body, sliding his erect cock between her thighs, up against the wet heat between her legs. She was warm and so slick, and he expected his entry to be a simple thing, but she was much smaller than he'd expected. Much tighter.

And instead of a single, slow thrust, he pressed against her gently, with just enough pressure to slowly part her engorged folds, and even more slowly to work his way inside.

She arched her hips, pressing close to help, but he didn't want to hurt her, didn't want what had been a totally pleasurable connection to go south for either of them. "Are you okay, Em? I don't want to hurt you."

"More, Gabe. I want more."

"Put your arms around my neck." She did, and he rolled with her to his back. "Now you're in charge."

She tossed her long hair back and clasped his shoulders, positioning herself over the smooth crown of his cock. Bracing her hands on him, she slowly worked her way down his erection. Very slowly. So damned slow he was afraid he'd lose it before he was all the way in because he'd never felt anything so perfect in his entire life. He was gasping each breath and struggling for control by the time he bottomed out against her cervix and her warm little bottom rested on his thighs.

"Are you okay?" He palmed both her breasts. They were absolutely perfect. Not overly large, but nothing about Emeline was all that big. Except her heart. Damn, but she seemed to have such a strong sense of honor. She honestly cared about people. She was beautiful, she was so not what he'd expected when he'd boarded the plane last night.

"I am." She smiled and ran her fingers through his hair. He kept it short most of the time, but it had grown out over the past couple of months. In fact, he'd not cut it since early in the summer, before he and Jace took off on their annual survey of wild wolves. "I don't think I've ever seen you with hair this long. I like it."

"I was thinking I needed to cut it, but if you like it longer, guess that's something I won't have to worry about."

She cocked her head and frowned at him. "You'd let my opinion sway your decisions?"

She looked so cute when she frowned that he laughed. "Sweetheart, you are currently sitting on my dick and I want to move so badly I ache. At this point I'll do whatever you want."

She snorted. Then she covered her mouth and blushed. "That wasn't very sexy, was it?"

"Actually, it was. It made all your inside muscles tighten around me. I hope you realize you're killing me here."

She wiggled her butt against his thighs and tightened her inner muscles, teasing him. "I think I like the power of this position. I could sit here all day and have you at my mercy."

He wrapped his arms around her and had her under him before she even had time to squeak. "We were discussing mercy?"

"Oh. Yeah." She linked her fingers behind his neck and pulled herself close. Kissed him with a little tongue and a whole lot of hip movement.

"Let's talk about it later." He thrust his hips forward, careful not to hurt her, but her eyes went wide. He did it again, and then again and she got a dreamy look on her face that assured him she wasn't in any pain.

He picked up the rhythm, filling her with every thrust, and then he opened his thoughts once again.

And found absolutely nothing. She was locked so tight that nothing was getting out. "Open to me, Em. Let me feel what you feel. Sense what you sense. You'll get the same from me, I promise. It's the best part about sex, sharing what we experience.

She frowned, but he sensed her thoughts, the gentle stirring in his mind that told him she was trying. Why was it that Em, a woman who'd known from birth that she was Chanku, would have so much trouble knowing how things worked? Something was wrong. Missing, as if she'd missed a whole section of the learning process of who and what she was.

Definitely something to look into, but not now. Now it was all about feeling. About wallowing in the smooth slide between those velvet walls clasping him on every thrust, holding him as he pulled back to drive deep again. He adjusted his angle, trying to hit her clitoris on each advance and retreat, and he felt her arousal growing once again. The good thing about worrying about Em's pleasure was that it helped delay his own. He was still hanging on, still giving her the ride of her life and it was good. It was all good.

And then it got even better as he caught the first tentative contact of her mind with his, the sense of his thick erection sliding within the tight clasp of her vaginal muscles, the fullness that thrilled her so completely. He gave it back to her—the heat with each stroke, as if he plunged into liquid fire, the rippling slide of her powerful inner muscles enclosing him in a solid grip of surprising strength. He shared the feelings he had when her breasts rubbed against his chest and the taste of her flavors on his tongue when he leaned close and drew her nipple into his mouth.

She returned the favor, sharing the shock of sensation from nipple, to womb, to clit when his lips surrounded her nipple and he sucked the tip into his mouth.

All of it, Gabe's sensations and Em's, shared and shared again until there was no ending to Gabe, no beginning to Emeline. Until their thoughts fused in a maelstrom of sensation and texture, of desire and fulfillment. Gabe knew he couldn't last, wouldn't last from that moment when the coil of heat at the base of his spine exploded, encompassing the ache in his balls and the squeezing pressure encircling his cock. He gave it all up to Em, every sensation, every bit of touch and reaction, of arousal and need and the lightning-fast journey from impending orgasm to completion.

Em screamed and her back arched as she forced him even deeper. Her mental climax was a veritable firestorm of color, of heat and light and pulsing shadows and stars, shared with Gabe, as she hovered for one brief moment on the precipice.

But when they leapt, what should have been light and completion, a sense of the sublime, was scarred by darkness. By a roiling cloud that followed Em over the top and buried her in the deepest shadows of despair.

He lay on top of her, gasping for air, holding her close, protecting her from whatever that thing was that seemed to intrude on her climax. On his. A dark shadow unlike anything he'd ever experienced, but he'd also known this was something Em lived with. Something she'd always lived with, or at least for as long as she could remember.

He wrapped his arms around her and rolled to his back, taking her with him. She trembled against him, and he wondered if it was fear or the aftermath of what had been—up to the intrusion of that dark something—a most remarkable sexual and emotional experience.

• • •

She couldn't look at him, wouldn't look. It had been so perfect. Everything she'd ever dreamed, better than she possibly could have imagined. What she'd always thought of as okay sex didn't even rate as bad sex compared to what Gabe had just shown her, what he'd shared with her. It had been absolutely perfect, until the darkness.

Obviously there was something terribly wrong with her. Something that must have disgusted Gabe. He still hadn't said a word. Hadn't done anything but cover her with his big body, pressing her into the tumbled blankets so perfectly that he made her feel safe even when she knew she wasn't. That she hadn't been for a long time. Would most likely never be, but why? What was the darkness that haunted her? What it the reason her parents were so overprotective?

Gabe nuzzled the sensitive spot beneath her right ear and then kissed her cheek. "I hope you realize things can't go on the way they were."

She froze. Had it been that awful for him? Was she that awful, with her mind suffused in some unknown . . .

"Because I am not letting you go. Ever."

He rose up on his forearms and kissed her, but her mouth was open in shock and he took the kiss so much deeper than she knew he must have intended, but that didn't stop her from kissing him back, even though her mind was absolutely flooded with questions.

"What do you mean? That darkness in my mind. You had to feel it. It's always there, it's . . ."

"It's something we're going to fix if it's the last thing we do."

He cupped her face in his big hands and forced her to look at him. His dark amber eyes sparkled, and he had that sexy little half smile on his lips, and Goddess but his lips were sexy. Warmth surged between her legs and all her internal muscles clenched. All from Gabe's smile.

Well, that and the realization that he was growing hard again, still locked deep inside her where she could feel the subtle stretching as his arousal made itself known. Except she didn't want to be sidetracked. Not now. "How, Gabe? How can we fix something if we can't know what causes it?"

"We ask Eve." He kissed her nose.

"Eve's busy. She's a goddess, Gabe. We can't ask her stuff like that."

"Why not? Lily does, and she gets answers."

"Well, Lily's special. She also goes on the astral and has some sort of weird celestial wine and catches up on gossip with Eve because they're friends."

"Weird celestial wine?" He cocked an eyebrow and thrust his hips forward at the same time. "What brand is that? And what's the vintage? Astral date nine billion and twelve?"

"Ah!" She lifted her hips on a gasp of pleasure. How could he carry on a conversation when he was doing that? "Does it honestly matter? Oh . . . Gabe! Again . . ."

It was some time later when she was near her third orgasm of the morning that Gabe linked with her. She wasn't sure if it was a very smart idea, but what he was doing felt so damned good that she let herself go. Shared the sense of his rigid cock plunging deep and hard, the amazing shock of contact as he slid across her sensitized clit. This time she would see what was behind the darkness, discover what horrible thing lay hidden in her subconscious, rising up when she was vulnerable, when her defenses were down.

She felt the crest of pleasure rising, opened herself to whatever it brought, though she knew the darkness was there, knew it would somehow taint the sweetness of Gabe's loving. As she reached her peak and flew, the shadow leapt with her and so did Gabe, but he wasn't lost in sensation. Fascinated even as her body convulsed in pleasure, Em saw the darkness fade beneath a glowing light.

Gabe's light, pushing it back into the corners, lighting the darkness and rendering it powerless, shrinking it back to nothing more than a pinprick of impotent fear. Nameless fear, ineffectual for the moment, but not gone. No, it waited. If only she knew what it was, where it came from.

Why it waited.

Blinking against dawn's sunlight streaming between the window blinds, Em stared up at Gabe, lost in a sense of absolute disbelief. She'd seen it but still couldn't describe what he had done. Yet, whatever it was, she felt lighter, freer than she'd been for as long as she could recall.

"What did you do? You sent it away, whatever it was."

"Is. It's still there, but smaller. Weaker." He rolled off her and scooted back against the headboard. Then he easily lifted Em, pulled her up against his side and tucked her within the curve of his arm.

She snuggled close and wrapped her arm across his chest. "But what happened?"

"A long time ago, I asked Jace if he could teach me to heal injuries the way he does, going inside a person's body as pure energy and fixing what's broken." Gabe laughed and kissed the top of her head. "Let's just say it's a good thing you're not bleeding anywhere, because no matter what he tried to show me, I couldn't do it. But I remembered something he said, that sometimes what needs to be done to fix something that's wrong isn't at all complicated. It's common sense—following your gut instinct to do what feels right. Whatever it is in your mind that's messing you up is dark. I mean it's physically dark and noxious-looking, and no, I haven't got a clue what it is, but I figured that if it's dark, maybe all we need is light."

He shrugged and kissed the crown of her head. "It seemed to work. It didn't make it go away entirely, but I'm hoping it won't pop up next time we make love. Which reminds me. Did that feel as good for you as it did for me? Good Goddess, Em. I'm never going to see you as little EmyIzzy again."

"Well, that's certainly good to know. It's about time." She felt his chest vibrate under her arm as he chuckled.

"I agree. Ain't gonna happen. I'm a true convert to the new and improved adult Emeline Isobelle Cheval." He rolled over and kissed her again. She kissed him back but then she got the giggles. "Three times before breakfast, Gabe? You'll keel over from exhaustion and starvation."

"But don't you want to test what we just did? Make sure it holds for a while?"

Before she could answer him, Em heard Gabe's mobile phone chirping in the other room. "Hold that thought," he said, heading for the kitchen.

And didn't that man have a truly fine ass. Grinning, Em rolled over on her back and stared at the ceiling. This wasn't at all what she'd expected when she realized it was Gabriel getting off the plane. Not at all.

5

Gabe recognized Alex's ringtone, so he grabbed the mobile phone and flipped it to face view. "Hey, man. Why are you calling at the crack of dawn?"

"Crack of dawn? It's after seven. Annie and I want to know what's going on. Is Em awake?"

"She is now." Gabe laughed and thought of carrying the phone with its camera into the bedroom, but figured that might not go over all that well. "Why don't you guys come on over. We'll figure out something for breakfast."

"Sounds good. Twenty minutes?"

"Works." He saw Annie peeking over Alex's shoulder. "Hey, Annie. You still hanging out with this loser?"

"It's a tough job, Gabe. A struggle, but I manage. See you in a bit."

"She's got your number, Alex. You're a beaten man."

Alex glanced over his shoulder and sighed. "Yeah. Isn't it great?"

Laughing, Gabe ended the connection. Twenty minutes. He wondered if he and Em might just . . . she stepped into the kitchen, still all tousled and sexy, and wasn't this how their morning began a little over an hour ago? "Hey, Em. Alex and Annie will be over in about twenty minutes. Do you think we . . . ."

She burst out laughing. "No. Why did I know you were going to ask me that. I'm going to get a shower. Make some more coffee, okay? And check the GPS."

"Yes, ma'am." Grinning broadly, he saluted, but he watched her leave the kitchen, admiring the curve of her perfect butt and the way her hair swung against her naked back with each step. Only after she'd moved out of view did he follow her into the bedroom and grab his sweats. He pulled

39

them on and went back to the kitchen to check the GPS. Sissy was still in the same location. By the time Em was out of the shower and drying her hair over the floor heater, Gabe had bacon frying, the griddle heating, and pancake batter mixed. Alex and Annie arrived a few minutes later.

Even though Alex was a couple years older than Gabe and Jace, they'd all hung out together when they were kids. They'd been like any regular pack of boys, except all had the ability to become predators. All kinds of predators. Gabe often wondered how their parents had handled such a precocious group, but from a kid's viewpoint, it had been a charmed childhood. Aaron Cheval, Em's brother, had been one of their pack, along with Mac, Gabe's twin, Jack Temple and Connor Trent. All great friends and good, solid adults.

Of all of them, Connor had been the first to take a mate when he'd fallen hard and fast for Jack's little sister, Andrea Temple. They'd both still been in college, but Connor said that one day he looked at Andrea and knew she was the one. Alex and Annie had rediscovered one another this past summer around the same time Gabe's sister Lily had met Sebastian. Lily and Seb had married shortly after mating, but Lily'd never been one to mess around when there was something she wanted.

She'd obviously wanted Sebastian, but that had turned out to be an amazing match. Just like Jace Wolf and Romy Sarika. The whole group was beginning to pair off, though Alex and Annie were still holding back on the wedding. Annie's dad made no bones about the fact he wanted to walk his baby girl down the aisle, which seemed to be the only reason Annie'd refused to set a date. One more way, Gabe figured, for Annie to wrest control from her often overbearing but much-loved father. Alex didn't seem to care one way or the other. He and Annie were bonded mates and he obviously adored her.

Gabe finished making pancakes while Em filled Alex and Annie in on Sissy's story. "So that's it, for now," she said. "Sissy is still in the same place, and once we have breakfast we're going to see if we can get close enough to mindspeak with her. She's got the nutrients and it shouldn't be too much longer before she can shift. That might come in handy when we're ready to stage a rescue."

"So today, we're only verifying where they're being kept?" Annie clutched Alex's hand. She'd been held captive by Sebastian Xenakis's father for a brief time, slated to be a blood sacrifice until Alex and Sebastian led a rescue and saved her life. "I hate thinking of her being held against her will. Of any of those women being held."

Alex raised their linked hands and kissed Annie's knuckles. "We'll get them out, sweetheart. But Em's right. We don't want to rush it and risk any of them getting hurt."

"I know." She sighed. "I know you're right. That doesn't mean I have to like it." This time, Alex kissed her temple.

Gabe's heart sort of did a little flip, and he wondered how it would be to have Em depend on him the way Annie obviously needed and trusted Alex. He glanced at her and caught Em staring at him. The moment he caught her gaze, she blushed and looked away. Grinning, he took a sip of his coffee, but he was smiling at himself as much as he was at Emeline.

The concept of finding a mate hadn't even been on his radar until this summer, when he'd watched Jace and Romy fall in love. In the beginning, from his point of view as an outsider looking in, it had been fascinating, but removed from anything remotely connected to his life. Then, as the two had grown closer, he'd seen the changes in Jace, a friend he had always admired—a man he admired even more, now.

Gabe had wondered how he would feel if there was a woman in his life. Not anyone in particular, just some nebulous female of his imagination, but still a woman who might love him as much as Romy loved Jace.

One he might love and want to protect the way Jace was with Romy, or Alex with Annie. The change in his thinking this morning was huge, and it was going to take some adjustment, but suddenly his nebulous, imaginary female had a face. She had a personality, and a beautiful smile, and a body that raised his temperature to boiling.

Best of all, she had a name, and it was Emeline.

• • •

Alex and Annie cleaned up the kitchen, and Em got the beds made while Gabe took a quick shower, but it wasn't easy, keeping her mind off naked Gabe, especially while she was making his bed and fighting her inner wolf's feral desire to roll in the sheets he'd slept in. It was even worse when she made her own bed, ripe with the scent of their lovemaking.

In fact, it was a relief to load everyone in her little SUV, even if it meant listening to the guys complain about the tight fit while she drove across town to the financial district and CGI headquarters. After Em parked in the company lot, the four of them headed toward the apartment complex near the Embarcadero where the GPS signal had remained fairly constant.

They found benches in a small park beneath the apartment window. They'd agreed that Gabe would make contact, but all of them were linked with him when he called out to Sissy.

Gabe? I hear you. Where are you?

In the park, hopefully below your window. Can you look out and show me? There are four of us—Em and me, and our friends Alex and Annie. We're sitting on a couple of benches. Are all of the women there?

No. Russo took Janine, one of the girls, out early this morning. I don't know where. Gabe, I took the pill last night, but I think I'm allergic to it. My arms are itching like crazy today.

That was fast—and it's not an allergy. It means you're very close to shifting. You must have been close when you were captured. Just not close enough.

Oh. I had no idea. What do you want me to do?

Open your curtains, do something to show us where you are. The locator is not as precise as we'd like, but it got us this far.

"There." Em pointed to a window south of where they were sitting. Sissy had stepped outside onto a balcony, but she didn't do anything to show that she recognized them. She glanced their way, then quickly went back inside.

I hear someone coming. Don't let them see you, Gabe. If it's Russo, he'll recognize you.

We're going. Be strong, Sissy. Before we leave, I want you to meet Alex and Annie. They don't live far from here, possibly close enough to hear you should you call on them.

Hi, Sissy. I'm Alex Aragat, Annie is my mate.

Hi, Sissy. I'm Annie. Can you hear us clearly?

I can. How do I contact you?

Gabe answered. *Think our names and if we're within range, we'll hear you. Right now you're not blocking, and that's a good thing. Once we have you safe, we'll teach you how to conceal your private thoughts, but for now we need to be able to hear you should you need us. Don't worry, though. We won't snoop.*

He's here. I'm pretending to sleep.

Okay. If all of you are together at any time today, no matter how many of the men are there, let us know. And if you can, picture the inside of the apartment and where all of you are. We can see those images in your mind.

Okay. But not now. I can't talk to you and act normal with them. I'm sorry.

Don't be sorry. You're doing amazingly well. Be safe.

They headed back toward CGI with Em and Annie leading. The guys walked behind them, almost as if they kept guard. It was a new feeling for Em. A safe feeling. She glanced once more at the balcony where Sissy'd been standing moments ago. "She is so brave," she said. "She's been their captive for over five years, forced into prostitution, treated as nothing more than a commodity. I really admire her. I don't think I could ever be that brave."

Annie frowned, stopped walking and took both of Em's hands in hers. "Em? How can you say that? You are brave. What you did when we were kids? That took amazing courage."

"What I did? What are you talking about?" Em shuddered, but she didn't know why. She remembered her mom saying that when you shivered for no reason, there really was a reason. Someone was walking over your grave. But that was stupid, because if you were alive, you didn't have a grave. At least not yet.

Annie shot a quick glance at Alex, who merely shrugged, and then frowned at Gabe, who shook his head. "Don't any of you remember?" She stared at Em. "It happened when you were fourteen, the year that man snatched you from the mall in Kalispell. He held you for two days, I think. He was a serial rapist and everyone knew he'd taken you because they had the video from the mall security cameras."

"What? What in the hell are you talking about?" She didn't mean to sound so confrontational, but for whatever reason, Annie's stupid story scared the crap out of her. Shaking her head, denying it with everything she had, Em said, "Impossible, Annie. That never happened. Believe me, if something like that had happened to me, I'd remember, don't you think?" She pulled her hands free of Annie's as she laughed it off and started to walk away, but Gabe's hand on her shoulder stopped her.

"Annie, what do you remember about it?"

He guided them over to another couple of benches at the far end of the park. They'd almost walked out of the green space, but now Em was glad to have a place to sit. Somehow, what Annie was saying felt so wrong, almost as if it fed that darkness in her mind.

Annie glanced at the guys before she said anything, which struck Em as weird. The whole idea of telling a story that had to be a lie was weird, but she figured she'd have to listen, since Gabe and Alex definitely intended to.

Annie stared off in the distance. Gathering her thoughts for certain, but was it to make up a story or remember something that actually happened? Again, that unexpected shiver raced over Em's arms, down her spine.

Annie glanced at Em and shrugged. "For what it's worth," she said, "it feels very strange to be telling this story to you, Em. I find it so hard to believe you don't remember this. Anyway, four of us had gone to the mall. It was twelve years ago, in late winter. February, I think, and it was cold and snowy and we were all bored because it was too cold even for our wolves, so none of us had been out to run. It was you and me and Phoenix Wolf and Gabe's little sister Lucia. I was older, nineteen then, so I was the token grown-up. My job was to keep an eye on the three of you.

Your dad dropped us off. He had some errands to run, so he said he'd be back in a couple of hours. I was hungry and went to the food court, but you and Phoenix wanted to look at a couple of stores. They were in the same mall and you had your phones, and we were all perfectly capable of mindspeaking for a lot farther than the length of the mall, so I didn't think anything of letting the two of you go shop together. Neither one of you ever got into trouble. Ever. Anyway, Luci and I went to get lunch and you and Phoenix took off to check out some clothing shops."

Em shook her head. It felt like Annie was talking about a complete stranger. She didn't remember any of this. Not a bit. She shot a quick look at Gabe, but he merely shrugged and hugged her close against his side.

"Anyway, about two hours later, Phoenix caught up with Luci and me, and she was so pissed off at you. Said some hot guy had been talking to the two of you, and the next thing she knew, you'd taken off with him. She said she'd hung out, waiting for you to get back, but you never showed up, and that's when she came looking for Luci and me because it was almost time for your dad to pick us up."

"Annie, I don't remember any of this." Em realized she'd grabbed Annie's hands, and she had to force herself to let go, but she was having trouble catching her breath. It was like hearing a story about a person she didn't even know, but it terrified her. "What happened?"

"We couldn't find you, so I called your dad. He got there minutes later. I told him we'd lost you. He tried mindspeaking—we'd already tried—but you didn't answer. Anton showed up a couple of minutes later—Luci had called him. He and your dad shifted into their wolves and tried following your scent, but it disappeared in the parking lot, so we knew you'd been taken somewhere in a vehicle, but there was no sign of you. Nothing. We searched everywhere. Tala, AJ and Mik did a full Pack Dynamics–style search, but they didn't have any luck, either. The security camera showed you getting into a dark van without any plates, but there was no way to identify it, and even though the cops did an all-points, no one saw it. Then two days after you disappeared, you showed up on the front porch at Anton and Keisha's house in your leopard form, with your coat all covered in blood."

Annie took a deep breath and squeezed Em's hand. "Only it wasn't your blood."

Em sucked in a harsh breath. Why didn't she remember any of this? Her heart thundered in her chest and her toes and fingers felt numb. Frantically, she glanced from Annie to Gabe, then at Alex, who shrugged. "I was away at college. I remember hearing something about you that was bad, but none of the details. Gabe?"

"Not a word." He kissed the top of Em's head and nuzzled close against her dark hair. "I never even heard she'd been taken. I can't believe Luci's never said anything. She can't keep a secret from me about anything, and Lily's never said a word, either."

Em rubbed her hands together, chilled to the bone. Granted, it was early December, not yet noon, but San Francisco's winters were often warmer than average summer temps. It was already in the high fifties, and she shouldn't feel this cold. This frightened. "I don't remember any of this. None of it." She turned and faced Gabe. "Why don't I remember? No one's ever mentioned it; no one has said a word to me. But look at me." She held up her hands, both of them visibly trembling. "My body remembers. My brain doesn't. Why?"

But it explained so much. So much about the way her parents treated her, the way they were so overprotective. They'd made her life unbearable in their misguided efforts to protect her, but why had they kept it secret in the first place? And how? You didn't just wipe away someone's memories, so why didn't she remember? She should remember, damn it!

Gabe tightened his arm around Em and held her close. "Do you recall anything else, Annie? Did they find the guy?"

Annie nodded. "I remember Mom calling me. I was already back at school, but she called to tell me when they found his body about a week later. We'd had an early thaw and the weather had turned unseasonably warm. His landlord noticed the smell when he went to check on the rental because the guy hadn't paid his rent. I didn't get all the details from Mom, but there was an article in the paper that said it appeared he'd been gutted, but there was so much decomposition by then, the coroner couldn't tell if it was an animal attack or just a pissed-off bad guy."

Gabe squeezed Em's hand. She felt as if she moved through air thick as mud when she turned and stared at him. This all felt so terribly wrong. Unbelievable, and yet there was no reason not to believe what Annie was telling her.

Gabe brushed her hair back and cupped her face in his palms. "I imagine we can find the stories in the newspaper online. We'll look for archives from that month when we get home, okay?"

She nodded, but she couldn't help thinking that she didn't want to know. That whatever she discovered was going to be so terrible that it could destroy her. But Annie was still telling her story, and Em focused again on her voice as Gabe pulled her even closer against his side, protecting her. But from what? From the truth? She needed to know the truth, no matter how much it hurt.

"Anyway, there was evidence in the guy's rental. A lot of it, linking him to more than a dozen rapes and murders over the preceding couple of years, all since he'd moved to the area, so his death solved a lot of cold cases, and even some recent ones. I was already back at college and went on with my life, but it's funny, now that I think of it, that nobody ever mentioned it." She tilted her head and frowned at Gabe. "Didn't Luci ever say anything to you?"

"Not a word. This is the first I've heard of it. And as gossipy as our packmates can be, I'm absolutely stunned that we've never heard it come up. But Em?"

She raised her head. Stunned wasn't the word for it. She was beyond stunned. "What?"

"This might explain the darkness. Once we get Sissy out of this mess here, we need to take her to Montana and turn her over to the moms to get her straightened out. And once she's in good shape, I think we need to get your parents and mine and sit them down for a long, serious talk."

"Why your parents, Gabe? Mine are the ones who have to be lying to me. Keeping the truth from me."

"Yeah, but this has Anton Cheval written all over it. I have a strong feeling that whatever happened to you was buried, maybe even wiped from your memory, but your parents couldn't have done that alone."

"Your dad could have?"

Gabe nodded. "Damn right he could."

• • •

They walked over to the Marina District, where Alex and Annie were living in Lily's old house. It had originally belonged to Ulrich Mason, and a number of different packmates had lived there over the years. Gabe kept Em close against his side. Her silence worried him, but so did Annie's story. The implications of some kind of horrific cover-up had his Dad's name written all over it.

But his mom would never have agreed to something like this, wiping a person's mind of a memory. Possibly wiping the minds of the other kids involved as well. Could Anton have done such a horrible thing to his own daughter? Did Luci have any memories of what had happened when Em disappeared?

Gabe's stomach was tied into knots. He felt absolutely sick, not only for his father's possible involvement but for what this was doing to Em. He cared about her. He'd always cared, but not like this. Not at a level that had him wanting to take her pain. Wanting to hold her and make the darkness go away.

He knew he could do it. He'd done it this morning, but that was only temporary. Somehow, this was something that was going to take a much bigger fix to make it all better. They were almost to Alex and Annie's house on Marina. It had been a quiet, thoughtful trek from the small park to this broad avenue with the view of the bay, but he sensed Emeline's disquiet. Her thoughts were blocked to him, her natural shields strengthened by an obvious need for privacy while she worked her way through what had to be a horribly traumatic search for memories somehow stolen from her. Horrific memories, possibly taken to protect her, but memories that should have been hers. No matter how awful, no matter how traumatic, Em had a right to her past.

Especially since she had obviously survived some horrible, life-altering event. She was a beautiful, intelligent, and strong woman, but if her past had been stolen, those trying to keep her safe had done as much damage as the man who had kidnapped her. Not only had they taken away the fear, they'd taken that part of her strong enough to survive something terrible. Strong enough, it appeared, to kill the one who had hurt her.

Something like that was not only terrible, it was also life-affirming. Chanku were predators by nature. Strong, powerful predators, capable of killing to protect those they loved, and just as capable of killing to protect themselves. Obviously, Em had displayed that predatory nature, and rather than celebrate it, she'd been separated from it. The memories were either buried or destroyed, but taking that away from her was like amputating part of who and what she was. No wonder she had such a hard time opening to anyone.

Opening to Gabe. Part of her past was missing, and along with the evil that had been done to her, whoever had tried to help her had destroyed a very large part of who and what Emeline Isobelle Cheval truly was.

If his father was behind this, he needed to know that what he did was wrong. And then, somehow, they all had to figure out a way to fix what Anton had broken.

• • •

Taking the few broad steps up to Alex and Annie's front door, Em realized she couldn't remember the walk she'd made to get here at all. She knew she had to have walked many blocks, but it was all lost in her swirling thoughts, in her fruitless search for memories.

If what Annie said was true, Emeline had been involved in something horrible. Probably raped, at the very least assaulted and molested. But, and she had to believe this was the most important part, she had overcome her attacker, killed him, and made her escape. She, Emeline Isobelle, had done that. By herself. She'd never imagined herself as a woman strong enough to survive something truly awful, but she had. And instead of holding on to those memories, as awful as they were, she'd had them stolen from her. It was like stripping her of the most important part of who she was—a woman brave enough, strong enough, to survive something beyond awful.

And she'd still been a child. Deep inside, she was more than she'd ever dreamed. Stronger, smarter, willing and able to fight for her life. Able to kill someone truly evil. She was more like Sissy than she'd imagined. Strong like Annie. She'd always known she was Chanku, but she'd felt as if she never measured up, that she didn't have what it took to be a true member of the pack.

But she did and she was proud of herself, damn it.

But was she strong enough to face her parents? They paused at the front door. Alex and Annie had already gone inside, but Em turned and gazed at Gabriel, and in his eyes saw compassion, maybe love, and definitely admiration. "I can do this." She stood on her toes to reach his mouth and kissed him. "But I want you beside me when we face our parents. They might try lying to me, but they won't, not with you there."

"I'll be there whether you want me or not, Em." He chuckled and rubbed his nose against hers. "I wouldn't miss this for the world. I always thought you were such a tough little thing. Now I know you are. What they did to you was wrong. Obviously, we don't know for sure whose idea it was or if my father was actually instrumental in wiping your memories, but no matter who was responsible, don't forget that what they did was wrong."

He ran his fingers through her hair, brushed it back from her face, and stared at her for the longest time. Then he rested both hands on her shoulders and gave her a light squeeze. "You need to meet Romy Sarika," he said. "Jace's mate. She lived through hell for most of her life, but surviving it is what made her the woman she is today. Believe me, she's tough. So are you, but you've been handicapped by whatever was taken away. It may be a painful process, bringing those memories back, but I want all of you. Whole and complete, memories and experiences that are good or bad. Everything that makes you the woman you are."

She was smiling when they finally entered the house. She wasn't certain Gabe even realized what he'd said, or if he meant the words the way she heard them, but he'd said he wanted her. All of her, whole and complete.

Which was exactly the way she wanted Gabriel Cheval.

• • •

Sissy crawled back into bed after the four shapeshifters left the park. Her arms itched but she forced herself not to scratch. The last thing she needed was for Russo or any of the other men to question why she had a rash, and as long as she didn't scratch, nothing showed.

But she was different. So different, knowing who and what she was. She'd felt like a victim for so long, but now she knew better. She was stronger, smarter, more powerful than any of the men here. Even stronger than the women, but that meant it was up to her to keep them safe.

Once she could shift, then all bets were off. And she had people willing to help her. That was the best thing of all, the fact there were people like her, ready to help.

Sissy? Can you hear me? It's Annie. We're home now, and I wanted to make sure we could still connect.

Yes! She kept her eyes closed and had to concentrate on not grinning like an idiot, but she heard Annie fine. *I can hear you. Janine is still gone and I hear at least two of the men in the other room. Sounds like they're watching a movie. There are four altogether. Russo's still gone, then there's Jengo, Ralph, and Kamon. I'm not sure who's in the other room.*

Can you look around your room, maybe go out to the other parts of the apartment and look at things like the front door, the kitchen, that sort of thing, even the men, so we get an idea what we're up against. You don't need to speak to me. Look at your surroundings. Alex, Gabe and Em are in the link, and they'll see what you see. We need to know what we're dealing with.

Yeah. I can do that. I'll go make coffee, see if the guys want any.

Good. We're with you.

She got out of bed and grabbed her robe. Janine's bed next to hers was still empty and Russo was still gone, but Jengo and Kamon were in front of the flat screen watching stuff blowing up. Ralph, as usual, sat by himself near the front door. He always made her nervous. She'd noticed that Russo never left him alone with any of the women. She'd never seen Ralph do anything weird, but he had scary eyes, a frightening sense about him that made her skin crawl.

Like it wasn't crawling enough already. She went to the kitchen and, as she'd figured, the coffeepot was empty. "Hey, any of you guys want coffee?"

"Yeah. I want some." Kamon raised his hand.

Jengo just laughed. "Me, too, as long as Kamon's not making it. I value the enamel on my teeth."

"What enamel? That brown stuff?"

Jengo punched him. "Turd."

"Dipshit."

Ignoring them, Sissy grabbed the can of ground coffee and measured it out, but she made a point of looking around the kitchen, noting the second door into a hallway, the size of the room, the front door, barely visible on the other side of the living room.

Once the coffee was brewing, she went through the second door and walked down the hall to another bedroom, stuck her head in the partially open door and focused on Lindy, who was still asleep with her face covered in her wild mass of red curls. She slept all wrapped up with her girlfriend, Nina, whose hair was as straight and black as Lindy's was red and curly. They loved each other and worked as a team—there were a lot of men willing to pay more than double for two women.

The next door was Mary and Mbali's room. Mary still slept with the covers over her head—she hadn't adjusted well to her abduction a year ago. The continual trauma had left her almost childlike in her willingness to please, hoping that if she behaved she'd get to go home. All Sissy knew about her was that Mary called a little town in Indiana home, and the way girls got used up in this city, she'd always thought it was a good bet she'd never make it back.

Except now she had a chance.

None of the men lived here. Just six attractive young women who rarely saw their neighbors. They were quiet, respectful, always dressed nicely. Never flashy, nothing that looked at all cheap, though they were definitely sexy. Acceptably sexy. Sissy doubted that anyone in the entire complex realized they were sex slaves, hired out to the guys with cash. Held here by armed men who obviously worked for someone, somewhere, with a lot of power. A lot of money, and the political strength to get away with something this terrible.

She went back to the kitchen for a cup of coffee and then returned to her room. Hopefully, Janine would be home soon. With any luck, today might be the day she escaped from hell. She called out to Annie, to Alex, Em and Gabe. *Will that help you? You've seen the entire apartment and all the girls except Janine. She's due back in a couple of hours. That's when all six of us should be here at the same time, but not for long. We're rarely all here at once.*

Gabe answered. *We'll be ready, Sissy. Are you okay?*

I am. I'm alone in my room and the door is shut. I think I'm going to try and shift. Can you show me how?

This time Annie answered. *I'll do it. Concentrate on me, and I'll show you exactly what to do.*

She heard Em's soft laughter. *Don't forget to get naked first, or you'll tear your clothes. And take off any jewelry, because it will fall off. Got it?*

Got it.

6

It was actually funny, when Sissy thought about it later, how simple it had been to shift. The hard part was not charging out into the other room and attacking the three bastards guarding them. Instead, she paced around the room for a while and then thought to stand in front of the mirrored closet doors.

This first sight of herself, standing tall and proud on four long legs, was utterly fascinating, outshining even her wildest dreams. She was absolutely beautiful. Beyond beautiful with her pale gray coat outlined in black, with what looked like hints of reddish brown across her snout and mixed into her dark ruff. Her color vision was altered in this form, but color didn't matter. Not when she was so big and strong, when her teeth were sharp and white and her muscles rippling with power. She wagged her tail, a thick plume of dark hair along the top and almost pure white on the underside. It reminded her of a flag, but she realized it was also part of her voice, a means of communication. Fascinating. Absolutely fascinating.

She heard the front door open, heard Russo's gravelly voice, and she'd shifted back to her human self before she had time to think about it. She was under the covers, feigning sleep, when Janine opened the door and entered the room.

Sissy opened her eyes and grimaced. Janine had a horrible bruise across the left side of her face. Scooting up in bed, she grabbed her cup of lukewarm coffee and took a swallow. "What happened? Russo didn't . . . ?"

"No. It was the john. Ugly brute wanted to pass me around to his buddies, do some two on one. I said no, that he'd paid for one girl, one guy, and he got mad and hit me. Russo didn't show up until four of the

51

jerks fucked me, three at once with the john cheering. Turns out he got off on watching, not fucking. Russo beat the crap out of the guy and scared the rest of them off, but not before relieving them of some extra cash. Of course, I'll never get any of it, but it was nice to see the bastards get their nuts kicked in. They won't be screwing anyone for a while. Russo's got a mean kick."

"He's still a bastard." Sissy got out of bed and went into the bathroom, rinsed a washcloth in cold water and brought it back out. Folding it into a neat square, she said, "What do you want to bet he waited until the others had fucked you so he could get their money."

"You're probably right." Janine was stripping out of her clothes. "I need a shower. Have to wash their stink off me."

"Here. Put this on your eye first. That looks awful. Girl, we gotta get out of here."

"How? And go where?" She sat on the bed and stared at Sissy. "I wasn't like you, going to college, a chick with plans. I was living on the street, pullin' tricks, barely making it. There's nothing for me. Sometimes I wonder why I even try."

"You try because there is something for you. Something better. Go get a shower. You'll feel better. Any idea what the guys have planned for us today?"

Janine gazed at her out of one piercing blue eye. She held the cool cloth over the other half of her face. "Russo said he wants us all hanging around here for the day. There's some big convention in town tonight and he's got us all working, except for you. He said that rich dude that hired you last night wants you again tonight." She laughed, a bitter, sad sound. "If he's got any lonely friends, give 'em my name."

"You got it. Get a shower. I'm already cleaned up, but I need to get dressed."

Sissy watched as Janine closed the bathroom door behind her. *Gabe? All six of us are here. We'll probably be together for at least a couple more hours, but come soon if you can. We're rarely all here at the same time. There are four men—the three who were here earlier, and Russo's back.*

We're already close. Wear something you can get out of fast in case you need to shift. Annie's going to knock on the door—if anyone but you answers, she's going to be looking for her old friend Sissy. I want you out in the front room because she's going to recognize you and waltz on in, maybe flirt with one of the guys, hopefully get their attention long enough for the three of us to barge in and disarm them. The only weapons I saw were the rifle leaning against the door and the handgun tucked into Ralph's waistband.

Russo might be carrying, but Ralph is definitely the scariest. Kamon and Jengo are good with martial arts and they're fast. Be careful. A couple of the girls might still be asleep. Janine just got back—she's got a bad bruise on her face. Her john hit her and then passed her around to his buddies.

Is she okay?

She's tough. We all are. She'll be fine.

We're in the hallway. Go out to the front room.

I'm there. "Hey, Russo. What happened to Janine? Her face is a mess."

He sneered at her, looked her up and down as if he could see right through the robe she'd put back on. "The bitch was asking for it."

Sissy stared at him for a long moment. "None of us asked for any of this." Then she walked past him into the kitchen and filled her coffee cup. She heard someone knock on the door. Anyone coming to the door was a rarity, so it was perfectly natural for her to walk back into the living room.

Russo jerked his head toward the door. "See who that is and get rid of them."

She set her coffee cup down and walked over to the door just as the doorbell rang.

"I said, get rid of them." Russo stood right behind her.

Sissy opened the door, and Annie stood there with a bright smile on her face. She wore a sweater that looked like it had been glued to her body, and jeans that were just as snug.

When she saw Sissy, Annie squealed and jumped into her arms. "Sissy! I heard you might live here. Ohmygod, I haven't seen you in like forever." She stepped back and held on to Sissy's arms. "I've missed you so much. You just disappeared. It was like you'd never existed!"

Before Sissy had a chance to answer, Russo shoved in front of her, separating the two of them. "Who's your friend, Sissy?"

Annie wasn't deterred. She reached around Russo and grabbed Annie's hand, managing to get herself further inside while still standing in the doorway so the door couldn't be closed.

Sissy held on to Annie and refused to turn her loose. "Annie and I grew up together."

Annie flashed a big smile at Russo. "So, who's the good-lookin' hunk, Sissy? Is he the reason you've disappeared off the face of the earth?"

Russo immediately preened like an overstuffed rooster. Annie leaned out the open doorway, still holding Sissy's hand. "Alex! Em, come see who I found."

Kamon and Jengo had come to their feet. Ralph stayed in his chair, but he had his hand on his hip, much too close to the gun he carried. Grinning like an idiot, Sissy tried to block the men behind her as she warned the others. *Kamon and Jengo are right behind me. Ralph's still in his chair by the door, but his hand is on the pistol in his belt holster.*

Alex and Em barged through the open door like they owned the place. Alex grabbed Sissy up in a hug and twirled her around, and that's when Sissy noticed the huge brown and gold wolf beside Em. He walked straight over to Ralph and sniffed his hand, wagging his tail as if he approved of the odd little man. Ralph actually smiled and reached out to pat the wolf's head.

"That's the biggest damned dog I ever saw."

Gabe's voice burst into Sissy's head. *Sissy, on the count of three, shift and take out Russo. Try not to kill, but if it happens, it happens. Annie's going for Jengo, Em and I've got Ralph and Alex will take Kamon. One, two, three, now!*

She didn't have time to think, to be afraid, to wonder if she could shift. She just did it, throwing off her robe and shifting within a single heartbeat. Gabe lunged for Ralph as Annie dove over Sissy's wolf after Jengo. Alex spun past Russo, kicking high and fast, catching Kamon under the chin with one well-placed booted foot.

And Sissy did what she'd wanted to do for five long years. She went straight for Russo's throat.

• • •

Gabe stood on Ralph's chest and snarled. The man was so terrified he was babbling. Em had grabbed his sidearm and she stood guard over Jengo. Kamon was still unconscious. Alex was on the phone with the police. He paused talking long enough to tell them an ambulance was en route. The other women in the house had all come out into the living room, obviously confused and frightened by the shouts, the snarling and the blood.

Sissy stood over Russo, still in her wolf form. Gabe was so proud of her—she'd brought Russo down without killing him. He knew how hard it could be to control the wolf when everything was happening at Mach speed, but Sissy had done a perfect job. The man's throat was bloodied but not badly enough to indicate permanent damage—his major blood vessels were still intact. From the stench in the room and the stain on the front of his pants, he'd obviously had a little issue with bladder control.

Annie walked over to Sissy and stroked her back. "You did a great job, Sissy. Congratulations. It's not easy to bring a big man down without killing him."

Sissy snarled, and both Annie and Emeline laughed. Em said, "I know you wanted to tear his throat out, but think of the mess."

A spiky-haired blonde wrapped in an oversized robe broke away from the group and walked over to Em's side. "Is that Sissy? That wolf?"

"It is. Beautiful, isn't she?"

"How did she do it? How did she know?"

Em glanced at Gabe.

Tell her, he said. *But don't mention the mindspeech. Sissy, are you listening?* She turned her head and looked at Gabe. *Good. We try not to let anyone know we're telepathic. That's a Chanku secret, okay.*

I understand. Russo moved. She turned her attention back to the man, bared her teeth and snarled. He lay still.

"I saw Sissy downtown a couple of nights ago," Em said. "We can sometimes recognize our own kind, and I suspected she was Chanku. She is. She'd actually suspected it herself, before she was kidnapped, and had taken the nutrients that helped her body make the change. We gave her more of the pills, and she made her first shift today."

"How do you know if you're, you know, like you?"

"I was born to Chanku parents, so I've always known, but if you don't know, it usually starts with dreams of running in the forest, dreams so vivid that you can smell the scent of the trees, hear the owls at night, smell game in the forest, feel the crunch of pine needles beneath your feet as you run. We think it's a genetic memory, something imprinted on our DNA. It's powerful."

Wide-eyed, Janine stared at her. "I know. I have dreams like that. They're all that keep me sane."

Em shot a quick glance at Gabe, and then another of the women spoke up.

"I have them, too."

Dark-skinned with long, curly black hair, she was slender and tall and totally confident amid all the bodies on the floor. "My name's Mbali. I've had those dreams since I was a little kid. Before my mother died, she used to say they were dreams the angels sent to keep us safe. Do they mean I can shift? Turn into a wolf like Sissy?"

Gabe shifted, standing tall and comfortably naked, though the women weren't quite sure how to take him. Em handed the gun to him and stepped outside, where she grabbed his clothes. He gave the gun back and slipped into his jeans. "I hear the sirens so the police and ambulance should be here in a couple of minutes," he said. "Mbali, we'll talk later, but yes. Dreams are a good indicator. Ladies, this was meant as a rescue of all of you. What these men have done is obviously illegal—sexual slavery is a crime, and they've held you against your will and forced you into prostitution. Even if you were prostitutes before you were captured, slavery is wrong. The police are going to question you. I want all of you to know that we can offer you a safe place to stay and help you get your lives back on track. We'll pay for transportation if there's somewhere you want to go, and if there's a chance that you might be Chanku, you can stay at our place and take the nutrients to see if you are indeed Chanku if that is what you wish. It's entirely up to you."

"Will you let me go home? Or at least call my parents? My name's Mary Ryder, and Ralph kidnapped me off the campus at Berkeley over a year ago. My parents probably think I'm dead. I don't have any dreams like you're talking about. I dream about my family and my little sister."

Em pulled her cell phone out of her pocket and handed it to the girl. "Go ahead and call them, and tell them once the police get a statement you should be able to fly home. We'll take care of the airfare."

Her whispered "thank you" was barely audible. She took the phone into the kitchen. Gabe grinned at the last two woman, a beautiful redhead with curly hair falling to her waist and an equally beautiful Latina with long black hair and dark, dark eyes. "Are you ladies okay?"

The redhead grinned at Gabe. "We're better than okay, though it might be nice if you lost the jeans. The view was a lot better before."

Gabe shot a quick grin at Em. She was scowling at the woman. "I think that's an issue you'd have to take up with my woman. I'm not sure she's willing to share."

What Gabe said seemed to change Em's mood. She smiled at him. "Your woman is fine with it as long as she gets to look, too. Touching though? That's another matter."

"That's good to know." He was chuckling when he turned as three police officers entered the apartment.

"Alex? Alex Aragat? What the hell are you doing here?" One of the cops stepped over Kamon, who was beginning to stir. "What the hell's going on?"

"Detective Bandy! Good to see you. These six young ladies have been held prisoner and forced into prostitution by the four gentlemen on the floor. We discovered that the one with four legs, standing on the big guy, was Chanku, and the only way to rescue her was to rescue all of them. We thought you might appreciate the help."

"I do. In fact, I'm beginning to appreciate it more all the time. Is that Russo Allende?"

"His name's Russo." Alex glanced at the girls. "Anyone know if that's his last name?"

The blonde stepped closer. "I think that's it. We only heard their first names. Russo, Kamon, Ralph and Jengo."

"That's okay. In fact, it's better than okay. I thought I recognized all of them. We've got all their last names on file. This is quite a haul, Aragat. There's a hefty reward for Allende, and Ralph Alonzo as well. Human trafficking, drugs, counterfeiting . . . the list goes on. Need to check on the other two, but might be something coming for them as well. We'll make sure you get it."

"Actually, it goes to the women."

"We can do that. Do you mind calling the wolf off Allende? We need to read him his rights."

"It's okay, Sissy." Gabe glanced at the policemen standing beside him. "Here. This was Ralph's." Gabe passed the handgun to the cop and then walked over to the wolf. "You were absolutely fantastic, Sissy, but you can go ahead and shift. The officers will take over now."

She stepped away from Russo and shifted. A couple of the officers and all of the girls gasped. Em handed her the bathrobe she'd left on the floor, and she quickly wrapped herself in it and walked over to stand with the other girls.

Bandy stood there, shaking his head. "Ya know, I've seen you folks do that at least a dozen times, and it still blows my mind. It looks impossible."

Gabe laughed. "According to all the laws of physics, it is. Luckily, I'm not all that good at physics. Look, we've offered the young women a refuge of sorts—they can stay at our complex over in the Sunset as long as they need. We've got plenty of empty apartments. We think two more of them are Chanku, so we'll want time to give them a chance with the nutrients, but the other three young women can choose to stay with us or do whatever they like. CGI will be more than happy to help them out financially so they can get started back to a normal life."

The paramedics had arrived and were slapping bandages on Russo's throat, but it appeared that Kamon and Jengo were going to the hospital first. Gabe noticed the EMTs had them cuffed to the stretchers before they took them out of the apartment.

"I don't get it." One of the younger police officers glanced up from cuffing Ralph. "What's in it for you guys? Why are you willing to help? They're just whores."

Em started to speak up, but Gabe was already down in the officer's face. "You, sir, are an ass. These women were kidnapped off the street and forced into prostitution. They've been held against their will as sexual slaves by these lowlifes. Any one of these young women could have been someone important to you—a sister, a girlfriend, a wife. They had no choice, and no recourse but to do what these bastards told them to do, or end up dead. If that's how you think of perfectly innocent victims of sexual predators, you have no business being in law enforcement."

"He's right, you know." Detective Bandy waved one of the other cops over. "Jenkins, go with pretty boy here and get these two booked. Keep them in a holding cell until I get down there. I'll get statements from everyone here."

Mary walked out of the kitchen. Her face was streaked with tears, but she was smiling when she handed the phone to Em. "Thank you. I just talked to my mom and dad. I told them I'd be home as soon as I could get there, but probably not for a few days." She looked at Gabe, and he realized she was absolutely beautiful, now that she didn't look terrified. "If you don't mind, I'd like a couple of days before I leave. I have to see if I can start feeling normal again. I'd like to go with everyone to your place if you don't mind."

"You're more than welcome. Let's see what Detective Bandy needs, and then we'll get all of you settled."

. . .

Alex and Em left to go over to CGI. They got Em's SUV and Alex borrowed the big van that belonged to the company so they could get everyone and their belongings moved to the Sunset house. It was another couple of hours before the police finished their initial questioning and said they all could leave, with instructions to keep in touch.

At this point, Gabe wanted nothing more than sleep, and he intended to do that sleeping in Em's bed. Running with the pack in Montana the night before seemed at least a lifetime ago, and it was already dark by the time they reached the Sunset house and got everyone settled.

Annie ordered Chinese takeout delivered from the Platinum Duck, since they all agreed that Em's walk to the restaurant for dinner was the beginning of the rescue, but by the time the food was delivered, it was almost impossible for Gabe to stay awake.

They sat around the big trestle table in the kitchen with cartons of food covering the surface. Em grabbed a bottle of the nutrient pills out of the cupboard and held them up. "If any of you think there's a chance you could be Chanku, go ahead and take one of these. You'll need to take them twice a day, at least until you shift. Usually takes a week to ten days. If you're not sure but curious, you're welcome to try them. Nothing will happen to you if you're human. You'll only notice changes if you're Chanku, but once those changes happen, there's no going back. You won't be human ever again."

Sissy, Janine and Mbali each took one. Lindy and Nina turned and glanced at each other and then shrugged and held out their hands. "What the hell," Lindy said. "I don't think I am, but damn I wish I could shift."

Nina punched her shoulder. "But what if you are?"

"Then I will be the happiest woman at this table. I think it would be so cool." She popped the big capsule in her mouth and washed it down with a swallow of her wine, and then turned to Mary. "Aren't you going to take one?"

She shook her head and blushed. "I can't. I know I'm not Chanku, but even if I were, my parents belong to a church that teaches that the Chanku are from the devil. I don't agree, but I'd hate for my parents to think that's how I was. It's going to be hard enough for them to accept that I've been working as a prostitute for the past year."

Em shook her head. "It's not like you had a choice, Mary. I hope your parents won't hold it against you or think you've sinned."

"I don't think they will. They sound excited about me coming home."

Annie reached across the table and covered her hands—Mary had torn her paper napkin into shreds while she'd been talking. "You ever feel the least bit uncomfortable, your parents or anyone gives you any grief—and this goes for all of you—Alex has programmed all our numbers into the phones he gave you guys. You just have to call and we'll fly you back out here so fast your head'll spin. We can always find a job for you here with CGI. It's a big company with good people."

Mary nodded, but she looked stunned by Annie's offer. The other women were eating and talking and laughing, telling stories about their time with Russo and the others. Mary ate and listened, but she kept stroking the mobile phone that Alex had given her. He'd picked them up for all six of the girls, but Mary seemed to be the only one with anyone to call. She'd spent most of the time she'd been here on her phone, catching up with her family.

Gabe watched her for a minute, wondering how she felt, knowing she was surrounded by Chanku. She didn't seem afraid, but he'd heard of churches preaching about the evil of the shapeshifters. That was one he'd never figure out, but he wasn't going to worry about it now. He needed sleep. Finally, he leaned against Em and whispered, "I'm going to bed. I want to sleep in your room. Is that okay?"

She turned around and surprised him when she kissed him. "I hope so, because I gave Alex and Annie yours. They decided to stay here for a couple of days because they don't want to miss anything. And yes, I put fresh sheets on the bed." Then she kissed him again, a little longer, a little deeper. He almost whimpered when he realized he was too tired to even consider reciprocating. "Go to bed. You're fading fast."

"Yes'm." He stood and saluted the rest of the group. "I need sleep. I'm too old to keep going for two days straight." He looked at Em and laughed. "I can tell I'm exhausted because I can look at you and imagine you naked, and merely want to sleep next to you."

Alex shook his head in exaggerated sympathy. "That's not just exhausted. That's dead, man. Go to bed."

"Dead's not good." He turned away and left the room, left all the chatter and laughter behind, but it was a damned good feeling, hearing that laughter. They'd not only rescued six young women, one for sure and possibly two others were Chanku. He needed to call his dad.

Then he thought about talking to Anton and realized that no, he couldn't call him, because if he did, he'd ask him what the fuck he'd done to Em. And that was not a question for Gabe to ask his father. It was Emeline's question, and both sets of parents needed to hear it. He stripped out of his clothes and crawled between the sheets. But he rolled over until he was on Em's side of the bed, where the sweet scent of her body lulled him into sleep.

• • •

Em wiped down the counters and made sure everyone had everything they needed. She was exhausted but still wound tight. It was almost midnight—the women had gone off to their beds and she headed toward hers. Alex and Annie met her in the hallway in front of her room.

Alex gave her a sheepish grin. "Em, can we sleep with you guys tonight?" He glanced at Annie. "We've gotten so used to being with the pack, well . . ."

Annie punched his shoulder. "The point is, it's lonely in that big bed with just the two of us."

Em gazed from one to the other and shook her head. "Yeah. I guess. I've never done that before. Slept with more than one person." She leaned close and whispered, "And I'm talking sleep. Gabe's the first Chanku guy I've even had sex with."

Annie giggled and Alex covered his mouth. "I was a virgin when Alex and I did the deed, so don't feel bad."

"I didn't think there were any female Chanku virgins." Em covered her mouth to keep from laughing. Goddess, she didn't want to laugh, but it appeared she and Annie had more in common than she'd thought.

"Well, there certainly aren't any now." With an exasperated look on his face, Alex grabbed Em's and Annie's hands and dragged them into the bedroom. He stripped off his boxers and pulled the tee Annie had borrowed from him over her head.

Em stripped down and got into bed beside Gabe. He grunted and rolled over, tugging her close against his chest. Annie snuggled up behind her with Alex on the far side. He wrapped his arm around Annie, and his fingertips rested on the lower curve of Em's breast. Gabe's heart beat a steady rhythm against her ear until Em felt cocooned in warm bodies, beating hearts and soft breaths. Annie sighed, Alex coughed. Then Gabe whispered softly, "Go to sleep, sweetheart."

And, just as simply as that, she did.

7

_____

It was still dark when Gabe awoke. He glanced at the bedside clock—it was barely six, so he rolled over and snuggled against Em. He vaguely recalled Alex and Annie coming in last night, but not anything after.

They all must have been exhausted. Gabe was still feeling his lack of sleep and he wanted another hour or so before they got up. If the weather was still nice, he wanted to take Sissy over to Mount Tam so she could run the mountain trails, but right now the bed and Em felt too good to think about running anywhere.

He closed his eyes, thinking of the thrill in store for Sissy, and how excited he was to be able to share it. And he wondered how long the other girls would take to change.

Unless they were making up the stories about the dreams, he had a feeling that Mbali and Janine were Chanku. This had been a good year for finding more—Sebastian and then Romy, and most recently Fen. All good people and assets to the pack. Each new member brought something fresh, and he wondered what Sissy, Janine and Mbali had to offer. And, if they might lead to others. Sisters, mothers, brothers—since the species followed the female line, there was always hope that each new discovery would lead to more. Too often, though, they were like Sissy—the single surviving child of a dysfunctional mother, a woman who'd never discovered her Chanku heritage. He didn't even want to consider the frustration, that constant sense that something important was missing, or at the very least, incomplete. The stories among his parents' generation were uniformly sad.

None of them had known the truth, not until someone in the pack had told them who and what they were. His father and Alex's dad, Stefan, had been the first, but they would have been lost without Alex's mom, Xandi, who forced them to see the truth, and Keisha, his own mother, who had saved Anton from his own personal demons.

No wonder they loved so powerfully. Gabe had come to realize he wanted—no, needed—that same kind of love. And he thought of Em, took a deep breath and inhaled her sweet scent, nuzzled his chin against the dark silk of her hair. This was all so new, this almost frightening emotional connection he was beginning to feel for her.

What if she didn't feel the same? And what if the darkness inside her wouldn't let her love him the way Gabe feared he already loved her?

His roiling thoughts scattered when the bed dipped on the opposite side from where he lay, and he heard Alex get out. A minute later he was back from the bathroom, but he crawled in behind Gabe.

"The girls are asleep. I know you're awake."

"I was planning to go back to sleep?" Gabe said it as a question, but he grinned into the pillow and rotated his hips against Alex's groin. It had been way too long, and Em and Annie were still out like the proverbial lights.

"Go ahead. I won't keep you awake." Alex stroked his flanks and slid his hands around to Gabe's belly, then lower, tangling in the hair at his groin, tugging lightly and then cupping Gabe's balls in his left hand. He slid his right hand beneath Gabe's flank and stroked his suddenly wide-awake cock.

Gabe bit back a groan. He didn't want to disturb the girls, and as isolated a life as Em had led, he wasn't all that sure how she'd take two men fucking in the bed beside her.

It's as good a time as any to find out, don't you think? Alex's chest bounced against Gabe's back with his silent struggle to keep from laughing.

Whether it's a good time or not, there is no way in hell I'm gonna let you stop doing what you're doing. Goddess but that feels good.

I'm stopping right now. Sorry. He slipped his right arm from beneath Alex's hip and gave a final soft squeeze to his sac. *I found some lube in the bathroom. Top or bottom.*

I'm fine right where I am. And he was, with Em snuggled close against his chest, her hair cascading over his arm, her lips pressed against the base of his throat. He felt each tiny puff of breath, the tickling flicker of her eyelashes against the side of his throat as she dreamed, and he wondered what her dreams were, if they were good or bad.

Alex's fingers slipped between his buttocks and he shivered when one well-lubed fingertip pressed against his sphincter. He clenched his muscles, a reflexive action as that same finger entered, slowly opening him, relaxing the taut ring. Alex added a second finger and then a third until

Gabe was gently panting with the strain not to fight entry, not to awaken Em. His heart raced with the thrill of Alex's touch, with the knowledge of what was coming.

The pressure was subtle at first, but he breathed deep and slow when he felt the broad crown of Alex's cock putting gentle pressure against his ass. He pressed back, bearing down to allow Alex in, and felt the stretch, the sharp burn of entry. He imagined the sound when Alex passed through the straining ring of muscle—he knew it was entirely silent, but in his mind there was a subtle pop as everything suddenly relaxed and Alex slid deep inside, past that sensitive barrier of nerves, a long, slow, steady push that didn't end until Alex's groin rested against Gabe's buttocks.

The two of them paused, both breathing deeply as Alex fought for control, as Gabe struggled to hold still, not to disturb Em.

It didn't work. Em raised her head, blinking owlishly in the half-light, and then she smiled. "Is Alex doing what I think he's doing?"

"Alex is," Alex answered.

Gabe chuckled. "Sorry, babe. I was trying not to disturb you."

She nuzzled his throat. "I'm not disturbed." Then she scooted lower in the bed and planted a kiss on his belly, just above his cock. When Gabe groaned, she moved a bit lower and licked the full length of his erection.

Let me know if I do it wrong. I've never done this before. She wrapped her lips around the crown and circled it with her tongue.

"Oh, Goddess . . . did you have to tell me that?" Groaning, Gabe managed to get out a simple thought as Alex pulled halfway out and then went deep again. *Doing great, Em.*

Alex, why do I get the feeling he doesn't want to discuss technique? This time she cupped Gabe's balls in one hand and held the base of his cock with the other. And then she sucked him deep inside her mouth, all the way to her fist.

Gabe could only whimper, but Alex was laughing when he answered, "He doesn't?"

The bed dipped. Annie got out on her side, walked around the bed and then crawled in behind Alex. "You know I hate it when you play without me."

Alex cursed, and drove hard into Gabe. "You were asleep, Annie. Goddess, woman. How do you expect me to last when you do that?"

"I don't." She giggled as Alex bit back a curse. "You should try this on Gabe sometime, Em, when he's topping one of the guys. Play with his balls and he'll be like putty in your hands."

"It's not just the balls . . ." Alex took a few deep breaths. "She's got her finger up my ass. Crap, Annie. You used to be such a sweet, innocent young thing."

DARK REFUGE

"Corruption is so much more fun. Like that, Alex?" He cursed, and Annie laughed and said, "How ya doin', Em?"

Can't talk with my mouth full.

At that point, Annie started giggling, Alex's strokes went from slow and deep to short and fast and Em squeezed Gabe's balls and swirled her tongue across that most sensitive part of his cock, the tiny, nerve-rich frenulum where the foreskin attached to the glans.

Gabe tried to pull free of Em's grasp as his orgasm hit, but Alex was on the downstroke and Em kept her lips closed tightly around the upper half of his cock while she rhythmically squeezed with her fist resting on his groin. And damn, but she was gently rolling his balls in her other hand, and there was no holding on. No way, nohow. He groaned and gave in to the pleasure as she sucked him deep and swallowed every bit of his ejaculate.

They lay there in a sweaty, messy heap, the guys gasping for air, the girls laughing about how easy it was to make a guy come, whether he wanted to or not. Gabe turned his head and glanced at Alex, still sprawled across his back. "We shouldn't have to put up with such insolence."

"I agree. Don't worry. They know payback is coming, but they also know we're going to make them suffer first. A lot."

"Ooh . . ." Annie scooted off the bed. "I am so scared." Then she headed toward the bathroom.

Em leaned close and planted a kiss on Gabe. There was something undeniably sexy about tasting himself on her lips. "I'm not," she said. "In fact, I think I'm looking forward to it."

And then she sauntered after Annie with that long black hair swinging across her perfect butt, and it came to Gabe like a high-voltage shock. There was no way on earth he was ever going to let her go.

He glanced at Alex, who'd finally rolled to one side and was still blowing like he'd run a mile. "You're outta shape."

Alex rolled one eye at him and grunted.

"How did you know, Al? You know, with Annie? How did you know she was the one?"

This time Alex laughed out loud. "I hadn't seen her in years. One afternoon I was in Kalispell and three big bruisers had her cornered. I didn't recognize her, but she was obviously a woman in trouble. I fought them off, and then I realized it was Annie." He rolled his head to one side and grinned at Gabe. "Ever run into a brick wall? That's how it felt. I just knew, and there was no way I was letting her go. Luckily, it turned out she'd had a crush on me for years, so she didn't fight me off too much."

"That must have been some scary shit when Aldo Xenakis kidnapped her."

65

Alex spun around and sat on the edge of the bed. "I still can't think about that without breaking out in a cold sweat. She's really special, Gabe. She makes me a better person. I can't explain it."

Gabe pushed himself up against the headboard and nodded. "I know. Crap, Alex. Em makes me feel the same way, like I can do anything because she thinks I can, and I don't want to disappoint her."

"Exactly." He glanced up as the girls came out of the bathroom. Both of them were wrapped in towels and had wet hair. They threw their towels on the floor, stood over them and shifted to wolf, then back to their human forms, only now their hair and bodies were dry.

"I have to remember to tell Sissy how that works." Em grabbed a warm robe and pulled it on. "C'mon, boys. The day is growing old and we need to get everyone fed and at least Gabe and me up on Mount Tam with our newest packmate. Sissy needs to go for her first run."

Annie slipped Alex's T-shirt over her head and followed Em out the door. Alex laughed and punched Gabe's shoulder. "Yep. That's the same look I used to get on my face around Annie."

"Used to?" Gabe shook his head, laughing. "You've still got it. C'mon."

• • •

Sissy couldn't believe she'd slept so well last night. She lay there in bed, feeling loose and relaxed, which was hard to believe after all the trouble she'd had falling asleep. She'd been so wound up all evening after their rescue, her body practically twitching with excitement, and the knowledge of who and what she was had kept her head spinning in circles. She was Chanku, an alien species with an almost unlimited life span, with the ability to shift into a wolf at will. In fact, she could become any number of predatory creatures, once she learned how, but for now a wolf was just fine.

Someone knocked on her bedroom door and she jumped, and then she started giggling. She was safe here. Safe, for the first time in forever. She opened the door and Em handed her a steaming cup of coffee.

"C'mon, lazy. We're going for a run."

"Thanks." She took the cup and inhaled the wonderful smell. This was obviously much better than the coffee the guys had bought for them at the apartment. She took a sip. Delicious, but she shook her head. "I can't run. I don't have any running shoes."

"No, silly." Em turned away and headed down the hall toward the kitchen. "Your wolf is going to go run. Alex, Gabe and I are going to take you over to Mount Tam. It's a beautiful day, and it shouldn't be too crowded, but even if it is, the people around here know we're not going to hurt them and they leave us alone. You need to eat first, though. You'll burn a lot of calories."

"Annie's not going?" Sissy followed Em into the kitchen. Annie was scrambling eggs in a huge frying pan. This place was definitely designed for a crowd.

"Nope." Annie turned around and pointed to an empty seat. "Sit. I'm bringing you breakfast. You're going to need the calories today. I'm staying here with the girls, we're going to talk about options for the ones who aren't Chanku, possible jobs, that sort of thing." She set a plate mounded with eggs and bacon in front of Sissy and went back to the stove.

Sissy stared at the pile of food for a moment, along with the big pill on the table beside it. "Will I have to take these every day?"

"Nope." Gabe slid into a chair beside her and Em took the one across the table. Alex wandered into the kitchen, but he stopped to kiss the cook before taking a seat next to Em.

Gabe scooted over and made room for him. "After a couple of weeks," he said, "all the changes in your body will have been made, and while you might crave the nutrients on occasion and want to take a few pills then, once you're Chanku, you're that way forever."

. . .

Sissy thought about that later, when Em pulled her little SUV into the parking lot on the northern end of the Golden Gate Bridge, the fact this was her new reality. She wasn't human, had never been entirely human. She was Chanku. A shapeshifter.

She got out of the car and stood beside the door, taking deep breaths of the clean air. The rugged slopes of Mount Tamalpais loomed high above them and she thought of the last time she'd hiked here, the day Russo darted her and turned her from a young college student into a sex slave. She'd been studying to be a teacher because she loved working with little kids.

Maybe she could do that again. She'd already gotten her degree and was in the credential program. She wondered if the Chanku sent their children to public schools, or maybe taught them in private schools. She'd have to ask. Soon. She stretched her arms over her head, then bent to touch her toes. The Pacific sparkled in the sunlight, but the December air had a real nip to it. She was too excited to feel cold, too wound up to sit still.

Gabe and Alex both crawled out of the backseat, moaning dramatically about their long legs and lack of space as they stripped out of their clothes right there in the nearly empty parking lot. It made sense now, why they'd worn nothing but old sweats and sandals, but they tossed everything into the backseat and then shifted.

Sissy did the same, feeling a bit exposed here in the lot on the side of the road, but she undressed quickly and threw her clothes inside as if she'd always done such a thing, standing naked in a public place. She shifted, calling up her wolf so naturally that it felt as if she'd always done this. She sniffed noses with Alex and then Gabe, and would have laughed if she could when Gabe raised his hind leg and peed on the back tire.

Does that make it your car now?

Gabe merely gazed at her over his shoulder for a moment before he answered. *Actually, I'm thinking of taking Em shopping for a grown-up-sized car. This thing's a joke.*

"It's not a joke," Em said as she tugged her sweater over her head. "It's a practical, economical car, perfect for driving in the city. And you get to wash the tire when we get home."

Sissy stepped away from the car and trotted to the edge of the parking lot. She was shivering, not from the cold but from the desire to run, to experience the feel of the well-packed trail beneath her paws, the myriad scents teasing her sensitive nostrils. She'd not felt free for much too long and her body thrummed with excitement. Not only was she free, she was going to run as a wolf.

Everything seemed fresh today. The sky was crystalline blue and so clear she could see boats that had to be miles away, their dark silhouettes barely visible above the horizon. She stood at the edge of the lot, staring at the broad expanse of ocean until she heard Em locking up the car.

Sissy turned in time to see Em shift. It was the first time she'd seen Em's wolf, and her pale gray coat was marked almost like a leopard's with a fascinating pattern of tiny dark rosettes.

She must have given the keys to Gabe before she shifted, because he had them in his mouth. Sissy wondered if he was going to carry them as they ran, but then she followed Em, Alex and Gabe as they trotted across the parking lot to the trail that led around the flank of the mountain. Gabe went straight to a large fallen log and dug into the soft dirt near the end. He dropped the keys into the hole, covered them carefully, and then he looked straight at Sissy.

Are you ready?

I am.

Let us know if you get tired. You're not used to running on four legs, and we don't want to wear you out.

Just try. She couldn't hold still a moment longer, so she yipped and took off, spinning away and racing up the trail. Dirt flew from beneath her sharp nails and she felt as if she could run forever. Her legs were strong, her big paws so nimble, her nails digging into the hard trail to give her the perfect traction for speed. Gabe nipped her flank and ran past her, and then Alex raced around the other side. Em stayed on her flank, though Sissy was certain she could have passed her without any effort. They were accustomed to running—she was fast, too, but there was too much to see, too many things to sniff and taste.

Smells were sharper, the sounds in the grass unbelievably loud. Quail burst out of some wild lilac bushes, scattering madly out of the way as the four of them ran past. She saw every detail of their escape—the mad rush of their wings and their little black topknots—with total clarity.

Then there were the ground squirrels beside their mounds that zipped down into their holes the moment the wolves came into view. Though she'd eaten a huge breakfast, Sissy's nose twitched at the scent of the little rodents, and she realized she wasn't the least bit grossed out at the thought of catching and eating one. Or maybe two.

I never thought I'd look at something that was little more than a furry rat and think "snack."

Em's silent laughter had Sissy's wolf grinning. *I guess that would be an adjustment. I've always thought they were tasty, though their little bones get caught in my teeth. I prefer bigger game like deer or elk, but it's been ages since I've hunted them.*

We'll be heading to Montana in another week or so, Gabe said. *Definitely before the winter solstice celebration. You'll have a chance to hunt then. Big game, in the snow. Now, that is real hunting. C'mon.* He veered off the trail and the rest of the small pack followed. *This is one of my favorite runs,* he said, circling down past the Marin Headlands to Bonita Cove. *My wolf likes running across the beach more than I do as a human. You're going to love this!*

The tide was out and the sand packed hard. They played at the edge of the water, splashing like kids in the foam before lying on the sun-warmed beach to watch the big container ships sail under the Golden Gate. Sissy gazed at the big ships and then turned and stared into Em's beautiful green eyes. *I can't believe this is my life. This is the most amazing day I've ever had.*

Thank you for letting us share it with you. Em glanced at Alex and Gabe, including them. *We've always known what it's like to be Chanku. You remind us how special this life is, how lucky we are.*

I hope Janine and Mbali are Chanku. They've both become good friends. I don't think that Lindy and Nina are, but I wonder about Mary. She wants to go home so badly, but I know she's adopted and she told me one time that she never felt as if she fit in, that sometimes her family seemed like they were totally unlike her. It makes me wonder.

It's a decision you can't force on someone, Sissy. No matter how right it is for you, each of us is an individual. That's one thing we believe very strongly in—following our own desires, living our own lives. Making our own decisions about things that are important to us.

But when she said it, Em stared at Gabe, and he returned her look while something passed between them. Sissy wondered what she was missing. Something had happened to either Em or Gabe, something that somehow took something important away from one or both of them.

She had no reason to think like that, but the feeling was much too clear to ignore. She wasn't sure why she suspected anything so weird, but she did, and the feeling stayed with her until they finally turned and headed back to the parking lot.

8

"This is so strange, to be sitting here in Em's car, driving back into town after running along the mountainside as a wolf. Does it ever stop feeling weird?"

Gabe caught Em's eye in the rearview mirror and grinned. "For us, Sissy, it would feel weird to go to Mount Tam and not shift and run. We've always been this way. I'm wondering, though, if you're noticing anything else."

"You mean like, if I don't get laid in the next ten seconds I'm going to explode?" She slapped her hand over her mouth and went about ten shades of red.

Gabe snorted and burst out laughing. Alex doubled up in complete hysterics. Em grinned, shook her head slowly and kept driving.

"Oh, shit. I can't believe I said that out loud."

Gabe grabbed a handkerchief out of his pocket and wiped his streaming eyes. "It's okay, Sissy. That's sort of the answer I was going for. You actually nailed it. That's part of being Chanku. What we've neglected to tell you is that we're creatures who essentially are ruled by an overactive libido, and the need for sex is particularly strong after a shift. You learn to control it to a certain extent, but it's always there, sort of bubbling below the surface." He laughed out loud. "Except when it explodes. I honestly didn't think about how you must have felt last night, especially after your first shift. Were you able to sleep okay?"

She kept her hands over her face and mumbled, "Yeah, after I found the vibrator in the nightstand beside the bed. I need to replace it."

Alex stared at her, openmouthed. "You mean you wore it out?"

She lifted her head, turned and glared at him. "No, stupid. I used it. That's not something people generally pass around."

Em stopped laughing long enough to answer Sissy. "Alex, behave.

71

Sissy, if you take the batteries out of it, I can run it through the dish-washer. That sterilizes everything, but it's not a big problem. We don't get any sexually transmitted diseases and you'll find that, now that you've changed enough that you can shift, you'll rarely get sick. Our immune systems are pretty amazing. I bet you've never gotten an STD from pull-ing tricks, have you?"

"No." She hadn't and now that she thought about it . . . "Lindy and Nina had to go into the clinic a couple of times, but none of the rest of us. We're all careful about using condoms though."

"You don't have to be. Not anymore. You can't get pregnant unless you have sex in your wolf form, and then only if you consciously choose to release an egg."

Gabe chuckled. "Or two, as the case may be. There are quite a few twins in the pack, including me. My brother Mac and I were Mom's sur-prise for Dad."

"Actually," Alex said, "I think Lucia was a bigger surprise." He leaned forward so Sissy wouldn't have to turn around. "Gabe's mom de-cided she wanted one more baby, and his dad wasn't all that excited about the idea. But Chanku are a matriarchal society, and baby Luci was a re-minder that Mom has last call on those decisions."

"Yeah, but you'll notice she's the family favorite and definitely Dad's little princess. Lily, Mac and I all spoiled her rotten, but Dad's the worst. When he caved, he caved entirely."

"I miss Luci," Em said. "Will she be in Montana when we go back?"

"She should be." Gabe and Alex both sat back as Em turned off Nine-teenth and headed toward Sunset. Gabe couldn't wait to go back to Mon-tana, especially since they were bringing at least a few more Chanku into the pack. The downside was, what was this trip going to do to Em? He hated to see her relationship with her parents brought into question, but it was hard to imagine a good ending to this mess.

Alex leaned forward again to include Em and Sissy. "I just talked to Annie. She and the girls are at the mall on Nineteenth, but they're getting lunch there so we're on our own. I hadn't even thought of that. We proba-bly should have hunted while we were running."

Sissy turned and shot him a grin. "I'm still not sure I'm ready to eat raw rodents."

Alex shrugged. "We could have chased down a few rabbits. There's more meat on them. I saw a couple of deer up on the hill." He sighed and held the back of his hand to his forehead. "I think I'm growing weak. Starvation is setting in."

"I think you'll survive until we can pick up some takeout." Gabe shoved Alex's shoulder. "Big baby. Actually, Sissy, we try not to hunt larger game in public this close to the city. In Montana, we've got thousands of acres of forest and can hunt whatever we need, but down here we're forced to act more civilized, which means no killing large animals that leave a bloody carcass. It tends to upset the bird and bunny people."

"Wonder how they'd taste?"

"Alex?"

"Yes, Gabe?"

"Behave."

They stopped long enough to pick up hamburgers and fries at a drive-through before heading home. Em hit the door opener and drove directly into their underground garage. Gabe and Alex grabbed the bags of hamburgers and fries, and Sissy went on ahead with Em to set the table.

She was standing at the table, staring at her hands, when the guys opened the bags and piled the burgers on a plate in the center of the table. "I can't believe these were paws a short time ago. I mean, I know it happened, and I still can feel the absolute rush of running, but it's too bizarre for words."

Em took a seat across the table from her. "I really enjoyed my run this morning. I travel all over Asia, and we're not as protected there as we are here, so I rarely shift and run in public places. There are a few areas where we have pretty large landholdings, but poaching is a huge problem, and since I'm usually the only wolf there, I don't feel safe enough to run on my own. Today was special. And you will get used to it, though I don't think any of us ever takes our ability to shift to other forms for granted."

She grabbed a hamburger. So did everyone else. The only sound was the occasional moan of pleasure from the joy of gorging themselves on junk food, what Alex often referred to as ambrosia.

In spite of their hunger, Gabe could tell it was hard for Sissy to concentrate on her meal. She couldn't sit still and the scent of her arousal was wafting straight for his nose.

"I think I need to be excused." She pushed her chair back from the table, but Alex covered her hand with his.

"Where are you going?"

She blushed. "I think I need to find that vibrator. This is killing me."

"We thought you'd join us."

She frowned, and Gabe wanted to kick Alex for not explaining what he was talking about to her. "Sissy, Alex, Em and I are going to get naked and fuck like bunnies," he said. "We thought you'd want to join us."

Sissy spun and she glared at Alex. "What about Annie? She's my friend. I don't cheat with my friends' significant others. I'm sorry, but . . ."

"It's okay." Alex was grinning, but at least he looked a little embar-

73

rassed. Gabe glared at him and Alex dipped his head. It wasn't fair to tease Sissy—this was all way too new for her. He glanced at Gabe. "I'm sorry, Sissy. I'm giving you a bad time by not telling you what I mean. I'm not being fair, and I'm sorry. Annie's my bonded mate. When you and Gabe and Em and I are all doing whatever we do, she'll be in my head, sharing everything. Chanku are openly polyamorous, which means we have sex with others in the pack that we're not mated to. This morning I topped Gabe while Em kept the rest of his boy parts entertained. When Annie woke up, she joined us. No one thought anything of it. Everything is different than with humans."

"How's that?" Sissy was still glaring at him. "A lot of human men and some women love to have group sex, but partners who are excluded still get hurt."

"Not for Chanku. There's no jealousy, and even if our mates aren't physically with us, they're not excluded. Not when your bonded mate is in your head and knows everything you're doing. Annie was with me on our run today, even though she was shopping with your friends. She knows what we're planning, and she approves. And if they get back and we're still at it, she might join us."

"But . . ."

"I would never cheat on Annie, Sissy. I love her. She's my better half, and without her I'm not much." He stared at the table a moment and then raised his head. "Truth? Without Annie, I'm nothing, and she knows that. She also knows that there is no woman anywhere who could ever take her place. Sex for Chanku doesn't hold the taboos that it has for the human population. It's just another bodily function. You eat, you sleep, you shit, you fuck."

Alex's laugh had a hollow sound to it that made Gabe ache inside. Damn how he wanted what Alex and Annie had.

"But connecting with Annie? Linking our minds when we make love? Sharing what's deep inside? That's what's important. That's not something we do with anyone else, because that's where the intimacy lies. That's what makes our mates so special to us. They're the ones who know us inside and out. We have no secrets from our mates. They know our good points and our faults, and they love us anyway. I could screw a dozen women, give each of them pleasure and thoroughly enjoy the experience, and yet it wouldn't have the intimacy of a single word from my mate. It's up to you, Sissy, but whatever you choose, be assured that I'd not be cheating on Annie." He grinned at Gabe. "And Gabe wouldn't be cheating on Em."

Sissy frowned and stared at Em, but she asked Gabe, "Are you and Em mated?"

He turned and smiled at Em. He loved watching the color rise across her face. "Not yet," he said. "I'm still giving her time to warm up to me."

• • •

Much later in the day after what had easily been the best sexual experience of her life, Sissy was helping Annie in the kitchen, and she told her what Alex had said. She still felt guilty. To have a man make love to her with such close attention to detail was an entirely new experience, but she couldn't handle it if there were any secrets, if Alex had lied about Annie's true feelings of her man with another woman.

Annie shot her a big grin that totally dispelled the shadows. "Isn't he great? Sissy, everything Alex says is true, though he left out the most important part. I've loved Alex since I was a kid, and he had no idea how I felt. I avoided him, avoided the pack for years because I couldn't handle the pain, the knowledge that he didn't love me. But then when we got together as adults, the love was there and it was spectacular. Does it sound awful that I love him so much I want to share him?" She laughed, but her eyes sparkled with what looked suspiciously like tears.

"No." Sissy shook her head, fully aware her tears weren't even suspicious. No, they were flowing down her face, dripping off her chin. These people were amazing. So kind and selfless and absolutely good. She wanted to be like Annie. Wanted to find the kind of love that Annie had.

But it would have to be someone like her, a shapeshifter. A man who understood that when he loved her, that even though there might be sex with other partners, she was the only woman in his world.

• • •

Friday evening, just over a week since she had first spotted Sissy in Chinatown, Em flopped down on the comfortable old couch in the sunroom on the third floor. She'd felt a need for some quiet time, if only to digest all that had happened over the past few days. Sissy, Janine, Nina and Lindy were downstairs in the kitchen watching television and talking about their meeting with the district attorney earlier in the day. All four men were being held without bail and it appeared they were going to be charged with human trafficking and sexual slavery along with running a prostitution ring.

There was also some gossip around the station that someone high up in local politics had been implicated in an active human trafficking ring, but the investigation on that was going to take time. Detective Bandy had told Alex what he knew, but it wasn't much. Still, anything that would stop crimes against both men and women was good.

There wasn't a formal living or family room in the building because every usable space—except for the big central kitchen—had been turned into separate suites for pack members. The top-floor sunroom with its western wall of glass and a full view of the Pacific was the only gathering place outside the kitchen.

Right now Em was really glad no one else was gathering here.

She'd heard Alex and Annie come in a few minutes earlier. They'd ended up moving a bunch of their stuff from the Marina house because they missed being part of a pack, and there were enough of them here to constitute a pack. Gabe was working late tonight, but Em had taken the week off to help the women get settled, and in case any of them found out they were Chanku and wanted to shift. So far, only Janine and Mbali had noticed any changes, and both of them had scratched their arms raw. She fully expected at least one of them to shift by tonight.

Nina and Lindy weren't sure what they planned to do, but neither had felt the least bit changed by the nutrients. Lindy had been a CPA who sidelined as a beautician and Nina had majored in accounting and business at Stanford before she was kidnapped. Both of them had excellent taste in clothes and had done some of their own designs. Gabe had tossed out the idea of them opening a shop as partners.

They'd told him they had dreamed about doing that but lacked the capital.

Gabe and Alex were discussing going in as silent partners, something that had both Lindy and Nina working on a business plan and checking out available shops.

The only mystery—and the reason Em had come up here to think— was Mary. She was so very shy and she kept to herself, though she spoke by phone daily with her family. Still, she'd shown no interest in going home to Indiana. Em suspected that Mary was taking the nutrients, even though she'd denied any interest in them. Em remembered that her adoptive family's religion was fairly conservative and preached that shapeshifters were created by the devil. Mary had said more than once that she didn't want to know because she couldn't be what her parents hated.

Em and Annie had tried to explain that she couldn't change what she was, that if her parents truly loved her, they would accept her no matter what. If only there was a way to guarantee such a thing. She couldn't imagine having parents turn away from you over something you couldn't change.

Which made her think of her parents, and the darkness that was so much a part of her. A huge gap in her teenage life that had to have been caused by her parents. Thinking about it made her feel ill, but until they had all six of the women settled, Em couldn't consider going home.

She heard someone coming up the stairs and turned as Annie stepped into the room.

"Hey, Em." She held up a full bottle of chardonnay in one hand and a couple of glasses in the other. "You hiding out up here?"

Em scooted over and made room on the couch. "Not really. Well, maybe." Smiling, she shrugged. "I dunno. Just thinking. Thanks for bringing the wine. That's actually one of the things I was thinking of. You must have read my mind."

"Sort of." Annie set the glasses on the table and pulled the cork out of the bottle. "I can tell you're worried about something, but not what . . . or who." She shot a quick glance at Em and then focused on pouring the wine. "I hope it's not Gabe."

"Not Gabe. Mary." Em took the glass, tapped the rim to Annie's and took a sip. "I'm sure Janine and Mbali are close to shifting. Tonight, maybe. Nina and Lindy don't seem to have a drop of wolf in them, but I think Mary could be Chanku. Sissy's the one who told me what she suspected, and I've been watching for clues. The bottle of pills is going down faster than it should since Nina and Lindy quit taking them. I think Mary is taking them as well, in spite of what she said about her family."

"She's been wearing nothing but long sleeves. I haven't seen her scratching at her arms or legs, but she spends a lot of time alone in her room. I heard her telling her father she wasn't ready to go home yet. I think he's been pressuring her."

Em nodded. "Gabe had a good idea. He thought we should ask Mary if she'd like us to invite her family here. Pay for their flights, treat them as guests. Be on our best behavior." She grinned at Annie. "You'd be in charge of Alex."

"Oh, Goddess! That's so unfair." Annie chuckled. "Actually, if we can get Alex to act like a grown-up, it's a great idea, though personally, I prefer him as a cocky teenager." She laughed. "I missed that period of his life, and mine, too. With Alex, though, I think his inner sixteen-year-old remains alive and well. But as far as Mary's folks? There's room for them to stay here, and it would give them a chance to see that she's okay, and maybe get past some of their issues with shapeshifters."

Em rolled her eyes. "Or not."

"I know." Annie stared out the big window facing the Pacific. "It's hard to fight serious lycanthrophobia, especially when that's the message you hear in your place of worship, but it might work."

Em faked a shudder. "I cringe every time I hear that word: lycanthrophobia. You know it means 'fear of werewolves,' don't you?"

"I know. I absolutely love the word!"

Annie actually giggled, and that had Em laughing with her. "And?"

"Crap. You made me snort my wine." Still giggling, Annie grabbed a tissue and wiped her face. "Lycanthrophobia." She drew out every syllable. "It's so much fun to use it because it drives Anton absolutely nuts. The minute you find a place to use it in a sentence, our dear alpha puffs out his chest and proclaims in a voice that would fill an auditorium, 'The term does not fit us. Unlike werewolves, we are not ruled by the phases of the moon. We shift at will and can become many different predators.'"

"Yipes! You sound just like him."

"That good, huh? Maybe we need a new term. Chankuphobia? Of course, that one could come back and bite us in the butt. Besides, it wouldn't be nearly as much fun around Anton. Anyway, back to Mary's parents. You'll tell her first, won't you? Before actually inviting them?"

"Definitely. By the way, I like Chankuphobia. Run that one by Anton next time you see him." Em stroked the stem of her wineglass and stared at the pale wine. "As far as Mary, I'm the last person to approve of making decisions about another person without that person's approval."

"I imagine you would be." Annie went back to staring at the view out the window, almost as if she couldn't face Em. "I still feel terrible that I'm the one who told you. I'm so sorry."

"C'mon, Annie." Em leaned close and hugged her. "Please, don't be. Gabe and I already knew there was something wrong, that I had some serious missing memories along with a few other hang-ups. Your information assured me I'm not crazy." She chuckled and took another sip of her wine. "At least not certifiably crazy. Not yet, anyway. You helped me identify the source of some scary stuff I've been dealing with, though not the reason my memories were so obviously wiped. I've tried to remember, and there's nothing there. Nothing at all, but your information has been pivotal to my sanity. Believe me. I was afraid I was going crazy."

"You're as far from crazy as any woman can be. Of course, that's not saying all that much, is it?"

Em couldn't stop grinning at Annie. Finally, she couldn't stand it. "I am so goddess-be-damned glad you and Alex are here. Seeing the two of you together makes me feel good. This is the closest I've been to being part of the pack since I was a kid. I've felt so isolated for so many years, but I had no idea why. Now, knowing so much of my past has been kept from me, I can finally understand. Having you guys around is wonderful."

She listened for a moment to the laughter from the kitchen. "Having them here is good, too. But I'm still worried about Mary."

Annie sipped her wine, a thoughtful expression on her face. "Have you tried mindspeaking with Mary? If she's been taking the nutrients, she might hear you."

Such a simple thing. "No. I haven't. But I will." She pictured Mary, thought of her personality, her vocal voice, and called out to her mental voice. *Mary? It's Emeline. Are you okay? I've been worried about you.*

Em? I can hear you! I'm afraid, Em. I'm so afraid. Help me, please?

"Shit. C'mon." Em set her glass on the coffee table, hiked up the skirt on her sarong and tore out of the room, taking the steps three at a time down to the second floor and racing down the hallway to Mary's room. Annie was right on her heels.

The door was shut, and when she tried the handle, locked.

"Move. I'll get it."

Em stepped aside while Annie landed a well-placed kick beside the handle. The door bowed without breaking, but the latch slipped free and the door flew open. Em raced in first, but it was dark in the room and she scrambled for the light switch.

She flipped it on, and an overhead lamp lit the room. A tan and black wolf cowered in the corner, shivering in fear. "Oh, sweetie." Em knelt beside her and wrapped her arms around Mary, hugging her tight. Annie slipped out of her clothes and shifted, sniffed noses with Mary and then lay beside her, resting her chin on Mary's back.

"How long ago did you shift?"

I don't know. A couple of hours, maybe? I really didn't think I was Chanku, but just in case, I took the pills. My arms started itching a couple of days ago, and I think I was ready to shift yesterday, but I was afraid. Today when I called my dad, he told me I had to come home, that I was being corrupted by staying with you, that you were evil, but I know you're not. I was so angry that I hung up on him, and then suddenly I was a wolf and the phone kept ringing and ringing and I couldn't shift to call him back. He's going to hate me. He already hates what I am, that I was a prostitute, even though I didn't have a choice. This will be even worse, but he still doesn't know I'm one of you. What am I going to do? Why can't I shift back?

Em continued stroking her head, projecting as much calm as she could. She kept her voice low, soothing, yet very matter-of-fact. "I imagine you can't shift because you're scared, and once you relax, you'll be fine. As far as your father, Gabe had an idea we wanted to ask you about. We thought we'd offer to pay for your family to fly out here to see you, see what we're like. I don't think we're all that scary, and I know you aren't. You're such a beautiful wolf, Mary. I can't wait for everyone to see you." She kept stroking the wolf between her ears, speaking softly while Annie calmed her with the sense of pack, the knowledge she wasn't alone.

It didn't take very long. In a couple of minutes, Mary was lying naked on the floor with Annie beside her and Em stroking her hair. She looked up and burst into tears. Annie shifted and she and Em both hugged Mary. They sat that way for a long time. Then Annie got up and went into the bathroom, wet a clean washcloth and brought it out. She handed it to Mary before picking her scattered clothes up off the floor. She dressed quickly and left the room. She was only gone a couple of minutes, long enough for Em to find a robe for Mary and the two of them to get comfortable on the bed where they could talk.

Annie walked in with the wine bottle and three glasses this time. She handed one to Em, another to Mary and set her own on the dresser. Then she poured half a glass for each of them, raised hers and said, "To the newest member of the pack. Welcome, Mary."

"Definitely welcome. I am so glad you're one of us, Mary." Em raised her glass and they each tapped the rims together and took a sip. As she tasted the wine, Em reached out to Gabe and told him what had happened. From the besotted look on Annie's face, she knew her friend was sharing with Alex.

Em was never so glad to see anyone in her life as when Gabe and Alex walked through the door into the bedroom a few minutes later.

9

Gabe pulled Mary into his arms for a warm, welcoming hug. "Thought you were going to pull one over on us, didn't you?" When Mary blushed and hung her head, he stepped back and gently said, "Welcome to the pack, Mary."

"My turn, buddy." Alex hugged Mary and planted a big kiss on her cheek. She blushed even deeper and scrambled back onto the bed with Annie and Em.

Gabe shot Em a grin and elbowed Alex. "Watch it, Aragat. Mary, I had no idea you could shift. I don't think you have any idea how exciting this is for the pack. Finding new members is always time for a celebration."

Gabe remained next to the bed where the three women sprawled, each with a celebratory glass of wine. He was so proud of Em he felt as if he might burst. Was there anything she couldn't handle? Still smiling at Mary, thinking of what he'd like to be doing right now with Em, he said, "What color is your wolf?"

Wide-eyed, Mary turned and stared at Em. "I have no idea. I was so terrified when I shifted that I never even thought to look in a mirror."

Em and Annie burst out laughing. "It's okay. You can shift again and look, but to answer Gabe's question, you're an absolutely gorgeous tan and black wolf. You're marked sort of like a German shepherd, but the dark saddle on your back isn't as pronounced. Definitely striking."

This time, Mary was smiling. It changed everything about her appearance. Gabe had thought of her as pretty before, but the smile changed everything. She was absolutely stunning.

"Gabe, we were talking about your idea, about bringing Mary's family out for a visit. What do you think? It might be even more important, now that we know she's Chanku."

He focused on Mary. "Do you think they'd come?"

"I don't know. I can ask."

Her phone rang. "Dad" showed on the screen. Gabe picked it up off the nightstand and held it so Mary could see it. "Or I can invite them," he said. "What do you say?"

Mary nodded. "I can't talk to him. Not yet. Tell him I'm busy. In the shower or something."

Gabe answered the phone. "Mr. Ryder?"

"Who's this?"

"I'm Gabriel Cheval. One of the people who rescued Mary. I think she's in the shower right now. Can I take a message?"

"Is my daughter okay? She hung up on me and wouldn't answer the phone when I called back. She said you people are shapeshifters. Have you done something to Mary? I don't trust you."

"Just a moment. Let me turn the video feed on so you can see me. I've nothing to hide." He pressed an icon, and Mary's father's face came into view. He was a good-looking man who appeared to be in his early fifties, dark hair, some gray at the temples. And he looked really irritated.

Gabe smiled into the camera, but he toned it down enough that he didn't show too many teeth. Not a good idea with someone who hated shapeshifters, no matter how much his mother loved his smile. "Okay. There—got it. For what it's worth, Mr. Ryder, she was kidnapped by human males and rescued by Chanku, but that's beside the point." Though he did give him a couple of beats to let that sink in. "There's something I wanted to suggest to you, something I discussed with Mary tonight. I told her I'd like to invite you and your family out to visit for a few days. You can see your daughter, see how well she's doing, and get to know us."

Gabe glanced at Mary and smiled before adding, "We're good people, Mr. Ryder. We're not evil, and we have nothing to do with the devil. We rescued your daughter and five other young women because they were prisoners of some criminals. We weren't rescuing Chanku, we were rescuing young people in trouble. I will have airline tickets delivered to you by courier within the hour if you would consent to a visit. If you like, you and your family can stay here at our apartment complex in San Francisco where Mary is staying, or I will make reservations for you downtown at the Mark West. We'll cover all your expenses. Take your time to discuss this with your wife if you wish, and I'll have Mary call you back as soon as she's able."

There was a long pause. Finally Mary's father said, "I don't know what to say."

"Nothing for now, Mr. Ryder. You should discuss our offer with your family, including Mary. She can let me know what you decide, though I do hope you choose to make the trip out here. I think you'll be surprised by what you discover."

Gabe ended the call, glanced at Mary and shrugged.

She had her hand over her mouth, but as soon as Gabe showed her the phone was off, she exploded in laughter. It took her a while before she could talk. "Oh, Gabe. How could you?"

"What?" It wasn't easy to look innocent, not when he was feeling pretty impressed with himself. He glanced to his left, where Alex was doubled over, laughing hysterically, and focused again on Mary. "What'd I say?"

"'You'll be surprised by what you discover'? I can't believe you said that! Should I meet him at the airport as a wolf?" And she went off again in peals of laughter.

Em and Annie were holding on to each other, giggling uncontrollably.

The door opened, and Janine led Mbali, Sissy, Nina and Lindy into the room. "What's going on?" She looked from one to the other. "We could hear you guys all the way in the kitchen, even with the TV on in there!"

"Mary shifted." Alex shared a quick look with Gabe. "And then her father called."

"God, Mary." Mbali grabbed Mary's hands. "What's he gonna say when he finds out you're a shapeshifter?"

Mary used the bedspread to wipe her streaming eyes. "I don't know, but Gabe invited him and the rest of the family to come visit, so he could get to know that shapeshifters weren't evil. He didn't tell him I was Chanku." She glanced at Gabe and started laughing again.

The five girls stared at one another as if they were all nuts. "What's so funny about that?"

Gabe shrugged. "I merely mentioned that he might be surprised by what he discovered. That's all."

"Oh, Gabe. You didn't?" Mbali glanced from Gabe to Mary. "He did, didn't he?"

"He did." Mary slid off the edge of the bed and stripped off her robe, standing unclothed in front of all of them without any sense of embarrassment. She glanced over her shoulder at Em. "I want to show them, and I figure I'd better get used to being naked on occasion."

Em grinned at her. "Go for it." She grabbed Mary's phone. Mary shifted and Em snapped her picture. "So you can see what you look like with your human eyes. Our color vision isn't as precise as wolves, so mirrors only give us part of what the world sees when we shift."

Mbali got a funny look on her face, stripped off her clothes, and immediately another wolf stood beside Mary. She was dark gray with reddish tips to her fur, black tips on her ears and tail and a dark mask across her face.

"What the hell . . ." Sissy grinned at the two wolves, slipped her robe off and shifted. Then she, Mbali and Mary went through the entire routine of sniffing each other from nose to butt.

Laughing, Em took more pictures. Janine glanced at Em and looked ready to cry. "I can sense it, like I'm ready to change, but whatever I need to know to do it isn't clear yet."

Nina and Lindy stood off to one side. "Not me," Nina said. She poked Lindy in the side with her elbow. "What about you?"

"Nope. What you see is what you get."

Alex wrapped his arms around Janine and hugged her tight. "Tomorrow. Don't be surprised if you wake up as a wolf. I can sense it in you, so you must be close."

"How do you sense it? Do I smell bad?"

He leaned over and took a deep, dramatic breath, then coughed and made gagging noises. Janine took a swing at him and he ducked, but at least she was laughing.

"Actually," Gabe said, "there is a scent, but it's a good smell, not a bad one. And you have it. You didn't yesterday, so in spite of the fact that Alex is a jerk, he's right. It means you're close. I'm surprised we didn't notice it in Mary, but I didn't know she was taking the nutrients, so I wasn't looking for it, either."

Mbali, Sissy, and Mary shifted and got dressed, and once again the room was filled with young women. Chattering, laughing, happier than Gabe had seen any of them since the rescue, they headed back to the kitchen. Em and Annie stared at each other a moment and then started laughing again.

Gabe looked at Alex and shrugged. Alex shook his head. "Haven't got a clue," he said.

Em caught Gabe's eye. "Annie and I were talking about this earlier, showing up in Montana with four new Chanku."

"It's going to be like taking a litter of puppies home and dropping them off. Hey, Mom. Look what I found! Can I keep 'em?" Annie hugged her knees. "I'm hoping it'll take Dad's mind off me. He might have enough to do he won't try and micromanage my life. At least for a couple of weeks."

"Dream on." Alex flopped on the bed next to Annie. "Your father will always be like that, but he does it because he loves you. I imagine I'll be every bit as bad once we have pups. There's going to be a wedding at the winter solstice. The last I heard, everyone who mated over the past few months is going to marry. Romy and Jace, Ig and Star, Sunny and Fen. What about us, Annie? Will you marry me? I've asked you before because I love you, and I'm going to keep asking you until you say yes."

He raised his head a moment and whispered, "Goddess, I sure hope she loves me." Then he took hold of both her hands. "By not getting married, you're letting your dad control our relationship simply because you know that's what he wants. But I want it, too, Annie. You are my mate, for now and for all time, but I want you as my wife, too. I like the sound of that. Mrs. Annie Aragat."

Annie was staring at Alex with stars in her eyes, so much love flowing between them that it made Gabe's heart ache. He glanced at Em, she stared at him, reached out and took his hand, tugged to give herself leverage and slipped off the bed. Annie and Alex were so caught up in each other, he didn't think they even noticed when he and Em slipped out the door.

He sort of hoped she'd head toward the kitchen, where the girls were talking and laughing. He'd gotten in from work and hadn't had dinner, but she didn't go that way. Instead, she led him to her room, the one they shared. And once they were inside, she carefully locked the door behind him.

"Make love to me, Gabe. Please?"

He didn't say a word, but he carefully unbuttoned his shirt and kicked off his shoes. Unsnapped his jeans and slipped the zipper down, shoved his pants over his butt, down his thighs until they pooled on the floor and he stepped out of them. And the entire time, his gaze never left Em's dark eyes. Her mind was closed to him, her thoughts a blank wall, but he knew that watching Alex and Annie together had affected her deeply.

Just as it had affected him. He hadn't imagined, on that flight from Montana to San Francisco a week ago, that he would be meeting his destiny here. Hadn't realized that little Emeline Isobelle would have grown up into the perfect woman for him. It hadn't hit him hard and fast, the way it had hit Alex, hadn't knocked him off his feet the way Romy had affected Jace. No, Em had been more subtle, almost as if he had to see through the layers of his memories of that little girl, peel them away and discard them in order to see the woman she had become.

She stood there, hands clasped at her waist, slim body wrapped in a pale blue sarong, the kind of garment that so many of the women preferred around the house, her caramel skin and long black hair a perfect counterpoint to the shimmering ice-blue silk. He stepped closer and untied the knot where she'd gathered the fabric between her breasts, slowly unwrapped the fabric and let it fall.

He stepped back so he could see her, all of her, as she stood with her eyes downcast, her long hair tumbling over her shoulders, curling in soft waves all the way to her hips. Her beauty took his breath, aroused him and terrified him, that she might not love him the way he loved her.

"You are so beautiful, Em. So perfect." He cupped her face in his palms, aware of the subtle swish of blood coursing through her veins, her thundering heart, the scent that told him she was aroused and waiting, that she wanted him, that she wondered as much as she wanted.

She obviously wondered what he was thinking, but it was only fair. Just as she had closed her thoughts to him, Gabe had hidden his away from Emeline. He kissed her. A light meeting of lips, the soft, slick slide of his tongue across her mouth. Then he pulled back far enough to focus on her face, on her dark amber eyes. On the slick surface of her lips.

"Do you have any idea what you've done to me?"

She tilted her head, still watching him. Still wondering. He sensed her curiosity and her arousal. His was evident—there was no hiding the erection curving up from his groin so hot and heavy and ready for her—but Em's feelings were a mystery. He couldn't read her. That was okay, for now. There should be questions. Only a few, since his desire for her was blatantly evident.

Finally, she frowned. "No," she said. "I have no idea."

"You should." He kissed her again, then pulled away before she could return the brief touch of his mouth to hers, but he cupped her bare shoulders in both hands. Anchoring her, or was he anchoring himself?

"I love you, Em. I'm not even sure exactly when it happened, but it's lodged in my heart—you're lodged in my heart. For what it's worth . . ." He grinned at her, and then winked. "I like the feeling. A lot."

She tilted her head and stared at him, holding the pose for much too long as her eyes filled with tears, as the tears spilled out and down her cheeks. Had this been a mistake? He couldn't have misinterpreted her feelings that much. Or had he? "Em?"

She stepped into his embrace, wrapped her arms around his bare waist, pressed her face to his chest and sobbed. He hugged her close, rocking her gently side to side while she cried. He tried seeing her thoughts, but her barriers kept him out. He hoped they were happy tears, feared they weren't, but he had no idea what made her cry.

Or why she kept him barred from her thoughts. He opened to her, let her see his love for her, the way her tears terrified him, but she merely held him tighter and cried harder.

This certainly wasn't how he'd expected her to react, not when he finally admitted something he'd never said to another woman. When Em showed no sign of stopping, he picked her up and walked around the bed to the far side of the room, where there was a big, overstuffed chair. He sat down with Em in his lap, his arms wrapped around her as she curled against his chest. Shivering, pressed against him like a lost and frightened pup.

And still she wept.

"Sweetheart, if you don't let me in, if you can't tell me or show me what's wrong, how can I make it better?" Brushing her tangled hair back from her eyes, he kissed the tears, kissed her cheeks, her lips, the warm silk of her hair. "Is it wrong for me to love you, Em? Is that why you're crying?"

She shook her head against his chest and drew a deep, shaky breath. Then another, and another, until the harsh, wracking sobs had ended. He grabbed some tissues out of a box on the table beside the chair. She took them and dried her eyes, wiped her face, blew her nose. She shuddered and, once again, buried her face against his chest.

"Will you tell me what's wrong, Em?"

Her voice came to him, halting, unsure. He'd noticed over the past few days she'd used her mindspeech with him less and less, but at least now she was trying.

I didn't mean to lock you out. I can't always control my mental barriers, and sometimes they lock down when I don't want them to. I think it's all part of whatever happened to me when I was younger. Can you hear me now? I was trying to open to you, but I couldn't. I'm okay using mindspeech with everyone else, but it's gotten harder, not easier, with you.

I hear you fine. You're open now. Can you show me what's wrong?

I don't want to. Gabe, I feel so flawed. What if there's too much wrong with me to fix? You don't want someone like me. I love you. I love you so much it makes me ache inside, but I'm so afraid that all my problems, all the crap in my memories, all of that will destroy whatever feelings you have for me. I couldn't live with that. I can't live with loving you and then watching you walk away.

He sat there, holding her, loving her, and yet absolutely stunned. Not that she loved him. He'd almost been certain she loved him, but what she'd said hurt. Hurt with a level of pain he'd never experienced, to find that Emeline had so little faith in his love for her. How could she honestly believe he would walk away from her over whatever crap was in her background?

Knowing she doubted him, though, that she didn't trust him with her heart, left him cold and aching inside. He wasn't sure how to answer her. Didn't know what to say, and yet he was well aware that by not answering her, he was proving himself untrustworthy. So he did the only thing he could think of. He opened his thoughts, his heart, his pain. He didn't know how to tell her, how to say the words, so he did the next best thing. He let her into his deepest thoughts, into his hopes and dreams for their future, all those private things he'd thought of over the past week. It was frightening to open himself so completely, but it was worth it if it would make her understand how very much he loved her.

• • •

She was a damned fool, but her heart was breaking and Gabe wasn't even fighting for her. She'd opened up to him, told him her fears, and he hadn't said a word. He'd held her close, his arms a comforting band around her body, but he'd not said a damned thing. He'd looked at her like she was the biggest loser on the face of the earth, as if she was too weak to deal with whatever was going on in her head, and maybe he was right. Maybe she was a loser. Maybe she was too weak. That's probably why she couldn't remember anyone making her forget. Probably because no one else had done it. What if she'd totally screwed up her own memories? She'd probably had a total meltdown and did it to herself.

"Em? Look at me."

She snapped her head around, and he was right there, lips close enough to kiss, but she looked away from his mouth and buried the thought of how much she wanted their lips touching, pressing together, tasting each other, and all that was left was looking into his eyes. He had such beautiful eyes, with lashes so thick and dark. She blinked, and no, she really had seen them sparkle. They were filled with tears. But why? She was the one who was all screwed up, not Gabe.

"Do you hate me so much that you're going to block me entirely?"

What? Why would he even think that? "I don't hate you. I told you, I can't always control my shields. I'm not trying to block you right now."

"And yet, you are. I've been trying to tell you how I feel about you. How much you hurt me by what you said, but you're not even trying to hear me. I love you, Em, but if you're going to give up and let whatever happened in your past rule your future, then, you and me? It breaks my heart to admit it, Em, but we don't have a future. I always thought you were a fighter. You've always been a fighter. Even when Aaron and I teased you, you gave it right back tenfold, but I guess you've forgotten that. If you're not willing to fight for us, for what you and I should have together, then maybe you don't love me enough. Maybe I was dead wrong."

He lifted her out of his lap and set her in the chair. He grabbed a blanket off the end of the bed and tucked it around her, and then walked around the bed and picked his clothes up off the floor. He didn't look at her, though he paused with one hand on the doorknob. "I'm going to get something to eat. I worked late and missed dinner."

He didn't even put his clothes on. He walked out of the bedroom with everything tucked under his arm and left her there, stunned, totally speechless, her heart shattered into a million pieces.

10

_____

"I guess she doesn't love me the way I thought she did. Damn, Alex. I gave her everything I had, but it wasn't enough."

Gabe stared at his reflection in the big window. He'd sat out on the front step until the cold sent him inside with no more answers than he'd had when he walked out of Em's room. He'd done the only thing he could think of—he'd grabbed his dad's bottle of cognac and asked Alex to meet him up here in the sunroom. He'd actually brought the bottle home from the office tonight, prepared to tell Em how much he loved her, maybe to celebrate a potential mating.

Looked like that wasn't going to happen.

"Just what did you give her, Gabe? From what you said, she was blocking you, whether intentionally or because she can't control her shields around you. So, yeah, you might have spilled your guts, but if she had everything shut down, she doesn't know that. She's had a pretty traumatic week, when you think about it. She's been hiding from the pack for years, knowing she had something missing in her past and afraid of what it was, thinking it was all because she was somehow flawed, she's dealing constantly with her estrangement from her parents, in the last week we've had a fairly wild rescue of six young sex slaves, four of whom have turned out to be Chanku, and to top it off, she's fallen in love with the son of the pack's alpha."

"That doesn't—"

Alex held up his hand. "Yes, it does. We're not nearly as feral as the general public would like to believe, but there's enough wolf in each of us at all times that we still have a hard time meeting Anton's eyes, we still do as he asks and I imagine we will always see him as our leader. Does anyone question that? No, especially Em's father, who has idolized Anton since he rescued Oliver so many years ago."

Gabe chuckled. "Actually, I think Oliver switched that idolatry to Jace's dad when Adam helped Oliver get his balls back. Dad got knocked down a notch below Adam."

Alex laughed and sipped his cognac. "Well, there is that. Point being, in an odd, subliminal manner, most of the pack see you and your sisters and brother as quasi-royalty, Em included. Why do you think Lily and I didn't end up mated the way our parents hoped? We've always loved each other, but it would never work because she's such an über-alpha bitch to my wolf that there never would have been any balance in our relationship. Sebastian is her equal in magic and balls."

Gabe shook his head and laughed. "Nah. There's not a man alive with bigger balls than Lily."

"I didn't say bigger, I said equal, but we're getting off point here, Gabe. You know what I noticed the most about what you've told me?"

"No, but I have a feeling you're going to tell me."

"Damned right I am. I almost had Annie dragged away from the chickfest in the kitchen when you said I had to come up here, and that's a great lead-in to what I want to say. Everything you've said comes down to one thing—you're making this all about you. Not what Em's dealing with, but how you're not dealing with Em. She's just discovered that a terrible thing happened to her when she was younger—a terrible thing she has no memory of. It's all pointing to something that was done to her by her parents or your father, and possibly all of them, working in collusion. She doesn't know. There's a huge chunk of her childhood that's missing, and it sounds as if it's a horrible thing she's lost. I think you need to give the girl a break. That is, if you really love her. If you don't, it's time to walk away before you get yourselves in any deeper, but if you love her, you damned well need to convince her that you're in this for the long haul, that no matter what, you're not walking away." He stared hard at Gabe for a long, telling moment, before softly adding, "The way you did tonight."

Gabe couldn't look at Alex. Not yet. Instead, he stared into the amber liquid in his glass and thought of how many times as an older teen, as a young adult, he'd stared at a glass of his dad's cognac while listening to his father as he helped Gabe work through whatever was bothering him, what might be hurting him. Now Alex was sitting beside him, and while the liquor in the glass was always the same, he hadn't expected the same level of advice from Alex.

What Alex had said was every bit as thoughtful, as sincere, and as perfect as what Gabe would have heard from his father.

And, as often happened when his father reached a conclusion, Gabe felt like an ass. An ass who owed Emeline an apology. He raised his head and found Alex staring at him. His dark eyes were troubled, the smile that always lurked at the edge of his lips not anywhere in evidence, and Gabe had a feeling that Alex was afraid he might have damaged their friendship with his honesty.

He hadn't. If anything, he'd strengthened it. Gabe swallowed, not all that surprised at the lump in his throat. Emotions were never easy, especially strong emotions between longtime friends. "Thank you," he said. "You're right, and I needed to hear that. I did exactly what she was afraid I'd do, didn't I? Sucks to be so predictable, ya know?"

"Yeah, Gabe. I do." He chuckled softly. "I've been guilty of male predictability on more than one occasion, and if you ever tell Annie I admitted that, you will die."

Annie just heard that. Thank you, Gabe. I've been trying to get him to admit it for months now.

Go away, Annie. Male bonding taking place.

Yes, dear.

She left them with the sound of a slamming door. Gabe glanced at Alex, but he couldn't hold it, and it took a long time before either of them could stop laughing.

• • •

Em thought about joining Annie and the girls in the kitchen. Their laughter carried down the hallway and left her feeling more outside the pack than anything else ever had. She couldn't sit in her room and cry all night. That was a waste of energy. Gabe was gone. He'd done exactly as she'd expected—walked away rather than stick it out with her.

She didn't blame him. Not really, though she was beyond disappointed and wondered if she'd ever find another man like Gabe, except it had to be one who loved her enough to stay. A person couldn't change who they were, what they were. Gabe deserved better than her, and it was a good thing that he'd figured that out before they got more involved.

She left her room, went downstairs and out through the door to the garage. She'd laughed when she first moved in here, to see a wolf-sized doggy door into the garage, but it made sense. They could get in out of the rain and shift, dry off and dress before ever going inside. It made it equally convenient for going outside, and right now Em needed to run. Needed it more than she ever had in the past.

She connected with Annie first. They always tried to let someone know when they were leaving, especially when going out for a run. *I need some me time, Annie. Gonna run in the park. I'll be back in a few hours.*

Sounds wonderful, and I'd go with you, but I think Janine's getting ready to shift. And don't worry, I can handle it. Go. Run an extra mile or two for me, will ya?

You've got it. It was so easy to connect with Annie. With Alex or even Mary or Sissy. Why couldn't she open up to Gabe as easily as she did with everyone else? Hopefully, things would be clearer after a run. Her wolf was good at that, at figuring out what her human side often turned into a hugely convoluted puzzle.

She left her sarong hanging on a hook beside the door, shifted and slipped outside. The door was well disguised, leading into the backyard, and the gate had a latch she could easily flip with her paw. Once out on the street, it was a short run to Golden Gate Park. This late at night it should be almost empty, and the homeless who sometimes camped in the park knew not to fear the wolves. Those same wolves often returned as humans the next day with food and money and offers of work. They were actually quite popular.

With that thought in the back of her mind, Em trotted down the side-walk, crossed Lincoln Way and slipped into the heavy shrubbery along the south edge of the park. She had no destination in particular, but the need to connect with her wolf was stronger than anything she'd felt during all her years of travel. In fact, she'd never experienced such a power-ful need to run on four legs, to see the world through feral eyes.

One week with Gabriel Cheval and she was losing it. It would almost be laughable if it didn't break her heart. She trotted through the woods at a comfortable pace, steering clear of the bison paddock, where her scent tended to have an unnerving effect on the huge beasts. She'd unintention-ally caused a stampede when she was new to the city, running too close and upwind of the small herd one night. They'd raced in panic from one end of the enclosure to the other until she'd gotten far enough away that they no longer scented her.

The next day, when she'd told Lily what had happened, CGI made a huge donation to the group responsible for managing the herd. It had eased some of Em's guilt, but not all of it. It still bothered her, to remem-ber how heartless she'd felt over such a stupid mistake. Now she headed northwest, far from the paddock, through areas where the park was wilder, the trees and shrubs closely spaced. She needed to feel the forest around her, even if it was only an urban park. It wasn't Montana, but any-thing had to be better than sitting alone in her room, almost within touch of Gabriel Cheval.

• • •

Gabe went straight to Em's room, but she wasn't there. He stopped at the kitchen, but she wasn't there, either. Annie and all six of the young women were celebrating Janine's shift, which must have happened while he was upstairs with Alex. Gabe hugged Janine and stood by more patiently than he felt while she shifted again so he could see how beautiful her wolf was.

She was definitely gorgeous, and absolutely unique, unlike any other in the pack. Snow white fur with brilliant sapphire blue eyes, but the edges and tips of her ears and the final half of her tail were black. No shade from white to gray—a black so complete it was a startling contrast against the pristine white of her coat.

He stood there, gazing at her, thinking of this small pack Em had led him to, how beautiful and unique each of them were. Even Nina and Lindy, while not Chanku, were good people, but where the hell was Em? He forced himself back to the present. "It looks like it was worth the wait, Janine. You're unique and beautiful. All of you are. I can't wait to show you off to the pack. I bet Em absolutely flipped when she saw you."

Annie gave him an odd glance. "Em left before Janine shifted. About an hour ago. I thought you knew."

"No. I was with Alex."

"Ah . . . the male bonding thing, right?"

Gabe nodded his head. "I'll go find her."

"I think that's a very good idea."

With Annie's solemn words ringing in his ears, Gabe trotted down Sunset toward the park. Em's scent was fresh and it was easy to follow her on a relatively quiet night like this. He didn't search for her mind. He tried to tell himself he didn't want to frighten her, but the truth was, he didn't want her to realize he was looking for her.

Obviously, she was trying to get far away from him, something Gabe hadn't had to deal with before. Women inevitably wanted to get closer. Of course, there'd never before been a woman who mattered.

Em mattered. That was obviously why he'd screwed this up.

He was such an idiot. An idiot and a complete ass, but at least her scent was growing fresher and easier to follow, and with any luck he'd get a chance to make amends, to attempt to fix what he'd broken. Her trail cut through heavy shrubs, away from the bison paddock, and he remembered Lily telling a story about EmyIzzy running too close to the bison herd and causing a stampede. Obviously that lesson stuck, and it made it easier to follow her, knowing she ran in the general direction of Ocean Beach.

As her trail grew stronger, Gabe took more care. Not that he was actually trying to sneak up on her, but . . . He stopped and raised his nose to the air. She was close, but the breeze coming off the Pacific was distorting the direction of her scent, so that he wasn't quite sure which way she'd gone. North along the coast, or was she circling south to head back home? It was close to one in the morning and he was exhausted. Today had been busy at work, as he'd wanted to finish up some last-minute projects before they all headed north to meet up with the pack, but following Em's trail had his adrenaline pumping and all his senses on high alert.

Even so, he was hoping she'd chosen the southern route, but he had a feeling she wasn't going to make it easy on him. And wasn't he doing it again? Seeing Em's pain from a perspective that was all about him. Goddess but he hated it when Alex was right.

But he hated even more what he'd done to Emeline.

Then it came to him, the place where she was headed, and he hoped he was right because, with any luck, he should be able to catch up to her. He raced through the park, to the northwest corner where Fulton hits the Great Highway. There was no traffic and he didn't see Em, but her scent here was strong and he knew she wasn't all that far ahead.

The walking trail took him along the coastline, above the Cliff House and the Sutro Baths, and then he saw her, trotting along the road that eventually led to Point Lobos. Wolf Point . . . how apropos, and so perfectly Emeline.

He caught up to her above the remnants of the baths. She didn't acknowledge him, though her ears flattened a bit. She was still pissed off. He didn't blame her. He was pretty upset with himself as well.

He stayed on her flank, following too close for sanity's sake. Her wolven scent enveloped him, a rich aphrodisiac that was tying him in knots. He thought she was headed to the lookout at the top of the hill, but she turned off the trail and followed a narrow path that led them down to the rocky beach. The tide was going out and the surf was low, but the natural phosphorescence of the waves leant a ghostly light to the area.

There was no one else around, and the night was cold, though not freezing. The wind had died down and the only sound was the slow rumble of waves against the rocks, a sound almost entirely obscured by the thundering beat of Gabe's heart. Even the sea lions were quiet tonight.

Em stopped beside a section of old concrete foundation and shifted. She sat on the flat surface and wrapped her arms around her knees, tossed her hair back and shoved it out of her face. She looked so terribly sad that Gabe wanted to wrap his arms around her, but he stayed in his wolf form. Em cocked her head to one side and said, "You can't hear me, can you? I've been trying to speak to you since I first realized you were following me, but you didn't hear me at all. When you first got here, we could at least communicate with mindspeaking, but even that's lost. I was trying to tell you to go home, to stop following me. Why are you here?"

Gabe shifted and sat next to her. "I'm here because I love you. Because I'm an ass, and Alex was right."

She sighed. "I hate to admit it, but he usually is. What was he right about this time?"

He bumped her shoulder with his. "At least we're agreeing about something."

She laughed. "That you're an ass? Yeah, I think we can agree to that. What else?"

"Plenty, I imagine. When I got upset, it was because I'd turned the entire problem around and made it all about me. It's not about me. Whatever is going on with you, whatever happened to you when you were a kid, is all about you, but it's something both of us have to fix. And then when I left, it was because I didn't know what to say, how to fix what I'd screwed up, and rather than crawl and tell you the truth, I chickened out and left. I was wrong, Em, and I'm so damned sorry. I want to be someone you can count on, not the kind of flake that walks away from the woman he loves because he doesn't know how to fix things. Will you give me a chance? And if I screw up, will you tell me before you order me to get lost?"

This time, she actually leaned against him. "I can do that. I'm sorry, too, Gabe. I do love you, but I get so frustrated when I can mindspeak with anyone else, but not with you. I've never heard of anything like this before. It has to be tied in to whatever happened to my memories, but I don't know how to fix it."

"I have an idea, but I don't know if you'll go along with me or not." It had come to him while she was talking. It might work.

"What? We won't know until you tell me."

"Do you love me, Em? Enough to put up with me even when I'm a jerk, because I can't promise that I won't screw up on occasion."

Laughing softly, she shook her head. "Gabe, I loved you even when you were a rotten teenager who took great pride in being an absolute jerk. Since before that, when you used to carry me around on your shoulders and tell everyone what a big boy you were. That's what hurt me so much. I thought you were ignoring me, even ridiculing my problem, but it was because I didn't hear when you were speaking to me. I thought you were . . . oh, hell. I don't know what I thought."

He hugged her close and kissed the top of her head. "Do you love me enough to be my mate? To agree to a lifetime with a total jerk? Because I'm afraid that's what you might be getting. I wish I were a better person, but I'm exactly what you see. I'm never going to be anything like my dad."

"Thank goodness."

He sat back, shocked by her answer. Everyone in the pack loved his dad. At least that's what he'd always thought. "Why? You're always talking about how much you admire my dad, that you love him."

"As the pack's alpha." She laughed. "I've always figured your mother was a saint for not murdering him years ago."

Now she made sense. "You're not the only one. Mom's pretty amazing, but he's been a wonderful father. Disappointed, I think, because only Lily appears to have inherited his magic, and then she's so much better than him that his ego has had to take a bit of a backseat to her abilities. Em, all I can do is promise you that I will do my best to be a good mate and a good husband, and hopefully someday, a good father, but you haven't agreed, and you're making me nervous. You know, I've never told anyone other than my mom and dad that I love them, so, in order not to make this all about me and stay within my comfort zone, I'm really hangin' it out here."

Em grabbed both his hands and leaned back, laughing. "Gabe, the moment you walked out of the room, I knew it was too late, that I already loved you so much there was no going back. I think we could be so good together, but how are we going to do this? Mating means a bond, and it's all mental and emotional. What if we can't connect?"

Do you hear me now?

Her eyes went wide. *I do! I hear you perfectly.*

Let's go back to the park. To that wild area near Mom's garden. That's always felt like a holy place to me. Are you okay with that?

I am. But what if it doesn't work?

We're going back to Montana in a couple more days. If our folks can't help us, we'll get Lily to take us to talk to Eve.

She can do that?

She can. And so can you, or me, or any of us if it's important. Eve always listens, and this is important, Em. It's the most important thing either of us has ever done. C'mon.

He shifted, and so did Em. And then she followed him along the trail, back along the edge of San Francisco to the park. And there, beside a garden Gabe's mom had designed and built so many years ago, they faced each other as lovers, as friends, as wolves.

11

Em was content to follow Gabe back along the walking trail and through the park to the garden his mother had designed. Such a beautiful, peaceful spot, it had been the true birthplace of the pack, bringing together Gabe's parents and cementing their relationship with Alex's mom and dad, and later connecting the four of them with Ulrich Mason and the original men of Pack Dynamics.

Then, a few years later, it had brought in six new members, disenfranchised young men and women attracted by the strange grasses Keisha had chosen—the same grasses native to Tibet that had given all of them, at one time or another, the ability to embrace their Chanku genetics and become the shapeshifters they were meant to be.

It seemed only right that she and Gabe would choose this spot to mate, though she still couldn't believe he actually wanted her. She kept waiting for him to say he'd changed his mind, that she was much too damaged, that he didn't love her enough to claim her for all time.

Her love for Gabe wasn't in doubt. She'd loved him forever, but since she'd given up on his ever returning that love, it still didn't feel real. Right, but not real. Not yet.

Mating wasn't something anyone took lightly. What if he'd made a mistake? What if whatever had happened, whatever had left that huge blank in her memories, wouldn't allow the merging of their minds in the connection that was imperative to the mating bond? Wasn't it all about the memories? About learning everything there was to know about your mate?

She knew so much about Gabe already, and yet so very little. They'd been children together, and yet they'd spent barely a week together as adults. Both of them had changed. She kept thinking this must be a mistake, and then she almost laughed when she realized her anxiety had set up a loop in her head—*we don't know each other anymore, what if it's a mistake, what if I'm too damaged, does he love me enough, do I love Gabe enough, and at least that was an unqualified yes, but what if Gabe*—round and round, the same questions stumbling over one another until she was ready to either scream or laugh hysterically.

They reached the garden with the beautiful stones and the bench beneath the trees, and the bronze plaque dedicated to Sherpas who'd died long ago. Gabe sat on his haunches and watched Em as she trotted into the grassy area near the heart of the garden. She stopped a few feet from him, wondering why he looked at her with so much concern.

Can you hear me?

She nodded her head.

Good, because I've been listening to you the whole way over here, which is a good thing and a bad thing. It means we're connecting the way we should, but it also tells me you're filled with doubts. First of all, I love you. I've never felt this way about any woman. Once we're mated you'll have full access to what I'm thinking and feeling, and all of your worries are going to be gone. My only concern is that the bond might bring back memories you don't want. We know you were kidnapped, that you were probably raped. We know your kidnapper died a horrible death, and the killer was most likely your wolf. That the memories have been hidden is a given. That they have been totally erased is not as clear. I love you so much, Em. I don't want our mating bond to bring you pain. What if everything comes back? What if it's more than you want to know? There might have been a perfectly good reason for locking those memories away.

There's never a good reason for stealing someone's memories. Never. If they come back, then I will deal with them. Maybe I'll be able to find out what happened, who did this to me, maybe I won't. But Gabe, if all I discover is that you are my bonded mate for all time, I'll be content. I love you. I've loved you for what feels like forever, but I never dreamed you might love me. I think I'm afraid you'll change your mind.

Too late for that.

She turned to run but he was much too quick. His heavy jaws came down on the thick fold of skin between her neck and shoulders, and he held on, grasping her middle with his powerful front legs. He was such a sensitive lover in his human form, his speed and bestial savagery was a shock, but it had the desired effect. She planted her feet to support his greater weight, turned and snarled at him with her ears back, and lifted her tail to one side.

Obviously her wolf wasn't concerned with foreplay. She felt the sharp stab as he entered her, the immediate response of her body as he thrust forward, finding her opening with unerring accuracy and sliding deep. The mating knot followed, tying them physically as her mind sought his, searching for the emotional mating that made each Chanku coupling unique.

Only as wolves, and only with their chosen mate, could the link succeed. Em wanted to cheer when she felt herself falling into Gabe, into his past, his childhood, his needs, his fears, the things that made him happiest, and the powerful love he felt for Emeline Isobelle. She couldn't believe she'd ever doubted him, not when his love surrounded her, held her close, and filled all those places she'd ever thought were empty.

· · ·

He'd wanted to be gentle, wanted to treat her with respect and love, but his wolf had other ideas. Yet when he clasped her body to his, when he entered her in a single powerful thrust and almost immediately tied the two of them together, he knew this was what Em wanted. What both of them needed.

The physical tie was beyond amazing, but the mental link that followed was the closest thing to perfection he'd ever experienced. The memories he found in Em's mind were the things he remembered, and the beautiful little girl had loved him even then. He'd need to apologize when this was over, because he'd been such a clueless idiot. He'd had no idea how she felt.

How seriously she loved. He could have stayed there forever in her memories of such an idyllic childhood, but just as no child stays the same age forever, Em continued to grow. He was there when she and Luci plotted to lock both Gabe and Aaron in one of the barns, and wanted to laugh at her attempts to explain what they'd been up to when Anton had caught them.

And then, on a day like any other, he was in her mind when she and Luci and Phoenix Wolf went to the mall with Annie. With her when the man turned from charming and friendly to dangerous human predator, when he held a gun to her back, took her by the arm, threatened to kill Phoenix if Em didn't tell her friend she'd be back in a few minutes.

He felt her terror and wanted to stop, but their bodies were tied and their minds caught in the mating link, and he couldn't pull free, couldn't stop what both of them were living through as the man forced her into his van and covered her face with a smelly cloth.

And that was where her memories stopped. She struggled against Gabe, against the mating knot holding them together, and Gabe tried to calm her but she was hysterical. Trapped in her wolf and totally out of control, snapping and growling. He shifted to set her free and the power of their link forced the shift on Em, but the woman in his arms was crazed with fear, incoherent and panic-stricken. She looked at him, eyes cat-green and filled with horror. He had no idea where her mind was or what she saw, but he opened his thoughts to catch her and hold her close.

He was fully linked to Em when she lost it.

She screamed, an unholy shriek of pure terror that turned into a leopard's cry. Her fear was a weapon, a blade that pierced his heart, exploded in his mind. He was only vaguely aware he was holding a panic-stricken snow leopard as both of them fell.

• • •

"I could tell you stories about Alex . . ." Annie took another swallow of her wine and rolled her eyes. They'd all ended up in the sunroom with the lights of the city glowing between the house and the Pacific, and smaller lights far out to sea where huge cargo ships and passenger liners moved slowly across the horizon.

Alex leaned over the back of the couch. "You could, but you won't, because I know stories about you that are every bit as good."

She tilted her head and met his lips, and as much as she loved having all the girls around, right now she just wanted Alex.

"Holy shit. What's that?"

Annie broke away from Alex, glanced briefly at Sissy, who'd been the one to shout, and then stared at the glowing apparition beginning to take shape in front of the window. Ignoring the gasps of shock from the girls, Annie said, "Eve? What are you doing here?"

"Is the pack okay?" Alex was around the couch and standing in front of Eve before their goddess could answer.

She nodded. "The pack is okay. Gabe and Em are not. They need you. They're unconscious at Keisha's garden, and I fear it's my fault. Hurry. Take a car, and be careful. There are other predators awake tonight. I'm going to them."

She disappeared and the questions flew. Annie was already slipping on a pair of shoes. "Later. We'll explain it when we get back. I want you guys to stay here. That was Eve, our goddess. We'll tell you more after we get Em and Gabe."

She followed Alex down the stairs. By the time she got to the garage, he already had the company van started and the garage door open. There was no traffic this late at night, and they reached the park within a couple of minutes, parked illegally and raced across the grass to the memorial garden.

Eve's glow lit the area around the monument. Gabe and Em lay close together, both of them naked. Alex knelt beside Gabe and checked his pulse, then Em's. "They're breathing, but something's clawed the hell out of Gabe's chest."

Annie lifted one of Em's hands. Her fingernails were bloodstained and broken. "Em. Let's get them in the van."

Still kneeling, Alex lifted Gabe like a child in his arms, and struggled to his feet with the heavy load of a man who weighed every bit as much as he did. "Stay with Em. I'll be right back."

Annie nodded as he left. She turned to Eve. "What happened?"

Eve sat beside her and ran her fingers through Em's hair. "They mated, or tried to, but during the bonding, Em's memories began coming back. Not all of them, but enough to trigger the block that's been in place since she was taken."

"Why were her memories blocked? That's not right."

"It's not my story to tell, Annie. Alex is coming back, and I can't hold my form here any longer. We'll talk when you're all in Montana. Thank you, and Alex and Em and Gabe for finding the four who are Chanku. I had no idea. Sometimes I feel such a failure."

Eve began to fade before Annie could wrap her thoughts around her strange comment. Her fading fingers brushed Em's face once again before she disappeared completely. Alex showed up right after she disappeared, lifted Em and walked with Annie back to the van. He didn't ask about Eve.

"We have to go to Montana," she said, "now that the girls have shifted. Eve said we'd talk there. Whatever happened tonight was because Em and Gabe were trying to mate. The mating link triggered Em's memories, but the kidnapping memories were blocked as we suspected. Somehow, accessing those memories is what knocked them both out. I hope they're okay."

Alex paused while Annie opened the back door on the van. "Gabe wanted to bring Mary's father to visit," he said. Carefully he lay Emeline down across the middle seats, and then checked on Gabe. He hadn't moved. "We'll have to let Mary know that the visit will have to be delayed. I don't want her left here alone with her family." Alex went around to the front and got in.

Annie took the passenger seat and they headed back to the house while Annie kept watching both Gabe and Em. They didn't seem to be in any distress, but their lack of consciousness was frightening.

So were the deep, bloody scratches across Gabe's chest, and the blood caked beneath Em's fingernails.

The girls met them in the garage and carried Em upstairs to her bedroom. Annie took Gabe's feet while Alex looped his arms around Gabe's body, lifting his head and shoulders. It was awkward and hard to carry him, but he was still unconscious when they reached Em's room.

They lay him on the bed beside Em. Annie lifted Em's hands and sighed. "I don't want them to awaken to Gabe's bloody chest and Em's bloody fingernails." She went into the bathroom and rinsed two clean washcloths in warm water. Handing one to Alex, she went to work on Em's hands. Alex cleaned away the blood and washed the slashes on Gabe's chest.

"She didn't do all these scratches. Look at her nails. Em keeps them clipped short. These are deep. They're going to leave scars without stitching. Do we have any strips? That might hold them together long enough for them to start healing."

"I'll get them." She found a box of the tiny bandages with the really good glue. They wouldn't stay on once Gabe shifted, but at least they should hold the cuts together while he slept. She helped Alex put the worst of the wounds together, and then finished cleaning up the mess. He was right, though. The slashes across his chest were much too deep for Em's fingernails

They were still unconscious when Annie pulled the down comforter up over the two of them.

"I'll stay with them," Alex said. He looked horribly tired and very depressed. "Why don't you go down and explain who Eve is and as much as we know about what happened."

"We don't know much." She walked around the bed and looped her arms over his shoulders. "I love you so much. You're a good man, Alex Aragat, and I want very much to be your wife. So, in case you were wondering, yes. I do want to marry you at the winter solstice celebration." She kissed him then, and when she left the room, it felt so good to know she'd left him smiling.

All six of the girls waited in the kitchen, sitting at the long trestle table with cups of hot chocolate. When she stepped into the room, Sissy stood and went over to the stove. "We saved you some. Whipped cream?"

"Oh, yeah. After tonight? You might want to make it a double."

Sissy grinned at her and gave the mug of steaming chocolate two big shots of whipped topping and then sprinkled tiny chocolate bits on top. "I'd put a shot of brandy in it, but I'm afraid you'd do a face plant on the table."

"You're probably right. Thanks." Annie took the mug and grabbed the chair at the head of the table with three of the girls to her right and three to her left. "Okay, I know you've got a million questions, but let me tell you what I know that happened tonight, and maybe that'll answer some of them. It actually started earlier in the week when we learned that Em has a big blank area in her memories. It's as if she didn't exist during part of her teen years, but I remembered an incident when she was kidnapped by a serial rapist, escaped after a couple of days and showed up at her parents' house covered in blood. It wasn't hers. About a week later, the body of a man was found in his rented house. He'd been eviscerated by a large animal of some kind, at least that's what the coroner finally decided, though he'd started to decompose, so it was hard to tell."

"Em?" The shock in Mbali's voice was echoed by the looks on the rest of the girls.

"Most likely, but we don't know if there was any follow-up by the police or not. Em doesn't remember any of it. She and Gabe love each other, and tonight—and we don't know why they chose tonight—they decided to mate. Mating for Chanku is a forever thing, so it's not a decision they would have made lightly. It's also unique in that we can only mate with one of our own kind, and the bond will only happen if we mate in our animal form. Most of us can become other kinds of predators, but as far as I know, the mating usually occurs as wolves. During the actual mating, a mental link forms that essentially shares whatever is in your mind—it's like downloading your brain's hard drive into your mate's brain's hard drive—but it creates a powerful link of such intimacy that you are forever bound to that person. Alex and I are mated. I know that he's sitting beside Em and Gabe right now and he feels terrible because he loves them and wants to help, but there's nothing any of us can do until they awaken. That's part of what a link does. It gives you constant access to the one you love. Anyway, something went very wrong when Gabe and Em mated, and we think it has to do with those missing memories."

"Will they be okay?" Sissy looked as worried as Annie felt, but she'd really connected with Em, which made perfect sense. Em was the one who'd found her and saved her.

"We think so, though we need to get them both to Montana, where they have family and we have healers who might be able to help."

"Who was the ghost?" Mary glanced at the others and then focused on Annie. "That was so bizarre. You called her Eve? Like in Adam and Eve?"

Annie laughed. "That's actually sort of funny. We Chanku have a unique relationship with our goddess and the Mother. The Mother is the ultimate ruler and she appears very rarely. I think the only one who occasionally hears from her is Sebastian Xenakis, the guy who's mated to Gabe's older sister, but our first goddess was named Liana. She screwed up and let the mate of one of our packmates die before our time. His name was Adam and his mate was Eve, and that was purely coincidence. When

Eve died, the Mother was totally pissed off, and she booted Liana off the astral plane, which is pretty close to the veil that separates the realms of the living and the dead. Then she put Eve in Liana's place. That's the woman you saw. She was once a living, breathing person who had only discovered she was Chanku a couple of years before she died. She became our goddess, and Liana is actually mated to Adam now, and is much happier than she ever was living on the astral. Eve loves it, and loves her work as guardian to all of us."

"All of us?" Mary glanced at Mbali, Sissy and Janine. "Even the four of us?"

"Most definitely the four of you. She specifically thanked Alex and me for helping to find you. That's been a big problem, because so many Chanku, like you guys, have lost touch with their nature. They've become more human over the years as they lost the memories of who and what they are. Unless they've been exposed to the nutrients, and until they've had enough and have tried to change, Eve can't find them. We were only able to find the four of you because Sissy cried out with mindspeech and Em was close enough to hear her."

She smiled at Lindy and Nina. "I'm so glad we found the two of you, too. I hope you realize that Alex and Gabe are dead serious about backing your salon." She laughed, and there was a sense that, maybe, this was all going to turn out okay. For Sissy and Janine and Mbali, Lindy and Nina, even for Mary. "In fact, I think they envision an entire franchise, once you guys figure out what you're going to call it."

She finished off the rest of her sinfully sweet chocolate, pushed her chair back and stood. "Ladies, it's been a wild night and I need sleep. I have a feeling I'll be calling in sick tomorrow. Oh, and one more thing. Eve wants us all in Montana as soon as we're able. Mary, did your folks decided to come for a visit?"

Mary stared at her toes for a moment, then raised her head and shrugged. "I never called Dad back. He'll probably be pissed, but I shifted and then Mbali and Janine, and then all this with Gabe and Em. When do we go to Montana?"

"We'd like to leave as soon as Em and Gabe are able to travel. We can take the company jet, so it's not a long trip. Call your dad in the morning, tell him that a couple of our packmates have been hurt and we're going to have to delay their visit. Maybe once we get to Montana, we can invite them up there instead. For that, though, I'll need to speak with Anton. He's Gabe's dad, and our pack's alpha, the leader."

Mbali giggled.

"What?"

"Leader of the pack?" She laughed even harder. "The foster home where I was raised, the lady loved old music. She had a song she used to play about the leader of the pack. All us kids would run around making motorcycle noises."

Annie hugged her. "Probably best not to do motorcycle noises for Anton. He might not appreciate the humor." She chuckled though. Knowing Anton, he'd probably love it. "Good night, all. I'm outta here."

She went straight to Em and Gabe's room. Alex had crawled in behind Gabe, so Annie slipped out of her clothes and got into bed behind Em. Alex reached for her, clasping her fingers. *I love you,* he said.

That was all she needed to hear before sleep took her.

12

Gabe lay on his back, blinking at the sunlight pouring into Em's bedroom. Em slept, snuggled close against his side, one hand resting over his heart. His skin beneath her hand felt raw, but the pain wasn't enough to concern him. He picked up Alex and Annie's scent, but they weren't in the room. He couldn't see the clock without moving, and he didn't want to disturb Em, but he knew it had to be late because of the amount of sunlight streaming through the window.

He had no idea how he'd gotten here. Last night seemed so long ago, lost in a foggy haze of what might have been dreams, or possibly a nightmare. Darkness and screams and an enraged leopard, but it was all jumbled in scattered bits and pieces. He went back to what was a clear memory—going in search of Em after he'd been an absolute horse's ass. He remembered following her scent along the walking trail above the Great Highway, finding her above the Sutro Baths.

He'd asked her to be his mate. She'd agreed, but then what? Vaguely he recalled his mom's memorial garden in Golden Gate Park. Facing Em amid the sweet grasses that meant so much to all of them. He'd mounted her, and the memory left a hollow feeling in the pit of his gut. No finesse there, from what he could recall, but it was coming back to him, the way her body had supported his, the mating knot binding them together, and then the mental connection, that perfect synchronization of her memories to his.

And then . . . nothing. He had to believe they'd gotten close to the kidnapping. He vaguely recalled her memories of going to the mall with Annie, in her mind and her point of view, but that was how it worked when you accessed your mate's memories. It was as if you were them, if only for the brief, soul-deep connection, but beyond that? Nothing at all. Not until he awakened a few moments ago.

He rolled over and pulled Em into his embrace, held her close to his heart, listened to the small hitch in her breathing that told him she was awake. She rubbed her face against his chest, ran her tongue over something that burned like fire and his body jerked.

"Gabe? What happened?"

She pushed away and stared at him with a look of absolute horror. He was watching her eyes, but as she backed away, he realized her cheek was smeared with fresh blood. Quickly he lowered his gaze, stared at his chest. He was covered with deep, still seeping scratches. Some were held together with bandage strips, most were scabbed over, but where Em's face had rested . . . *holy shit.* He reached out, ran his finger along her bloodstained cheek, lifted her chin and kissed her.

I don't know, but it doesn't matter. You're okay. I'm . . . well, almost okay. He was careful to keep his mental voice upbeat. The last thing he wanted to do was frighten her. He was certain they'd had enough of a scare last night. He kissed her again. *I'm glad it's my blood and not yours. I love you, Em. I know we tried to mate last night, but it appears something went a little bit wrong.*

She touched his chest, brought her hand away covered in flakes of dried blood as well as fresh. "Gabe? You're still bleeding. Good Goddess, Gabe. What happened to you? Did I do this? Oh, Gabe . . . you're a mess. Something must have gone a lot more than just a little bit wrong." She tried to push herself away, but he held her.

"It doesn't matter. What matters is that you're okay. Alex and Annie slept with us last night. I don't remember coming home, so they must have come after us, somehow got us back here. I have no idea how they knew we needed help, but obviously we did. We'll find them, find out what's going on."

He kissed her, drew her taste into his mouth, breathed in her scent and swallowed the sounds she made. She was his, she was everything he wanted, but why the fuck couldn't he remember? He remembered the beginning of the mating bond, and when he'd tried to link with her, she'd been right there in his thoughts, the way she should have been. Even now, their connection felt the way it would if they were bonded, but they weren't. Not entirely. Still, he felt her pleasure, her love, her fear of what had happened last night.

Gabe? You guys awake?

Alex? Yeah, but it's important that you leave us alone for a while. A couple hours at least. Em and I are trying to figure out what happened.

Got it. Good luck. And then he was gone.

Knowing they wouldn't be interrupted made it so much easier. Gabe kissed Em again, and the more they kissed, the more she relaxed beneath him. Her body melted against his, all soft curves and warmth, and the sounds she made were the sounds of want, of need, of pure desire. She'd been shivering moments ago, so afraid of what they'd done, but now she felt like love. He kissed his way down her throat, across her collarbone and along the curve of her shoulder. Skipped to the sensitive, soft skin of her inner arm and then to the sweet curve of her breast. She arched against him, all sense of the lingering questions over last night lost in the pounding cadence of her heart, her sweet sighs and moans of pleasure.

He moved lower, kissing his way across the soft curve of her belly, around the dark thatch of curls at the juncture of her thighs. He teased her then, stopping to inhale her scent, to lap up the moisture gathering for him, but she was tugging at his arms, pulling him up and over her body, and he slipped so easily into her heat, finding her slick sheath and entering her carefully, slowly as her muscles clenched along the full length of his cock.

He knew she could take all of him, but she was still so tight, just as her wolf had been tight when he'd mounted her last night. Her wolf, and something more. Something teased at the edge of memory even as he fell into a comfortable rhythm sliding in and out of her. His thoughts were coming together as he recalled the fierce joy of claiming her as his mate, the wondrous montage of memories shared as they'd learned the small things about one another's childhoods.

He remembered the mall, her fear as the strange man led her away, and now he struggled not to share the moment when that cloth covered in what had to have been chloroform was pressed against her mouth.

She'd struggled, but the drug had taken away her will. The memory had terrified her until Gabe had done the only thing he could think of—he'd shifted back to his human self and he'd forced Emeline to shift with him. But she hadn't wanted to shift. She'd wanted to kill the one who took her. Lost in terror, she'd shifted once more.

He'd been holding a terrified woman who'd become a furious snow leopard in his arms. She'd clawed him, trying to escape. No wonder the scratches were so deep. No wonder they still bled. She would feel horrible, but he refused to hide the memory from her. She'd had too much stolen already. He would tell her, but not now. Not while they loved.

"Em," he whispered. "I love you so."

Her eyes had been closed, but she opened them and reached for him, stroked his beard-roughened chin, traced the contours of his lips. Then she cupped his cheeks in both palms and raised up to kiss him. He met her halfway, taking her mouth in a kiss of feral intensity, thrusting deep, his tongue tangling with Em's, his cock filling her, sliding hard against the mouth of her womb. They'd not completed their mating dance, and until they knew her truth, understood the depth of her pain, that would have to wait.

But he wanted her. All of her. She'd fought him last night out of fear. Now he wanted her fighting with him, pushing back the darkness and joining with him with everything she was able to give. His rhythm increased, hard and fast, his tongue in her mouth, his cock sliding in and out of her just as it had been when he'd taken her as a wolf. Feral, as far from the gentle loving they'd started as their wolves were from their human counterparts.

Em arched her back, crying out as she tilted her hips to meet him. Lifting her, Gabe sat back on his heels and she wrapped her legs around his hips, whimpering as he lifted her with each powerful stroke. Holding her close, telling her with every move he made, with every breath he took that she was his. No matter what had happened, she was not damaged, she was perfect, and he was never letting her go.

Their climax slammed into both of them without warning. Em's keening wail seemed to wrap around Gabe's shout of release. Her inner muscles clamped down on his cock, holding him deep inside, clasping him so tight that it felt as it had when they'd tied as wolves. Gently, Gabe lowered her to the bed without collapsing on her much smaller body. His arms shook from the strain of holding himself above her. Laughing, she reached for him and pulled him down to cover her.

He sprawled across her, laughing softly. "I feel like melted wax, but damn, Em. You feel good." He nuzzled her tangled hair and planted a gentle kiss on her cheek.

"Mmmmm . . ." She blinked lazily. "Now that we've got that out of our systems . . ."

"Give me a minute. I'm not through yet." He lifted himself on his forearms so he could look into her brilliant green eyes. At the same time, he thrust his hips forward, letting her know in no uncertain terms he was far from done.

She raised her head and nipped his chin. "Yes, you are. For now anyway." She sighed and lifted her arms to loop them over his shoulders. "Gabe, what happened last night? You realize you're still bleeding, don't you? I don't recall becoming a leopard, but I must have. The last thing I remember is you mounting me as a wolf, that memory of the man in the mall and the smell of that nasty rag he put over my mouth and nose, and then nothing."

"It was chloroform. I recognized the smell from your memories, but

Em, someone took those memories from you. I want to give them back to you so you can bury them yourself. What happened to you at the hands of that bastard was wrong, but trying to protect you from the truth was worse. Link with me. I want you to know what happened last night. At least as much as I can recall. You did become a leopard, but only for a very brief time. Mostly, you were just absolutely beautiful, a magnificently furious beast. And I think that beautiful creature is the one who saved your life."

He thrust his hips slowly, tightening the connection between them, both mental and physical. Taking her slowly to a pitch of arousal that would have her entire body thrumming with the energy of the two of them together. Similar to the mating link, but not entirely. He'd not be going into her memories, wouldn't force her to relive anything more than she was ready for, but once they were totally in sync, hearts pounding as one, breathing in and out at exactly the same rate, he linked their minds, using his to draw her in, to show her he would keep her safe.

And then he took her back to last night, to that time when they were tied together in Keisha's garden. When their minds and bodies were entirely aligned, but it was Emeline's memories guiding them.

• • •

This felt the same but not. Em saw her memories filtered through Gabe's recall of last night. She was in the mall, but not, talking with Phoenix, but their conversation was muted, the context not important. What was important was the good-looking guy who appeared to be following them.

Neither one of them was anything special. Just a couple of teenage girls hanging out in the mall, giggling, being silly and pretending to be older than they were. She remembered that fourteen was such an awkward age, especially for Chanku girls, who tended to reach puberty later than most humans, but she and Phoenix were beginning to have more awareness of that damned Chanku libido, which tended to show itself when they least expected it.

The man was cute, though, and he smiled at her when she turned and caught his eye. Then, a few minutes later he caught up to them, talking about the stuff in the window, asking where they went to school. The kinds of things another kid would ask, which would have raised a red flag except he looked fairly young and he was so cute and they were so terribly naive.

He glanced down, bent over and came up with a twenty-dollar bill. "Here," he said. "One of you must have dropped this."

She'd looked at Phoenix and shrugged, and Phoenix laughed. "Not mine. I didn't even bring a purse with me. No money."

"Here," he said, handing the money to Phoenix. "Why don't you go and get us all an ice cream?"

"Sure." Phoenix grabbed the twenty and ran into the shop across the way from the store where they were standing.

As soon as she left, the man grabbed Em's arm and something poked her in the side. "I have a gun in my jacket pocket," he said. "I will kill you and your little friend unless you come with me. Now."

She followed him, and when Phoenix came out of the ice cream shop with three ice cream sandwiches, Em turned to her and forced a smile. "I'll be right back, Phoenix." And then she tried to mindspeak, to tell her to get help, but she was so frightened she couldn't form the thoughts, so she forced herself to get control, to push the terror down where it couldn't strangle her. By then they'd reached his car, a black van with dark windows, and he shoved her inside and then covered her face with a smelly rag. She felt her gorge rise up, knew she was going to vomit, but then everything faded away. The man was gone, light was gone. She was gone.

Em knew, with a rational part of her mind, that this was a memory, not something happening now, and since she was seeing it through Gabe's mind, she knew he was right there with her, but it was still so scary her entire body tensed, her muscles tightening, including those in her vagina closing like a fist around Gabe's cock.

And it was Gabe's, though now she could remember more. That other man, forcing her, and they were her memories, not Gabe's. But Gabe was with her now. Protecting her.

It's okay, Em. If you don't want to go any further, you can stop right here, right now. I will never ask you to do anything you don't want to do.

I want to know, Gabe. As long as you're with me, I'll be okay. Hold me. Don't let go of me.

Never. I've got you, Em. For always.

He kissed her. Sweet, gentle kisses in time with his slow, easy thrusts between her legs. Loving her, holding her, doing exactly as he'd promised. Keeping her safe. Safe enough to hunt for those lost memories.

And once again, she was there, but the link with Gabe was strong, those memories like an old film she'd not seen in years. The scene had faded out and now it slowly faded in and she was conscious, alone in a dark room with something covering the windows so no light came in except a tiny sliver around the edge of one window. For all she knew, it was the only window in the room, but it told her it was still daylight and she wasn't starving or thirsty yet, so she couldn't have been out for too long. For some reason she thought of Gabriel Cheval. She wasn't sure why, but it was probably because she was naked. She'd had dreams of being with Gabe when she was naked, and she hated the fact that this sick bastard had been the one to take her clothes off her, but at least it meant that if she needed to shift, she wouldn't have to worry about her clothes being in the way.

She wanted to shift, but one thing they'd been taught as children was that if anyone ever took them, unless shifting would help them escape, they were never to let their captors know they were Chanku. Not only did it turn them into a valuable commodity for criminals, keeping their abilities secret could give them an important edge in case there was a chance to overcome the bad guys. Even children could be deadly predators.

She could mindspeak, though, and call for help. She called out for Anton. If anyone could hear her, it would be Gabe's dad because he was amazing, and really powerful. Her dad was pretty cool, but Anton was their leader, and there wasn't anything he couldn't do. She called out to him, over and over, but he didn't answer. She tried calling her mom. Then her dad.

Nothing.

She tried to reach Annie and Phoenix and even Luci, but no one could hear her and she was so afraid because she didn't know where she was or what the man was going to do to her, but whatever it was couldn't be good.

Hours passed, but in her link with Gabe it was mere seconds. The sliver of light in the window was gone when the man came to her room. She asked for her clothes, but he laughed. She really had to pee, so she didn't complain when he took her to use the bathroom, but then the sick bastard stood in the doorway and watched. Being naked in front of others wasn't an issue with the pack, so even though she was mad at him, she pretended he was one of the guys she knew, and then she could go. He smiled at her then, like she'd done something special, or maybe it was the fact she'd done what he asked. That really pissed her off, but it was obvious no one was going to rescue her. She had to figure out how to rescue herself.

The place he'd brought her to was built like a prison. There were bars on the windows and a row of locks on the doors in front and in back, including a bar across each of them so no one could break in. She noticed a hatch-like cover in the hallway ceiling in front of the bathroom. It had to lead to a crawl space between the ceiling and the roof, but once she got up there, if she could get up there, she had no idea if there were any vents or openings for her to get out of the attic area. She'd have to be patient.

He took her back to her room, and that was the first time he raped her. She'd had sex before, so it wasn't like she was a virgin, but she'd never been forced. From the way he acted, she figured he wanted her to be afraid, so she screamed and tried to get away. He liked that, but she wasn't afraid. She was absolutely furious and she wanted to kill him, but she didn't want to do it until she had a way to get free so no one would know she'd done it. She knew that killing was wrong, and if any of them did it while they were in their animal forms, it could make a lot of trouble for the pack. That was a lesson that had been drilled into all of them over and over again—don't do anything to draw bad attention to the pack, unless you had no other recourse, because it could hurt all of them.

She didn't want to do that. He raped her again that night, more than once, but then he let her have dinner and pretended that he really liked her. That was when she decided he wasn't just an evil man, he was crazy, too. She wondered if anyone would believe her when she told them the things he made her do, and again she thought of Gabe. Why now, when she was stuck with a madman, did she keep thinking of him? Probably because she knew she'd love doing all these things with Gabe instead of with the idiot who'd kidnapped her. Things that she loved doing with her friends and wished she could do with Gabe, but when the bad guy made her do them she wanted to puke.

It was the second day, and she knew she had to do something to get away. The man was awful. He hadn't actually hurt her, but she was Chanku. No one should be forced to have sex, but it didn't have the same taboos for her that it would for human kids. She asked him about that without giving her own nature away, asked him if he'd had other girlfriends, since that's what he'd started calling her. *His girlfriend.*

What he did terrified her, and everything changed. He pulled out a picture album she'd noticed earlier. He'd left it on a table, but she hadn't looked at it. She was glad then that she hadn't. It was filled with pictures of little girls and big girls, and even a few young women. Most of them were about her age, and all of them were dead. There were dozens of them, each with a name and a date written in thick, black pen at the bottom of the picture, and they hadn't been shot or anything. They looked like they were sleeping, except they were naked, and what she first thought were pictures painted on their bodies wasn't paint at all.

He'd carved things into their skin, and he'd either done it while they were alive and then he'd washed the blood off them, or he'd done it after they were dead and no longer capable of bleeding. She hoped it was the latter, feared it might be the former, and that made her think of the smelly rag. She could smell that same stench again, the one that had knocked her out.

He'd left the room, but now he was coming back.

She heard him moving quietly behind her. She didn't give it a thought. She shifted where she sat, and instead of choosing her wolf, she went for an even more lethal weapon.

She chose her snow leopard.

The moment she spun out of her chair, changed from compliant young girl to furious snow leopard, the man did two things: he dropped the smelly rag and then he pissed all over himself. He was naked and she wondered if he planned to knock her out and rape her while she was unconscious, and maybe cut her up then, but it didn't matter. She went for his throat, but she didn't kill him. She wanted him to know what she was doing, wanted him to suffer for all those little girls and big girls and young women he'd murdered.

She held him in a choke hold so he couldn't scream and then she disemboweled him. She'd heard her mother say that people were afraid of a leopard's bite but they forgot about their claws, especially the ones on their back feet. The best part was that he was still alive when she'd ripped him to shreds, so she bit him once more on the throat, crushing his windpipe. That way he couldn't scream anymore while he died, and that was going to take a while. She wanted him to have time to think about dying, about all those girls he'd killed.

The entire scene within her memories, even knowing Gabe was with her, took on a dream-like quality. She thought about shifting so she could open the front door and walk out of this horrible place, but she didn't know where her clothes were, so she went back to the hallway, jumped up on a table and shoved at the hatch cover in the ceiling. It popped free and she leapt from the table to the opening. There was a vented window at one end of the attic space and she shoved at it with her shoulder until it popped free.

It was dark again. She'd lost all track of time, but she stared about her, checking out the neighborhood from her perch in the attic, figured out which way the mountains lay, and jumped. It was only about fifteen feet to the ground, and she left the little house and the dying man behind and headed for home.

It was almost dawn when she got there, and for whatever reason she wasn't sure why she'd been away or why she was covered in blood. She knew, but it was all so ugly, that it was easier to pretend it never happened, so she curled up on Anton and Keisha's front porch and went to sleep. Gabe wasn't here—not in her memories. He was away at college, but it was almost as good, sleeping at his house. She knew he liked to tease her, but she also knew he'd take care of her. He always had, hadn't he?

She wished he'd quit calling her EmyIzzy. Such a stupid name for a grown girl. It was okay for a baby, but she hadn't been a baby for a long time. And after what had happened to her, Em had a feeling she was never going to be a kid again.

Exhausted, she let the link fade, sent the memories away until she was back in the midst of the blissful present. Gabe lay beside her with one leg across her thighs. She didn't remember him pulling out, but she still felt connected to him despite the fact they were no longer making love.

"Did I do it to myself? Am I the one who made me forget?"

"I don't know, sweetheart." He brushed her hair back from her eyes. "But if you were, it was probably the smartest thing you could have done. That doesn't account for the fact that no one else seems to know, either. Not Luci, at least. She's not one to keep any secrets, or at least she wasn't when she was a kid." He kissed her again, his mouth so sweet, the kiss so tender she almost cried.

Then she realized it was too late—she'd already been crying and her cheeks were wet from tears, but so were Gabe's. She brushed them off with her thumbs and kissed him again. "I guess we need to get up, huh?"

"Yeah. I don't know how long it's been since Alex asked if we were okay, but I told him to give us time. No idea how much time he's given us, though." He sat up and tugged Em upright to sit beside him. "You okay?"

She nodded, surprised at how good she felt. "I feel lighter. I know what happened and it was pretty awful, but seeing it filtered through your mind made it easier to accept. I'm glad I killed him."

"Me, too. Very effective. I'm guessing that the police found his album."

"I hope so, though I want to ask my folks. I'm so glad you helped me uncover the memories. I was so angry with my parents."

"I know. I was pissed at my dad, too." He laughed. "I'm glad I never said anything, but I still feel like I owe him an apology."

Laughing, Em stood and caught Gabe's hand. Dragging him off the bed, she glanced over her shoulder and said, "Well, let's not go overboard, okay?"

He threw an arm around her shoulders, and both of them were laughing as they headed in to take a shower. Em thought of the night they'd had, the fact they'd not really mated, and decided that was something they had to look forward to. Maybe, with any luck, if it wasn't too late, they could leave for Montana today.

13

Most of Gabe's bandages fell off in the shower, but Em made a point of replacing the ones on the deepest cuts. He said, "I think I could get used to this," as she carefully applied a strip to both sides of a particularly deep slash.

She raised her head and cocked one eyebrow. "What? Me trying to gut you?"

He laughed as she went back to her job. "Well, no. Not that. I like the attention, though."

This time she rolled her eyes and then kissed a spot above the bandage. "That's because you're male. If you're anything like Aaron, you'll whimper over the small stuff and be brave and stoic with the real boo-boos."

He slapped his hand over his heart. "You're saying these aren't real?"

Instead of the laughter he expected, she merely shook her head and stared at his chest. "I wish they weren't. I hate that I did this to you, Gabe. Will you ever forgive me?" When she looked at him, her eyes were swimming with tears.

"There's nothing to forgive. I think the mating bond took you back to the time when you killed him. You were fourteen years old when that happened, had been held by that bastard long enough to know you might not get out alive. I'm surprised that all you did was leave a few scratches, but I'm the one who needs to ask for forgiveness. I had an idea what we might find when we mated, but I thought I could handle it. I had no right to ask that of you. No right at all."

"Well, I for one am glad you did." This time she smiled openly at him. "I feel lighter, freer, than I've felt for so long I don't remember what freedom felt like, but I like it. I love you, Gabe. I can say it without any doubts at all. You've seen me at my worst and haven't run screaming from me."

"Never." He pressed his forehead against hers. "You ready to face the troops? They're going to want to know what happened."

"They need to know. I sure needed to know." She patted the last strip into place. "There, but put on a shirt, okay? I don't want them reminded of how stupid I was last night."

"I'll wear a shirt, but only because I don't want to ruin anyone's appetite. They're badges of honor, Em. I'm so proud of you. The person you are now and the brilliant and brave girl you were so many years ago. C'mon. What you went through and survived should tell you how strong you are. Personally, I find it terribly sexy." He leaned over and kissed her.

She laughed. "Gabe, I think you'd find an old sweatshirt sexy."

"Only if it's yours, sweetheart. Only yours." He wrapped an arm around her waist, and they walked down the hall to the kitchen, where a loud and rather heated argument appeared to have everyone involved.

• • •

Em stopped so quickly in the doorway to the kitchen that Gabe almost piled into her. Sissy was standing up at the end of the table, leaning forward and shouting at Mary, who sobbed, shoulders shaking, her head buried in her arms. Mbali screamed something at Sissy, but Janine had her arms around Mbali's waist to keep her from attacking.

There was no sign of Alex or Annie, and Lindy and Nina, the only non-Chanku in the room, sat close together at the far end of the table, watching everything with expressions shifting from avid curiosity to absolute terror. Gabe started forward, but Em shoved him back with a palm against his belly. At least she'd remembered that she'd already carved up his chest. She stalked into the kitchen and got right in Sissy's face. "Stop this now."

It wasn't a shout, but it worked. Sissy backed off, Janine let go of Mbali, and Mary raised her head. "Mary?" Em said. "What's going on?"

"She is such an idiot!" Sissy slapped the table, and Em turned and stared at her. She didn't say a word, but her expression could have filled a book.

Gabe leaned against the wall and watched.

Sissy hung her head. "I'm sorry," she mumbled. "But . . ."

"I asked Mary. Please sit down, Sissy. You too, Janine, Mbali. Mary, do you want to tell me here, or would you rather go in the other room?"

Mary shook her head. "Here is okay. Sissy's mad because I told my father what I am. He's disowned me. Said that, as far as he was concerned, I was dead, that I was better off dead."

Em merely nodded. Then she turned to Sissy. "And why is Mary's issue with her father your problem, Sissy?"

"It's not my problem, it's . . ."

"Exactly. It's Mary's and she will have to deal with it. Not you. Did she ask for your opinion?"

Sissy shook her head. "No."

"We'll talk later, okay?" Em stared at Sissy until the taller woman nodded. "Where are Annie and Alex?"

"They left about half an hour ago. Said they were going to get something for lunch."

"Good. I'm starving." She took a slow breath as if shaking off tension, and glanced at the four women. "Look, I don't know all the details and it's not my place to judge anyone here. You're all adults and should know how to act accordingly, but you're also pack, and Lindy?" She glanced at the two sitting as far from the shapeshifters as they could possibly be. "I'm including you and Nina in the group unless or until you choose to opt out, but packmates stick together. When there's a problem, we talk it out, find a way to work together. We don't always agree, but we find a way to get along. Shouting solves nothing, and for shapeshifters, it can lead to tragic results if arguments get out of hand and your predators take over. Another thing—when you get to Montana, you'll notice that the pack hierarchy is more powerful. Sissy? Did you notice the way you deferred to me?"

Sissy nodded and quietly sat down at the table.

"That happened because I'm what we call an alpha bitch, and that's not bragging, nor is it an insult. Essentially, my orders trump yours, but it's not something you can fight. It just is. The longer you're openly Chanku, the better your wolf will understand the way power within the pack works. It's not always age or anything you can put your finger on, but it's sort of the way things work in the BDSM world. There are dominants and there are submissives, and all different levels in between. My nature is dominant. I think yours is, too, but because you're new at this, your wolf hasn't learned to establish and hold on to authority. It will happen, but along with more power comes more responsibility, and yelling at an obviously upset packmate is a misuse of that power. You owe Mary an apology, though I'm not going to force it on you. It has to come from your heart, hopefully once you understand that what you were doing was wrong, even if your intentions were good."

"I know." Sissy stared at the table, let out a slow breath and raised her head to look directly at Mary. "And I am sorry, Mary. For what it's worth, all I could see was your problem through my baggage. My mother's dead, I never knew who my father was, and I couldn't understand why you would intentionally drive your father away."

Mary wiped her face with a paper napkin. She glanced at Sissy and smiled, but she spoke directly to Em, acknowledging the stronger wolf in the room. Gabe wondered if Mary even noticed how her wolf was directing her actions. "It wasn't intentional," she said. "I called him this morning to tell him about the change in plans regarding their possible visit, and before I said anything he yelled at me for taking so long to get back to him. I told him that two of the people here had been hurt, and everyone was busy because of that and we might be going to Montana so he'd have to delay his trip out here if they wanted to come."

Gabe slipped around behind the table and filled a glass of water at the sink, carried it over to Mary, and handed it to her. She took a sip and then wiped her hand across her face. Then she smiled at him before turning back to face Em. Gabe was so proud of Em. She was handling this with the same kind of grace and style his mother was known for. He had a feeling Keisha would approve of her future daughter-in-law a hundred percent.

Mary took another swallow of her water. "Anyway, he went ballistic, said that whatever happened to you was deserved, that you were all evil and I needed to get out of here now. He demanded that I come home, that he'd talked to the minister and they were going to hold a prayer vigil for me to cleanse me of all the evil from my year of sin."

She frowned as she looked at Em. "Year of sin? I can't believe he said that. I reminded him that I'd been abducted at gunpoint, held captive and threatened with death, that I tried to escape and couldn't get away, and I didn't see any sin in anything that I did. He said I'd lived as a harlot and if I'd done it by choice I couldn't come home at all, but he'd gotten special permission to bring me back into the church." She laughed, but it was a harsh, bitter sound. "I knew then that I couldn't go home. Not ever. And Sissy, that's why I told him the truth. I couldn't let him think I agreed with or approved of anything he was saying. I told him that I had taken the nutrients and that I shifted, that since I knew he wanted nothing to do with shapeshifters, I was no longer his daughter." She sucked back a sob, and this time she looked directly at Gabe.

"I told him I had a family here, people who loved me, who more than approved of me. That if he and Mom ever wanted to visit, they were more than welcome, but that, under the circumstances, I thought it better for me not to go back to Indiana."

Gabe let out a big breath. He hadn't realized he'd been holding his breath, but . . . poor Mary! "I'm sorry, Mary, but you're right. You have a family here and we do love you, though I know that's not going to take away the hurt from your father's comments. I'd suggest you give him a couple of days, call and let him know that the offer to bring them out to see where you're living still stands."

"Thank you. I'll have to think about that. Right now, my gut reaction is to say not in this lifetime." She shrugged, and then glanced toward the garage and smiled. "I think I just heard Alex and Annie come back."

Em laughed. "You did. It's that wolf hearing. Hard to sneak up on any of us. Mary, Gabe is right. You are officially family once you're pack. All of you are, including Nina and Lindy. We'll have to make you two honorary Chanku."

Alex walked in with bags of something that smelled really good, and Annie was right behind him with more. Mexican this time, and they spread out a feast along the table for everyone to share. It wasn't until after lunch, when Sissy and Mary, Mbali and Janine had talked out their differences, and all of them helped clean up the mess, that Gabe sat down and pulled Em into his lap so they could tell everyone what had happened.

Finally, Em leaned her head against Gabe's shoulder and kissed his chin. "So that's why we ended up sleeping until almost noon. Gabe and I need to go to Montana. We want to get his parents and mine together and find out what they know about my kidnapping. It looks as if I might have buried these memories on my own, but that doesn't explain why no one else has ever said anything about it. Obviously, traditional human-based psychotherapy isn't going to work with a mindreading Chanku patient, but I can't believe there was no therapy of any kind offered to me, that no one talked to me about what I'd gone through."

"But that's where Eve comes in." Gabe squeezed Em in a tight hug, and the look she gave him, the pure love in her eyes actually made him ache. She was his, but not. They had to complete the mating bond. Until then, a huge part of what they deserved with one another remained lost to them. It wasn't easy to break away from her steady gaze, and he had to force himself back to the conversation. All he wanted to do was grab Em up in his arms and carry her back to the bed.

He chuckled and Em smiled. She knew exactly what he was thinking because she let him see that her thoughts mirrored his. He focused on the rest of the group and wondered what they thought of the things he and Em, Alex and Annie all took for granted. Like a goddess who visited them in person.

"My father built a unique family room in our house," he said. "It has five walls, so it's shaped like a pentagram. Dad's a wizard as well as being Chanku, and he's used his magic to make the room more accessible to our goddess. It's not just the shape but the magic as well that makes it easier for Eve not only to visit this plane, but to remain on it for a longer time. We're hoping she'll be able to tell us more of what happened. The fact she wants all of us together in Montana to talk is important, and it's part of the reason we're hoping you'll all come with us."

"The thing is," Em said, "I know my parents lied to me, if only by omission, but someone messed with the memories of the other girls who were there. Not Annie's, but definitely Phoenix and Luci's. I'm sure it was done to protect me, but by hiding all that awful stuff, including that I killed a man to save my own life, they took away part of what makes me who I am. I survived, but because I couldn't remember it, I only had a vague sense of fear that never left me, a darkness in my soul that has changed my life, and not for the best."

She grabbed Gabe's hands with both of hers where they met at her waist, turned and gazed at him, smiling softly. "I could never love anyone, never even consider loving anyone, because I knew something was wrong. I've spent almost half of my life feeling damaged. Unworthy. I'm not. I refuse to feel like a victim because I'm more than that. I'm a survivor, but in order to complete the healing process, we need to find out what our parents know and what, if anything, they did to hide the kidnapping from me."

"So that's the reason Em and I have to go to Montana—because we want to complete our mating, and until we get this all straightened out, we're afraid to try it again." Gabe planted a kiss on Em's cheek. "But there's a multipurpose reason we want all of you to come with us. The winter solstice is coming up in eleven more days and it's a time of celebration for us. It's also a time to hold weddings and to bring new members into the pack. We want you to share the celebration with us as pack members."

"All of us who can get there try to be in Montana for whatever celebrations we're having," Em said. "I haven't been to one in eight years, so I'm excited to go."

Gabe leaned back and stared at her. "You haven't? It's been that long?"

"Yeah." She leaned against him and tilted her head back so she could look at him when she answered. The angle made her dark green eyes even more mysterious. "Once I went away to college," she said, "I always made excuses. Everyone was so happy, and I was so miserable, but I didn't know why. And the few times I'd tried to visit, my parents made me crazy." She shrugged and nestled back against his shoulder. "This time, though, they're not going to tell me what to do or how to live."

Gabe rolled his eyes and glanced at Alex. "Guess I don't get to boss her around, either. Ooof! Goddess, Em, you have such pointy little elbows. So, Annie . . . you and this guy going to get married?"

"Yes." Alex grabbed her around the neck and put her in a choke hold. "She already said she'd marry me, right, Annie?"

"Yeah, but I'm a woman. I can change my mind, and I'm still thinking about it. Let me go!"

"Never," Alex said. And then he kissed her.

That was about the time Gabe figured this meeting had officially ended.

• • •

Gabe walked up to the sunroom and found Nina and Lindy sitting together on the couch, poring over figures. "How's it coming?"

Nina raised her head and stared intently at him. "Are you and Alex serious? Do you have the money to front us for a salon? Because I really don't want to go to all this work and find out you've been stringing us along."

"That's why I came looking for you. Alex and I transferred the money into an account about an hour ago." He named a sum that had Nina gasping and reaching for Lindy's hand, so he figured that was a good sign. "It's in Alex and my names and you'll be added once we go over your business plan. I'm hoping you'll talk to Aaron Cheval. He's Em's older brother and a good attorney. He won't let you do anything that's not fair to you."

"But he works for you. Won't he want to set something up in your favor?"

Gabe laughed. "I wish. Aaron and I have been competing about everything since we were kids. He's going to be totally pissed off when he realizes Em and I are going to be mates, and hopefully getting married at the winter solstice. I imagine he'll be on your side, not mine, when it comes to negotiations."

He stepped over the back of the couch and slid onto the cushion beside Lindy. "I know you two don't know us very well, and you can't help but feel like outsiders to a certain extent because the other girls turned out to be Chanku, but for what it's worth, we do want you to feel as if you're pack. The six of you went through hell together, and that creates a bond that even genetics can't trump. Chanku Global Industries is known as a fair and honest company, and the honorable dealings and overall integrity that our board insists on are something we all believe in. I hope you'll trust us, but if you want outside advice, I'd suggest you find any legal firm you want to represent you, and we'll pick up their bill."

Nina glanced at Lindy. "We'll need to talk about it, okay?"

Gabe nodded. "I understand. Now, will you be okay here by yourselves? We need to take four new wolves out for their first run." He stood, and then realized they might like to go along. "You're welcome to come if you like, though it might be boring. We park at the foot of Mount Tam and take off from there. We'll probably be gone for at least a couple of hours."

"That's okay." Lindy gestured at the notepads they both had covered with figures. "That should give us time to get this put together so we have something to present."

He glanced at the figures, the notes they'd lined up in neat rows. "You certainly seem to know what you're doing. This is impressive."

Nina raised one dark eyebrow. "Well, I majored in accounting and business at Stanford before I was kidnapped. I was working on my master's in business. Lindy was already a CPA. Hair and nails are something we did for fun, and we're both interested in fashion and design. The fact that we both loved to sew and design clothes is what brought us together after we were kidnapped." She grinned at Lindy. "Well, that, and she's just too damned hot for words."

"Nina's right. We clicked right away as friends, and we're beyond sexually compatible. I fell in love with Nina the day I met her. We've talked about opening our own business ever since we were both kidnapped, so we already have a lot of ideas."

Gabe started for the door, but he paused and glanced at the two of them. They were both damned smart and so beautiful inside and out. "I hope you realize how sorry I am you're not Chanku. You both have so much to offer. We'll see you in a few hours, okay?"

Lindy turned and waved. Nina didn't even look up. She mumbled what sounded like "Bye," and kept working. Gabe headed downstairs. Em's voice popped into his head.

We're all in the van. Are you going to be much longer?

On my way. Em, I'm hearing you perfectly.

We might not be bonded mates, Gabe, but the darkness is gone.

There was such an open sense of joy to her mental voice, as if she'd never had those terrible shadows inside. *Do you want to try again? We'll have the others close by, in case there's trouble.*

Yes. I do, Gabe. This time, I think I might be ready.

He picked up her laughter as he climbed into the backseat beside Mary and Mbali. Janine, Sissy and Em had the next row. Alex was driving and Annie rode shotgun. They backed out of the garage, but traffic was heavy and it took a few minutes before Alex was able to pull out onto Sunset and head for the Golden Gate.

"Looks like the sunshine's gone for the day. We might get wet, ladies. I can't even see the top of Mount Tam."

"Should we have brought towels? I'd hate to get the inside of the van all muddy." Mbali stared at the dark skies and the way the ocean disappeared in the clouds lying on the horizon.

"No need," Em said. "One of the best things about being Chanku."

• • •

Alex drove beyond the parking lot where they'd taken Sissy running earlier in the week. He followed a road that wound along the eastern flank of the mountain until they found a small parking lot without any other vehicles. Gabe set up a privacy shade that looked like half a tent attached to the side of the big van, but it gave them a place to undress and shift in case other park visitors showed up. Saturdays weren't the best time for running wild, even on a day promising a cold rain, but they'd decided not to wait until after dark. Tonight they'd be packing up and getting ready to fly to Montana in the morning, and the new wolves were anxious to run.

At least Sissy was. She'd stripped off her clothes and shifted while still in the van, and now she paced outside, impatient to get going.

Gabe had given them a list of rules. She was surprised to know that wolves had rules, but he reminded her they might look like wolves, but they thought like humans . . . mostly. And it was important to act responsibly. Just because this particular parking lot was empty didn't mean the trails were empty. Mountain bikers and hikers could have parked in any number of places on the mountain. No sneaking up on hikers or bikers, and if there was an equestrian on the trail, they were to give horses and riders a wide berth.

There might not be a lot of wild wolves in the San Francisco Bay Area, but horses appeared to have the predators' scent genetically imprinted in the fear centers of their brains. Horses and wolves were not a good mix. Dogs on the trail were something else— some feared them, some wanted to play. Occasionally a hiker would scream and run away. They were not allowed to chase, no matter how much fun it looked like.

That one had all of them laughing. Some things were pretty obvious, though she wouldn't have thought of the horses if Gabe hadn't said something.

Finally, all of them had shifted and Alex found a place to hide the keys to the van. Then they trotted out of the parking lot—eight beautiful wolves in all sizes and colors. A few hikers on the trail stopped and just watched, others snapped pictures as they picked up speed and veered off the regular trail.

Chanku running in pairs were not unusual, but it was rare to see a large pack on the mountain in daylight. *We usually stick to the trails,* Gabe said, *but there are so many people out today I think we'll cut across the flank of the mountain and hit the higher regions. Then we can go back to running on the trails.*

He picked up the pace and they ran, all of them with tails flying and jaws wide to grab the fresh, rain-slick air. She'd wanted freedom above all else, but Sissy had never dreamed of freedom such as this, the way it made her feel, the way it sounded and smelled. It even had a taste—the taste of fresh air on her tongue, filling her mouth as she raced through the tall winter grasses. She glanced at Mbali, at Janine and Mary, and touched their thoughts.

There were no words. They ran with a single unifying thought—joy. This was freedom, this was the life each one had dreamed of, this was joy.

• • •

Alex and Annie took the girls higher on the mountain, following a rugged trail that might even give them a chance to chase a rabbit or two, while Em and Gabe split off toward Muir Woods. There were areas of the redwood forest there that were as private and primeval as if man had never stepped foot within its boundaries. For the past twenty years, an effort had been made—financed heavily by CGI—to reforest much of Mount Tam and return it to its earlier glory, before so much of it had been logged when California was young.

It's not Montana, but I don't want to wait. Gabe ran on Em's right flank, so high on her scent it was hard not to stop and take her right here on the trail, but then he remembered how their mating—or attempted mating—had gone last night, and he knew he wasn't going to waste this second chance. He'd not been a very thoughtful lover, but he'd underestimated the feral power of a wolf ready to mate. Tonight he wanted to take his time and savor his mating with Emeline. He loved her. He planned to love her for the rest of his life. There was no need to rush.

I don't want you to hold back, Gabe. The only thing not perfect about last night was the fact I tried to kill you. My wolf was perfectly happy with your wolf's form of foreplay.

The killing part was not good. Let's try to avoid that tonight. He nipped her flank to show her he was teasing, but then he added, *There wasn't any foreplay. That's the problem.*

For you, maybe. Not for me. I think that, at least as wolves, there's something very sexy about all that power.

He didn't answer her. He couldn't. He wanted her so badly it was all he could do to run without stumbling, without chasing her down and taking her here and now. No foreplay? He could do that. Whatever Emeline wanted.

14

They'd reached a heavily forested area on the north side of the mountain. Em's paws no longer pounded against a hard-packed trail. They'd entered an area where moss grew thick and the ground was covered in spongy red humus. Ferns filled the spaces between the trees, and dark strands of winter-burned vines looped among the branches. Though the rain had stopped, water still dripped from the trees and fog dimmed what little light could filter through the heavy growth. A few of the redwoods were massive, but many were only fifteen or twenty years old, freshly planted by CGI donations and hours of labor put in by many of the employees. It made Em feel as if this forest was pleased with the Chanku, with what they'd done to help renew what had been lost over the years.

It took her mind off what was coming, what she wanted with equal feelings of fear and wonder. They'd come so close to the mating bond, but close was a chasm of unbelievable distance, and the fear they'd never close that separation was a constant ache. She wanted more, and she wanted Gabe. She'd loved him forever, but that childhood crush, that sense of love was nothing to the depth and breadth of what filled her now. So much, so terribly raw and yet so beautiful. She looked at him and saw her future—the only one who would ever completely love and understand her because their minds would be forever linked.

As part of a pack, she'd been surrounded by mated couples, pairs so entirely in sync with one another that, while their individual personalities were unchanged, their connection to the one they loved was undeniable. She'd tasted that connection with Gabe this morning, when he'd taken her through the lost memories of her kidnapping. Her memories, but with

Gabe beside her, the memories—as horrific as they were—lost their power. She'd seen herself as a fighter, not a victim.

That simple act, that sharing of what had hidden dormant in her mind for so many years, had changed her. Was still changing her. He carried her burden, simply and easily. She was no longer alone.

Gabe took the lead with an obvious destination in mind. Em followed close behind, leaping over logs and rocks, twisting through dense shrubbery and finally slipping between the bare branches of a stand of willows growing beside a creek. There was a small meadow here, ringed by ferns and giant trees, the mossy ground lost in perpetual shadow.

Stopping in the center, surrounded by ancient trees, Gabe raised his head and sniffed the air. *There's no one around. It's private. Peaceful.*

Perfect. It's absolutely perfect, Gabe. It feels right.

You're not afraid, are you? I don't want to do anything that frightens you, that you're not ready for.

I love you, Gabriel Cheval. I have loved you forever, and I know that as long as you're with me, I haven't got anything to fear. You've always protected me, even when you didn't know it.

He approached her, standing almost nose to nose. *I saw myself in your memories, when you were that madman's prisoner. Your faith in me is humbling, but it's empowering, too. You make me a better person, Em. I want you. I love you. I will always love you. But just as strong is the knowledge that I need you. Already, I know I will always need you.*

She gazed into his dark amber eyes and admitted her truth, that she wouldn't have survived the kidnapping without the powerful sense of Gabe in her mind. *You gave me courage when I needed it most. I needed you then, I need you now and forever. I love you. I will always love you.*

Gabe stared at her for a long time, but he'd closed his thoughts to her and she wondered what was going on in his mind. Then he licked her muzzle as if they had all the time in the world, but it was obvious that tension had him strung tight. She remembered then what he'd said earlier, that he'd rushed their mating last night and he wasn't going to let that happen when they finally tried again to mate.

Em growled. Stupid man . . . didn't he realize she wanted him now? *Save the foreplay for later, Gabriel . . . for when I can appreciate it. My wolf has no patience. She wants you. Now.*

His laughter floated through her mind as she turned and braced her legs, ready for his weight. He mounted her, found her center and filled her in a single thrust. She opened her body, opened her mind to him until he filled her, body and soul.

His memories were there again, so much a part of her that she accepted them now as if they were her own. The connection went deeper as he filled her, tied with her, linked with her on a level known only to bonded mates.

This time, her memories began in the mall, as if she needed to face this horrible event again and see it through to the end, but now Gabe stood beside her. He was with her when she awakened in her captor's home, when the bastard raped her and she refused to fear him. It was obvious her fear was an act, that her anger outweighed any sense of fear. She knew the man was evil, knew he was a killer, but she also knew she had the ability to escape. That she would not die at this man's hands. She wasn't certain she'd have to kill him, didn't want to do anything that might come back and hurt the pack, and so she waited.

She wondered why no one had come to rescue her, why her mental voice didn't connect with anyone in the pack. Especially Gabe's dad. Anton Cheval was so powerful, he should have been able to hear her when she called out to him for help.

This time, she remembered something new. There was an alarm on the doors and windows, and she sensed the signal it constantly emitted. That might be what blocked her. She didn't know for sure, but something was keeping her from contacting her parents, her pack.

Then, on the second day when he came at her, when she'd been looking at his photo album filled with disgusting pictures of the women and girls this bastard had murdered, when she smelled that same chemical that had knocked her out before, Em realized that the only way to save herself was to act, and she had to act now.

She called on her leopard without thinking, but that was the animal she'd always felt most comfortable with, and when she killed him, she made sure he suffered as those poor girls had suffered.

And in their link, with Gabe completely tied to her, body and mind, she heard her mate cheering for her. Felt his pride in her quick thinking, in her ferocity. He congratulated her predator and made her proud.

Her memories skipped then, from Anton finding her on the front porch to her life after the kidnapping. There were no memories of import from that point on. Whatever had happened, however Em might have shut herself down, it was no longer part of who and what she was.

But their sharing went both ways, and she saw how lonely Gabe had been, how much he'd yearned to find the right woman. How he'd celebrated Jace and Romy's mating this past summer, two people he loved dearly, but who now loved each other above anyone else.

As it should be.

The best part, in Em's opinion, was seeing herself through Gabe's eyes. Seeing the love he felt, the sense that finally, this one woman was the answer to questions he'd hardly known to ask. She was part of his past, but she was all of his future. And as the memories spilled from one mind to another, the final connection that bound them forever, the mating bond that was so much a part of the Chanku pack, clicked perfectly into place.

Em wasn't sure when they'd shifted, but she was lying in the soft moss with the mist from the overhead fog beading up on her skin. Gabe was still buried deep inside her, his lips against the back of her neck, his arms wrapped beneath her breasts, their legs tangled together in love.

Em turned, nuzzled his throat, kissed the line of his jaw, and realized that she felt the link, the connection that was so much more than mere mindspeech. His thoughts were there in the background, and if she wanted to know what he was thinking, all she had to do was listen.

She listened.

There you are. Gabe's thoughts in her head were as velvety soft as a caress. She sighed and pressed closer. The mossy ground was cold, but he was like a stoked fire burning bright.

I am. And I intend to stay here. In your mind . . .

In my heart. Em, you are forever in my heart. I love you. I love everything about you, and I am so glad you're mine.

She thought about that, about staying here longer, reveling in the connection, the sense of peace she'd never experienced. But there were too many things undone. She sighed, and unwilling to break the almost mystical silence, used her mind instead of her voice. *Should we go back?*

We should. And we need to call our parents. Yours and mine.

I know. She laughed. "I was not looking forward to finding out what my parents knew and what, if anything, they did to my memories. But now, knowing you're going to be there not only as my longtime friend, but also as my mate . . . well, there's nothing to fear. Nothing at all."

"I dunno," Gabe said. "Your mom can be pretty scary at times. Your dad, too."

"Yeah, but you're bigger. Nothing to worry about."

Gabe stood and held out his hand.

Em grabbed it and he tugged her lightly to her feet. "I feel as if I should look different," she said. "But I don't think I do."

"You look different inside. The colors in your mindspeech were brilliant. I can almost feel their glow."

Em shifted first, but Gabe was right behind her. She picked up the scent of their small pack not all that far away, and with her ears pricked forward and her tail waving like a flag, she raced across the eastern side of Mount Tam with her mate staying close on her flank.

• • •

Gabe glanced at the clock in the kitchen and then turned to Alex. "This day's gone by way too fast. It's almost eight. Have you arranged for the plane for tomorrow?"

Laughing, Alex made a scene of collapsing into a kitchen chair as if he couldn't take another step. "C'mon, Gabe. I just got out of the shower. Sex with five women ain't easy, bud."

Shrugging, Gabe bit back a laugh. Alex actually did look wiped out. "Em and I are newly mated. We needed some quality time alone, and you said you could handle it."

"Oh, he handled it all right." Annie flopped down in the chair beside Alex. "Sort of like a pasha with his harem. 'Take me, my women. I'm all yours.'"

"Well, did he manage?" Gabe winked at Em. There was no need to say a word. She knew exactly what he was thinking, and that was the most amazing thing he could imagine.

Alex moaned and did a face plant on the tabletop. Annie got the giggles, but finally she said, "Let's just say they took him at his word . . . and they took him. I doubt it'll be a fantasy for the poor boy in the future. I sat back and watched while they wore him out."

Sissy and the rest of the women, including Lindy and Nina, walked into the room. Sissy picked up where Annie left off. "Well, we are professionals, you understand."

"Retired professionals, so we might have been off our game," Mary added. She was laughing, which told Gabe that today's run had been good for her. That, or not talking to her father.

Or having sex on her own terms for a change. Em tilted her head, grinning.

He kissed her. Or maybe the combination of all three.

This time I'm kissed him.

Nina took a chair next to Alex and slung her arm over his shoulder. He didn't look up. Lindy snuggled up beside Nina, who laid her head on Alex's back and said, "Next time, Alex, call me and Lindy. We'll help take the pressure off." She glanced at the four new Chanku, wiggled her eyebrows and said, "Right, ladies?"

There was laughter all around except, Gabe noticed, from Alex. His shoulders were shaking, and Gabe was tempted to ask him if he was laughing or crying. Then Mbali leaned across the table and patted Alex's hand. "He did his best, poor boy."

"Okay, ladies." Annie stood up and planted her hand on top of Alex's head, almost as if she'd decided to stake her claim. "Everyone has picked on Alex enough. Did anyone who was in our bed not have an orgasm?" She glanced around the table and nodded, acknowledging their lack of response. "Did anyone not have multiple orgasms? That was plural, by the way, as in more than one."

She looked from one relaxed and satisfied face to the next, smiled, and patted Alex on the head again. Harder this time. "S'okay, sweetie. Ya done good. Just don't try it again. You might hurt yourself."

He groaned.

They were all still laughing when Gabe and Em slipped away to her room to call Anton and let him know they'd all be arriving by lunchtime tomorrow. And that there were four new Chanku coming with them, along with a couple of human women who were as much pack as any non-shifter could be. "I'll bet you ten to one that Dad already knows we have four new members and that we're mated."

Em laughed. "What? Do you think I'm stupid? Of course he knows. Besides, you've told him you suspected more were Chanku."

Gabe slipped a shirt on first. No need to advertise the fact his new mate had almost killed him during their first attempt. Then he used the larger screen in his room to place the call. He and his dad could use mind-speech at this distance, but he wanted to make sure Em was included in everything, and until Gabe was more certain of the connection between him and his mate, he wanted to make it as easy as possible.

His mother answered, her beautiful face filling the screen and immediately making Gabe homesick. "Mom! It's good to see you." He tugged Em closer. "We've got news."

"Em? Are you and Gabe . . . ?"

Em merely nodded. "We are." She glanced at Gabe. "Finally."

Keisha's raised eyebrow had both of them laughing. "It's not funny," Gabe said. He glanced at Em and knew he could talk freely to his mom about what had happened. "A lot of really bad crap in Em's past came up. Something she had no idea was even there. We're flying home in the morning, should be there around lunchtime. We're going to want some private time with you and Dad and Em's folks. Can you arrange it?"

"Whatever you need, Gabriel. And Emeline, I am so thrilled to welcome you. You've always been our family, but this is better than I ever dreamed. You are the perfect mate for our son."

Gabe wrapped his arm around Em's shoulders and hugged her close to his side. "I agree, Mom. She's more than perfect. Did you guess? I was sure Dad would have figured us out by now."

"He knows now, because he's eavesdropping on our conversation, but no, he seems surprised, so I don't think he had a clue. He does tell me that you're bringing not one but four new members into the pack. Four of the young women you rescued are Chanku?"

"They are. Got a notepad? I want to give you their names." He rattled them off. "Sissy Long, Janine Cross, Mbali Jefferson, and Mary Elizabeth Ryder. Lindy Marlette and Nina Marquez are entirely human, but they were held by the same sex slavers and they're close to the other girls. We're bringing all of them with us tomorrow."

Gabe's dad arrived and stood beside his mom. "Congratulations to both of you, and welcome, Em." Then he switched topics fast enough to leave heads spinning. "Did you say Mbali? Any idea how common that name is, or what her background might be?"

This was so typical of his dad that Gabe almost laughed, and Em was biting back a grin. "No idea. Why?"

"We've done a lot of genealogy traces over the years, trying to find siblings or other female relations to pack members. I think Tinker's birth mother might have been named Mbali."

"Well, she's not old enough to be his mother, or even his sister, but we can see what she knows about her mother. We should be arriving tomorrow around noon. You can question all of them to your heart's content. Just be nice. They've been through a lot."

"I'm always nice."

"If a dog after a bone can be called nice, well . . ." Em laughed. "Sorry, Anton. We know you too well."

He focused on Em, and the look in his eyes almost brought Gabe to tears. "Emeline. It's been too long since we've seen you. You have no idea how happy you've made Gabe's mother and me. We never dreamed you might one day be even more a part of our family. We could not be happier to welcome you. Do your parents know?"

She shook her head. Gabe felt every emotion welling up inside her, and he leaned over and kissed her cheek before looking into the screen again. "We're calling them as soon as we get off this call, but I told Mom that we want to meet with you and Em's folks tomorrow. We have some important stuff to discuss."

Anton nodded. "Whenever you like. We'll wait until after you talk to Oliver and Mei about mating before contacting them." He gazed at them a moment longer and then smiled, a slow, sweet smile that clutched at Gabe's heart. His father was an emotional man who so often tried to hide his deeper feelings. He wasn't hiding them now.

"Gabriel, Emeline," he said, "you have made both of us very happy. We could not have imagined a better match than the two of you. We won't say anything until you arrive, though I'm not sure if Oliver and Mei might choose to announce."

Gabe shook his head. "It's okay, Dad. There's nothing secret about our mating. We've had enough of secrets. No more."

Anton stared at the two of them, his look more inscrutable than usual.

133

Then he nodded. "I agree," he said, but the sad smile he shared with Keisha spoke volumes. They said their good-byes and ended the call. Gabe kissed Em. "Ready to call your parents?"

"I am. I wanted to call yours first. I knew that was how they'd act when they found out. They've always been so accepting. My mom and dad? It's weird. Dad comes across as so self-assured, but sometimes I sense that he's filled with doubt, as if the person the pack sees is merely a façade. My mom adores him, but she treats him as if he's fragile. I don't think he is, but their dynamic seems sort of weird at times."

Gabe wrapped his arms around Em and hugged her close against him. "Think about it. We grew up on television shows and movies made by humans for humans. What did you think of them, when you were a kid? Did they make sense?"

She shrugged. "Not really. Luci and I thought most of the sitcoms were stupid. They didn't act like normal people."

"Actually, they did. That's how normal humans act. Not normal Chanku. We think differently, react differently, but we expect that because we know we're not human. Not entirely. Our parents didn't know that. They thought they were human, but they didn't react like normal humans. They had no idea they were perfectly normal for what they—we—are. We're Chanku. Our dynamic is totally different. Most of our parents grew up feeling like misfits."

"I never thought of that. I've known I was Chanku from the time I can remember anything. I was raised to be proud of who I am."

Gabe laughed and hugged her close. "Yeah, but I remember you and Luci playing like you were characters in some of those shows and acting so silly."

She rolled her eyes. "I remember. But we knew we were playing. It wasn't real. But what's this have to do with my mom and dad?"

"I think it's our nature to watch the human dynamic and try to make it our own. It's not ours. It never will be. We're not only ruled by our libido but by our pack status. Whether alpha or beta, or even omega, our personalities and our actions are shaped by our genetics as well as by birth and experience."

Em leaned against him. "So you're saying that weird is normal for us?"

"I'm saying that your dad is either a beta or omega personality. Your mom is definitely an alpha, so their dynamic isn't only about love, it's about who and what they are as wolves. Your dad is the only reason my father survived. You've heard the story, but I probably wouldn't be here if not for your father making sure Dad took care of himself when he was on his quest to learn more about our past." Gabe chuckled as he reached for the screen to call Em's parents. "In case you hadn't noticed, my father tends to be a little single-minded at times."

"Ya think?" Em tilted her head and gazed up at him. Her green eyes sparkled.

He chuckled, loving the scent of her, the feel of her warm skin touching his, the soft glide of her silky hair over his arms. "Does this feel weird to you?" He kissed her behind her ear and smiled at the shivers that raced beneath his lips.

"Oh, Goddess. Not one bit."

He sat back, laughing. "We need to call your parents before we get sidetracked."

"I know." She tightened the knot on her sarong, sighed and sat forward on the edge of the bed.

Gabe punched in the number, and Oliver's face was there, almost as if he'd been waiting.

15

"Hi, Dad." Em clasped Gabe's hand hard enough to shift the bones in his fingers, but he stayed back, still in the picture for Oliver, but not saying anything.

"Emeline! It's good to see you. Were you able to find the young woman?"

"We did. We ended up rescuing six women from a prostitution ring. They'd been held as slaves for years. Four of them are Chanku."

It took Oliver a moment to respond. "Four? You're sure?"

Em blinked and glanced at Gabe. *See what I mean?* "Of course we're sure. They've all had their first shift. We're bringing them to Montana tomorrow to introduce them to the pack. That's why I'm calling. To tell you that Gabe, Alex, Annie and I are coming home tomorrow and plan to stay until the first of the year."

"That's good, honey. I'll tell your mother. We'll get your room ready."

"Not necessary, Dad." She glanced at Gabe and shrugged. "Gabe and I are mated. We'll probably stay in one of the extra rooms at his mom and dad's. They're set up for guests and I hate to intrude on you and Mom."

Oliver didn't say a word. He stared at Em for a long, telling moment. Gabe held on to her hand, well aware she was visibly trembling.

Finally, he spoke. "Oliver? Do you have a problem with Em and me being mates? Because if you do, we need to know what it is and deal with it."

Oliver nodded. "I want Emeline's mother with me when we talk. She's gone to a movie with Xandi and Liana. They won't be home until late."

"Then we'll see you tomorrow and talk then." Gabe glanced at Em.

"We just got off the phone with my folks and they're going to have us all together for lunch."

"You called Gabe's parents first, Emeline? Why?" Oliver was obviously upset, but Gabe couldn't get a read on what was bothering him. He had no idea how to answer his future father-in-law.

Em didn't hesitate. "Because Anton is the pack alpha and Gabe's father. And we knew he and Gabe's mom would be happy for us. Obviously, you're not, but we'll find out why tomorrow. Good night, Dad." She reached over and ended the connection without giving Oliver time to respond.

"Well, that went about as well as could be expected." She blinked rapidly, but the tears filled her eyes faster than she could blink them away. "I just don't understand him. Not at all."

"I don't either, sweetheart." He wrapped his arms around her. Right now she needed a hug more than anything else. "Don't worry. It'll be okay. I love you, my folks are thrilled that we're together, and we're going home in the morning. Everything will make sense once we're in Montana."

"I hope so. But what if it doesn't?"

She looked so young, so absolutely heartbroken, and Gabe was glad that Oliver was over a thousand miles away. Any closer and he might want to chase the bastard down and knock some sense into him. How could any father possibly hurt his daughter this way?

"Does it matter, Em? I know he's your father and you love him, but you're not alone in this. Not now and not ever again. We'll figure out what's going on, and we'll fix it. Besides, you have me beside you, and I will always love you. I won't have any secrets from you. I promise I'll stand by your side no matter what happens."

She crawled into his lap and hugged him even tighter, and when she raised her head to look at him, her green eyes sparkled with tears. She sniffed and tried to smile, but it wasn't a very successful one. "That's one of the perks of this mating thing I hadn't thought through. I've always had to deal with things on my own, but you'll be there for me. My parents can't hurt me, not as long as I have you."

He held her close and let the sense of her, the feel of her body, the scent that was all Em's, the life and the light of her, fill his heart. He would always protect her. He'd never realized how much it meant to him to be needed by someone, and then he almost laughed.

Just like Alex said, he was making it all about himself, and how Em made him feel.

He had to think of what she was feeling. "They might hurt your feelings, but only if you let them. You will always have me, Emy. Always."

137

He kissed her and she practically melted into his embrace. She felt so good wrapped in his arms, pressed against his chest, that he actually trembled. So much emotion swirling in his mind, in his heart. He nuzzled the side of her neck, dipped his head and licked the valley between her breasts, loving the way she arched against him. "I had no idea how special it would be, to make love to my mate. Alex said it changed everything." He kissed her again. "But I didn't realize how or how much."

"It's as if everything is more." Em turned in his lap so that she straddled his hips. The silky length of her sarong slid high on her thighs so that the only barrier between Gabe's erection and the damp heat between her legs was the light pair of cotton pants he'd slipped on after his shower. "More. Brighter. So immediate when I feel your love in my mind as well as my body. I think I could get used to this, ya know?"

"Goddess, I sure hope so." Laughing, he kissed her again, and then again. It didn't take long to lose the shirt he'd put on earlier, or to shimmy out of his cotton pants with Em's help. It took a bit longer to undo that fancy knot she'd tied in her dress and tucked between her breasts. The sarong—a green one the shade of her eyes—actually seemed to slither away from her body until it pooled in shimmering green waves around their hips. He lay back and she stayed with him, the silk still sliding against his skin, Em still straddling his body, trapping his cock between her thighs, teasing him with her damp heat.

She ran her fingers lightly over the deep scratches still covering his chest. It had been less than twenty-four hours since their first attempt at mating had gone awry, and the worst of the slash marks were already scabbed over. He wasn't a very pretty sight, but at least they didn't hurt. Of course, as much as he wanted Em right now, he doubted he'd feel any kind of pain beyond the steady throbbing in his balls and the exquisite pain of a fully erect cock trapped beneath but not inside his woman's sheath.

Em leaned over and licked his chest with the very tip of her tongue, pausing to kiss the deepest marks, then making a trail to first his right nipple and then the left. Both beaded up into tight little points. She nipped the left one. Sharp teeth left a sharper sting that made his hard cock twitch and reminded him that he'd sorely neglected her breasts. Cupping her soft curves in his hands, he lifted their weight and teased the silky skin. She sighed and arched her back, driving her pussy down hard on his cock. Biting back a groan, he pinched and twisted the taut peaks of each breast, tugging just enough to sting. She whimpered and then sighed. He felt the small pain through their link, then the corresponding rush of feminine fluids as her body reacted.

She might be an alpha bitch, as tough as any woman he'd known, but there was enough of the submissive in her to react when he tugged at her nipples. He filed that knowledge away for future reference, but then Em rose on her knees and his cock rose with her. She came back down on him, taking him deep inside, surrounding him in wet heat and clenching muscles, and any concept of future anything was lost.

This was here and now and absolutely perfect. Worry about her parents, about the trip tomorrow, about anything beyond the sense of his mate loving him flashed out of existence with his first deep penetration inside Em's welcoming body.

The connection expanded, from the first tentative bits of sensation to a complete melding of minds, a link of their spirits from one to the other that was as powerful as their original mating bond had been. But the difference, Gabe realized as he lifted and turned Em, as he covered her body with his without breaking their rhythm or losing that physical, mental and emotional link, the difference was in the images that filled his mind, that filled Em's. Where the mating bond had taken their pasts and fused them into one singular memory, this bond, this link between lovers, was all about now. It was a step forward, not back.

A step through the purity of the moment, and a glimpse of their path together, into the future.

• • •

They lay there, panting as if they'd each run miles, but Em couldn't wipe the smile off her face. Their mental link was secure. She'd worried that it might be as tenuous as it had been before they'd finally finished their mating bond, that once they got off the high of the original link she'd regress to that same woman, sort of shuffling through the dark where Gabe was concerned, but they couldn't be closer.

She couldn't love him more. Rolling her head to one side, she looked directly into his eyes, their dark amber so filled with love she wondered if she should pinch herself.

Gabe chuckled. "If there's any pinching that needs to be done, I'll take care of it." He ran his long fingers over her breast and the nipple immediately stood up to meet them. "It appears they're well trained."

"Is that what you call it?" She dragged her fingers lightly over his chest, still careful of those horrible slash marks, but they both laughed when not only his nipples both stood to attention, but his cock rose as well. "Looks like you're trained even better than me." She leaned close, twirling her tongue around first one nipple and then the other. Then she began the slow slide down his body, kissing her way along his ribs, over one hip and finally reaching his cock. It was hard again, thrusting straight up from the nest of dark hair at his groin. She ran her tongue along his full length, licking from the base to the tip, swirled her tongue around the crown, tasting herself on him.

He arched his hips and groaned. She lifted her head and stared at him. "What are you thinking about when I'm doing this? You just blocked me."

He let out a big puff of air. "I didn't mean to. I was thinking about how good that felt, that you hadn't touched my balls and they were begging for attention, too, that as good as it felt, I wanted to be inside you again. Why? Just guy stuff." He laughed when she grabbed a pillow and whapped him with it.

"Okay, so what were you thinking?"

This time she sat back on her heels, but she made a point of cupping his sac in her palm and gently squeezing. "Actually, I was counting."

"Counting? I inspire counting during sex? I need to work on my technique."

"Your technique is excellent. I was trying to remember how many times we'd made love since our first attempt to mate. Since I gave you these." She touched one of the deeper slashes. It had broken open a bit during their lovemaking and a drop of blood showed near the deepest part.

"Not nearly often enough." He grasped her hand, tugged her fingers lightly away from the marks on his chest. "This happened less than twenty-four hours ago, Em. They will heal. They don't hurt, but they remind me of how brave you are. How much I love you, and how easily we could have never had this moment if you hadn't reacted against that bastard the way you did. I have these because, unlike all those other women he killed, you were tough enough to save yourself. In a lot of ways, I think you've saved me, too. We've been together as adults for such a short time, but already I can't imagine life without you."

She raised her hips, fitted him to her once again and slowly lowered herself over his cock. He slid deep inside her, feeling so perfect, she couldn't believe how she'd been afraid such a short time ago that he wouldn't fit at all. So many things had changed over the past week. This was the best. This amazing connection with a man who made her stronger, more self-confident, more the woman she was meant to be. He loved her enough to encourage her to be herself.

What an amazing gift.

Smiling, she rose and fell over him, opening her mind, her thoughts, her dreams to this man who had meant so much to her as a child. Only a few years older, she'd seen him as someone so much more than she was. He was older, smarter, braver. Now he was her mate, and she realized something even more profound—she might not be his age, though four years wasn't a big deal when one was almost immortal—but she was every bit as smart and as brave. She was his equal in those things that mattered.

And the thing that mattered most? Gabe loved her every bit as much as she loved him.

. . .

Sissy clutched Janine's fingers as the Chanku Global Industries jet circled in over the mountains and lined up to the private runway at the Chanku headquarters near Kalispell, Montana. She'd never even been outside of California before, and had definitely never flown in a jet. For that matter, she'd never flown in anything, so to take her first flight in a private jet with amenities most people never see was more than a thrill—it was absolutely wonderful in a terrifying manner. She just wished she wasn't so nervous.

Her life was so different. So far from what she'd been living a week ago that it was hard to believe she was the same person. Janine raised her head and shot her an impish grin. *I'm eavesdropping,* she said. *And you're not the same person. Neither am I. Mbali and Mary aren't either. We're shapeshifters. Can you fucking believe that?*

When you talk in my head, I can.

They were both laughing when the jet touched down on the runway. Sissy watched the ground speed by and then they were slowing and rolling toward a big hangar that held another jet and a couple of helicopters. Snow was falling—not a lot, but enough to hide the mountaintops—but she could see a cluster of houses at the far end of a huge meadow. A large van, more like a small bus, was coming toward them, and in a way that she'd not allowed herself to consider, it slammed into her that this wasn't merely a trip to Montana. This was a visit to the place where most of the shapeshifters lived. She was going to be meeting more Chanku.

People just like them, but from what she could see, Montana was nothing like San Francisco. She was so glad Annie had taken all of them shopping, because it was cold outside. Colder than she'd ever experienced before, and the sudden case of nerves wasn't helping. She was shivering, and her mind was spinning and she had no idea if she was just cold or had a serious case of nerves.

Leaning forward, she whispered to Em, "Too bad they don't serve drinks on this plane. It just hit me that we're here, that I've never been out of the Bay Area, much less out of California, I've never been in snow, and I've never been around a whole pack of shapeshifters."

Em grinned and patted her hand. "We're harmless, you're one of us, and I'm probably more nervous than you. We told my father last night that we'd mated and he was not happy. As in really not happy. If anyone should be a basket case, it should be me. You are not allowed to be a nervous wreck. My turn."

"Crap. I didn't know that, Em. I'm sorry." She squeezed Em's fingers, but she realized her own nerves had settled. "I think your goddess is on your side, though, so tell your father it's not up to him. That you're the one who loves Gabe and he loves you and that's all that counts."

"You're right, you know. Thanks, Sissy." Em turned to watch as Gabe unbuckled his belt and went to open the door and lower the ladder, then she turned back to Sissy. "I hope you find someone soon who completes you the way Gabe does me. We're not like humans in that way. Chanku do best when mated. I never imagined I would end up with him."

"I think sometimes that Gabe is as surprised as you. Your father will come around. If he loves you, he'll understand."

"I hope so."

They unbuckled their seat belts and Sissy walked to the back of the plane where they'd stowed their luggage. She gave Annie a big hug. "Thank you so much for the shopping trip. When you said it was going to be cold up here, I had no idea how cold you were talking about! It's a lot nicer facing all that snow with warm clothes and even warmer boots."

Laughing, Annie handed a bag to Janine and then reached for Sissy's. "Cold has an entirely new definition in Montana. San Franciscans think it's cold when the temps drop to forty. It's not really cold up here unless it's forty below."

"I'll remember that."

Sissy stood in the doorway while Gabe went out first. Damn, it was cold! The air actually burned her skin, and the nerves hit again when she realized where she was, why she was here. But Gabe glanced at her and waved her down the steps. He helped Sissy with her bags, and she was freezing by the time she got away from the plane and waited for the van. Gabe stayed there at the bottom to help everyone down and then herded them all together like a little flock of shivering ducks as the van pulled in close to the plane. A tall, handsome man with long, dark hair got out of the passenger seat. He was smiling when he reached for Gabe and hugged him.

Then he turned to Sissy and held out his arms. "You must be Sissy," he said. "I'm Anton, Gabe's father. Welcome."

He hugged her as if he'd known her forever. She hugged him back, but she had to force herself to close her mouth. Gabe's dad was gorgeous, and he looked even younger than his son. Obviously he knew what she was thinking, because he leaned in close and said sotto voce, "One of the perks of being almost immortal. None of that aging stuff."

She covered her mouth but couldn't hide the laughter. Anton merely lifted an eyebrow and grinned and all of her nervousness fled. Another man came around from the driver's side, and he looked so much like Gabe she took a startled step back.

He came up behind Gabe, looped an arm around his shoulders and hugged him. "What's this about you finding a mate on your trip? Sheesh, bro . . . we can't let you go anywhere."

"Mac! When did you get home?" Gabe turned and hugged him close, then stepped back with both hands on the man's shoulders. This had to be the twin brother he'd mentioned.

"Flew in last night. It's good to see you. Where's Em?"

"I'm here, Mac." She'd been standing behind the other girls talking, but she went into Mac's arms for a hug. "How are you?"

He stood back, looked her up and down and whistled. "Damn, Emeline. You're gorgeous. Gabe, I can see why you made it permanent so fast. You didn't want anyone else to have a chance."

Gabe was laughing, and obviously so proud of Em. "I'm not stupid. Do you think I'd let you see her when she was still free?" Then he spun Mac around. "Ladies, I want you to meet my baby brother. He got the brains, but I got the looks."

Janine raised her hand. "Uh, Gabe? He looks just like you. So where's that leave you in the brains department?"

"Smart ass."

Gabe flipped her off with his comment, and they were all laughing when Mac rounded them all up. "He also got the gift of gab," Mac said. "It's freezing—let's get these ladies close to a warm fire."

16

The huge buffet that Keisha and Xandi had prepared for the four new Chanku and their human friends was typical of the kind of welcome Gabe expected for new pack members. He stood back while Alex's dad organized the extra tables and chairs.

"Expecting a crowd?" Gabe laughed, moving in to help as Stefan struggled with one of the larger tables.

"You're kidding, right? Thanks. This sucker's heavy." Stefan grabbed one end of the table while Gabe lifted the other. "Anton gave your mom and my wife free rein with the preparations. They've been cooking all morning and still called in a caterer. There's going to be enough food for an army."

"Mom always says that sharing meals is the way to keep a pack strong and united."

"Really? Xandi says it's the sex."

"Well, that too." Laughing, Gabe helped Stefan make sure the table was aligned. Now all they needed were the chairs. He grabbed a couple out of the cart Alex had delivered to the room.

Stefan paused in mid-lift. "Congratulations are in order, I understand. You and Em?" He chuckled. "Never saw that one coming, but it definitely sounds right. She's a good kid, smart and strong. And beautiful." He turned away, as if he was considering more.

Gabe waited. Hoped he'd say something.

"I hope Oliver handles it okay."

"That wasn't what I expected you to say, but it's a good call." Gabe set the chair down and rested his hands on the back. "So far, from what we can tell, he's not handling it at all."

Stefan merely nodded. "It's not my place to comment, but your dad's concerned, and that's a good thing. He loves you, and his sympathies have always been with Emeline. He'll make sure things work."

"Sort of a cryptic message from you, Stef. I won't question you further—don't want to put you on the spot, but thank you."

Stefan nodded again, and then went back to setting out the chairs. More packmates were arriving and immediately pitched in to help. Gabe stood back and watched for a moment, enjoying the purity of love he felt within this room. No matter what happened, the pack hung together. They supported one another. He was getting the feeling that they had supported Oliver over whatever had happened with Em, but if he'd interpreted Stefan properly, there wasn't total agreement on that.

He stepped into the big kitchen, which was almost too crowded to enter. All six of the young women were here, along with Alex and Annie and at least a dozen other packmates, and the level of conversation ebbed and flowed, though it was still too loud to hear anything.

He spotted Lindy and Nina off to one side talking with his sister Lily and her mate, Sebastian. Leave it to Lil to make the only two humans in the room feel welcome. "Hey, big sis!"

"My baby brother! My mated baby brother! Congratulations!" She threw her arms around him and he lifted her off her feet in a tight hug. She was tall, but he was still a lot taller and definitely bigger. He swung her around a couple of times before setting her back on her feet, but he held her elbow until she caught her balance.

Lily glanced at Nina and Lindy. "Proof the brat's finally a grown-up. Used to be he'd spin me and set me down so dizzy I'd land on my butt. Thank you, dear Gabriel, for not making me feel like a fool in front of guests." She raised one eyebrow, so much like their dad, and glared at Sebastian. "Unlike some men we both know and love."

Gabe tipped an imaginary hat to Sebastian. "Thank you for taking on such an onerous duty."

"My pleasure." Sebastian smacked Gabe on the shoulder and they both cracked up.

Lily glanced at the women and rolled her eyes. "See what I have to put up with?"

"I wanted to make sure you two were having a good time." Gabe smiled at Nina and Lindy and then took a quick look at the kitchen, rapidly filling to bursting. "This crowd can be a bit overwhelming."

"It's great," Nina said. "Everyone's been so nice. Sebastian said he's interested in getting in on the salon we're planning."

Gabe raised an eyebrow when he looked at Sebastian, who merely shrugged.

"Hey," he said. "It's business. And look at these two. Even I recognize style when I see it, and Lindy designed both their outfits."

"I have a feeling Lindy and Nina are going to take over the world. Or at least make sure we're better dressed, with good haircuts." He hugged both Lindy and Nina, kissed Lily on the cheek and shook Sebastian's hand. "I'm sorry Em and I can't join you guys for lunch. We're eating with Mom and Dad and Em's parents. I have a feeling your party's going to be a lot more fun."

Lily nodded. "I heard there was an issue with Oliver. Don't worry. It'll work out. Dad's good, but Mom's the one with the muscle. She'll make it work."

"She always does, doesn't she?" He left the room, but not before stopping to give his mom a hug. "See you in the study in about half an hour, okay?"

She patted his cheek like he was still an eight-year-old, but it worked. There was something about his mom that inspired confidence. "Give Em a hug for me."

He kissed her cheek and grinned. "I've only got half an hour. That's about all there's time for."

This time Keisha raised her brows and smiled at him. "You're your father's son, Gabriel. You've always got time. Now go. I sense that little girl of yours is anxious and nervous. She needs you."

He'd noticed that same sense of anxiety, but the mating link was so new, he was still learning to interpret feelings. Words were much easier. But his mom was right. Em was already a basket case.

The sense had been growing since they'd gotten on the plane earlier this morning, so he'd taken her directly to his room and left her with plenty of time to get settled. He'd been gone almost an hour, and he needed to get back to her now. The mating bond had allowed him to sense an unusual fragility in his normally strong mate. It was more than obvious Oliver's strange behavior was the cause.

Gabe was ready to punch her father. The man hadn't made any attempt to talk to her, hadn't come to meet the plane, hadn't said a word. It made no sense.

Satisfied the girls were in good hands, he turned to leave, but Mac was there, waiting right outside the kitchen door. Gabe crooked a finger and led him through the dining room, down the hall to a small study their mom occasionally used. Today it was dark and quiet—a good place to talk to his twin.

"What's going on?" Mac stood there with his arms folded across his chest, and as always it gave Gabe the surreal sense of staring into a mirror. Probably why they were called mirror twins. "Mom and Dad aren't saying a word, Oliver's been holed up in their house since last night and Mei's sulking like a grounded teenager. Are they upset about you and Em?"

Gabe stuffed his hands in his rear pockets and let out a deep breath. "They are, but we're not sure why. Mac, do you remember about twelve years ago when Em was kidnapped? We were away at college, but did anyone ever say anything to you?"

"Em? Kidnapped?" He shook his head. "I don't remember that."

"Neither did Em, but Annie did, and she told us the story, how Luci, Em, Phoenix and Annie had gone to the mall and Em was kidnapped by a serial rapist who held her for a couple of days. She was raped and would have been murdered, but she shifted—took her leopard form—and killed the bastard. I know it happened, because it came out during our mating link."

He lifted his shirt and showed off the slashes on his chest. Mac's muttered "holy shit" seemed totally apropos. "Yeah, exactly. We waited, I walked her through the memories during a less stressful time and we were finally able to mate last night, but for whatever reason, her conscious memories of the incident were gone. There are no Internet stories about this guy that mention Em. He's there with the long list of his victims, but Em's not on it. And when the media talks about his death, all we could find was a reference to the fact that he was found dead in his home, badly decomposed, and cause of death was at first a suspected animal mauling but could not be definitively determined. Something's going on, but we don't know what. We think Oliver and Mei are involved in a cover-up, but from something Eve said . . ."

"Eve's involved?" Mac shook his head, the disbelief on his face almost comical.

"Yeah, or I might have bled to death. During our first attempt at mating, Em freaked when all the memories started coming out, and she shifted. You do not want to be having sex with a wolf who becomes a totally enraged snow leopard. Eve alerted Annie and Alex and they found us and brought us home. We were both unconscious and bare-assed in Golden Gate Park. As she said, there are predators there at night. We could have ended up dead, Em could have been raped. It wasn't a good place to be sleeping off whatever happened to us."

"Whatever I can do, let me know, okay? Em's amazing, not to mention gorgeous. She was a sharp little kid and a beautiful teen, but she's turned into a breathtaking woman."

"Thanks, Mac. I'll tell her you said so." He cocked his head and studied his brother, a quieter, more introspective version of himself. "And keep your hands to yourself."

Grinning, Mac saluted and turned away to head back into the dining room. "Good luck, bro."

"Thanks."

Luck. As if luck would help them. What the hell was going on? He went back to his room to get Em. She was changing clothes, but her hands were trembling so much she couldn't button her blouse.

"Sweetheart? You going to be okay?" As he talked, he sat on the edge of the bed and pulled her between his knees so he could do up the buttons. He left the top two open. No bra necessary with breasts like Em's, and she had an absolutely perfect, sexy cleavage. He leaned over, planted a kiss in the dark V between, and inhaled her scent. "I'd love to skip lunch and stay here with you." He rested his forearms on the slight curve of her hips and kissed her. "But we can't do that. Putting it off won't make it go away."

She sighed. "I know, damn it!" She turned away, spun around and faced him again. She was such a tiny thing that they were eye level with him sitting on the bed.

"This is so stupid, Gabe. What's going on with them? And why do I let it make me so angry, so . . ."

"Hurt?" When she nodded, he wrapped his arms loosely around her waist and rested both hands on her butt. She had an absolutely perfect rear, and the feel of those soft curves beneath his palms tempted him to start undressing her now that she'd covered up all the good stuff. "It hurts because they're your parents and you know they've lied to you. I have no idea why, Emy, but in the scheme of things, it's not important. What's important is that you and I are together, we're mated and no one can break us apart." He leaned close and kissed her. "How long has it been since you actually saw your parents?"

"I left for college when I was eighteen. I came back once, when I was nineteen. I lasted three days. That was the last time." She turned her head away, as if she was too embarrassed to face him.

"Em." He sighed. "They've never tried to bring you back? Never asked you to come home?"

She shook her head. "I think they were relieved that I didn't want to come back. Life had become a nightmare for me. I imagine it wasn't much better for them. Secrets are never good, and I had no idea why they were so overprotective. I fought it, we argued. I stormed out and since then our interaction has all been by phone or email. Aaron came to see me a few times, but he never said a word about them. I didn't ask."

He stood and gave her a good, long look. "Damn but you're gorgeous. Which reminds me, my brother said the same thing. He more than approves of our mating, and you, my dear, more than pass inspection. It's almost noon. I told Mom we'd be there early. I think she wants a few minutes to hug and cry without an audience."

Laughing, he tugged her fingers, and she followed him down the hall. They could hear laughter coming from the main dining room, where everyone else was already eating.

"Sure you don't want to go eat with everyone else?" She flashed him a grin and he wrapped an arm around her shoulders.

"I'd love to, but then we'd have my parents pissed off at us, too."

"Good point."

Gabe's mom met them in the doorway, and it was exactly as he'd predicted. She laughed, she cried, she hugged both of them and kissed Em and cried some more. Anton walked in a few minutes later and wrapped his arms around Keisha.

"Well, I'm certainly glad no one's dying. From all the tears, I thought . . ."

Gabe and Em started laughing, but his mom turned and stared at her mate long enough to have him blushing. Gabe leaned close to Em and loudly whispered, "I'd love to hear what she's saying right now, because whatever it is, she's got the pack alpha nailed to the floor."

Keisha turned and glared at Gabe. "And don't you forget it, bud." Then she laughed and hugged Em. "If you want lessons on how to handle these men, I'm available anytime. Just ask."

"I'll remember that."

Anton led them on in to the room he called the study but Gabe always called the pentagram room. Besides, what study had a fully stocked bar that stretched the full length of one side? It had been designed in this shape to make it easier for their goddess to appear on this plane. She'd said she wanted to talk, but Gabe wondered if she'd actually come.

They sat at the bar, and though it was early, Anton poured a glass of wine each for Keisha and Em and handed a cold beer to Gabe. He opened one for himself. Em glanced around and finally turned to Anton. "Are my parents coming?"

"They are. They'll be here in a few minutes. I wanted to wait until they arrive to ask both of you what happened this week to resurrect Em's memories. We thought they were buried forever."

"They were never completely gone." She glanced at Gabe; he smiled and took her hand. "There was always a darkness in my mind, an entire section of my teen years that I couldn't recall. I knew it was something that I'd forgotten, but I had no idea what it was. I just knew it was bad."

Anton nodded, then raised his head and smiled. "Here they are. Let's move to the table."

Em, relax, sweetheart. They're your parents and they love you. No matter what you might think, I will bet you that everything that happened, misguided or not, was done out of love.

I know you're right. Thank you. I think I'm ready.

He squeezed her hand and helped her off the tall bar stool. She turned and saw her parents for the first time in over seven years. Her mother smiled and held her arms out.

"I have missed you so much!" She grabbed Em and hugged her.

"I've missed you too. I've missed so much."

Mei finally turned her loose and turned to Gabe. "I am so glad you are together. I think Em came out of the womb loving you, Gabe. She idolized you when she was just a toddler, and the older she got, the more she followed you around. I used to worry that her heart would break when you went away to school." She held out her arms and hugged him. Gabe hugged her back, but her mental voice whispered in his mind as she held on to him.

Don't hate Oliver, Gabe. He's lived with his mistakes since Em left at nineteen and never came back. Thank you for bringing her back to us.

I hope we can get this worked out.

Me, too.

He stepped away and turned to Em's dad. Oliver had stayed by the door, and Gabe wasn't sure if he worried about his welcome or just didn't want any part of Gabe. Em raised her head and stared at her father.

"Hello, sweetie."

"Dad."

That was it. That single word, and when Oliver didn't respond, she turned and grabbed Gabe's hand. Anton was there beside her as well, and they walked to the table, where Keisha had already laid out their meal.

They sat, the six of them at the table, Anton and Keisha at each end, Gabe and Em on one side, her parents on the other. There was a plate loaded with sandwiches, another with pickles and peppers and different kinds of olives, and a big bowl of chips. What Gabe thought of as comfort food. He shot a quick grin at his mother and she smiled broadly. She'd guessed right, and he could tell she was thrilled he'd recognized her efforts.

"Go ahead and start," Anton said. As they reached for sandwiches, he said, "Mei and Oliver, you've always been part of my family, but now it appears we're linked even more profoundly. Keisha and I are so happy to have Em join us as Gabe's mate." He smiled at the two of them. "I can still see Em and Luci following Gabe and Aaron around, idolizing them when the girls were little, and then driving them nuts as they got older. I used to imagine the two of you as mates, but I honestly never thought it would happen. I am so glad you've proved me wrong."

It might be too soon to open up this particular can of worms, but he had to. Em was already trembling, and the longer they all pretended to get along, the worse she was going to be. He shot an apologetic look in his mom's direction, and said, "Thanks, Dad. We're mated, but it almost didn't happen. Uncovering a past Em didn't know she had was, to put it bluntly, a painful experience." He slipped his shirt over his head. Mei and Keisha both gasped. Em couldn't even look at him.

"Emeline's memories returned when we were in the midst of our mating link. She shifted into a snow leopard and did her best to gut me, and if Eve hadn't appeared and gotten Alex and Annie to come rescue us, it could have turned out pretty ugly. We were able to complete the mating bond last night after walking Em through some absolutely terrible buried memories, but we have a lot of questions, and we need answers. I think the four of you are the only ones who can tell us what happened twelve years ago."

"How did you find out?" Oliver's question sounded like more of an accusation than curiosity.

And Em told him. Told all of them how Annie had told her the story that she didn't remember, how it had triggered more of the darkness she'd never been able to get away from. They went through the entire process of discovery, including Em's time in the man's house. And while Em talked, Gabe watched her parents.

Mei was obviously shocked by the details, and Gabe wondered if she'd ever known the whole story. Oliver, though, seemed to shrink in upon himself. He couldn't even look at his daughter, he avoided looking at Anton and Keisha, and the one glance that Gabe caught coming his way was filled with such loathing that it raised shivers across his neck and arms.

That was unacceptable. He faced Oliver without malice, thinking only of what this was doing to his mate. "You look at me as if I'm at fault, as if whatever happened to Em is somehow something I've done. Why, Oliver?"

"She forgot. She didn't remember any of the horror she'd been through when she got home. She was smart enough to push it all into the background and she was fine. She didn't even have nightmares. She's a brilliant, beautiful young woman and she was doing great until you came along. You did this to her, Gabriel. So selfish that you had to push her, had to force her to confront a past better left in the dark."

Gabe merely nodded and silently cautioned Em not to react. She squeezed his hand so tightly the bones shifted. His father had remained silent and Gabe sent him a silent thank-you as well. This was his fight. His and his mate's. "The memories were there, Oliver, a festering, seething mass of darkness that has kept her from being a part of the pack since it happened. When I met up with Em last week, she had never run with a pack, had cut herself off from the family she loves, and had never even made love to one of her own kind. By fostering the loss of her memories, no matter how horrible they were, you have crippled your own daughter."

"That is not true." Oliver stood and planted his hands on the table, but he was absolutely furious. "You're lying, Gabriel. She forgot all of it. Until Annie told her what happened, she didn't remember anything. We made sure of that, and Eve helped us."

Gabe ignored Oliver's outburst. He turned to Em and held both her hands. *Do you want to explain what it was like? How you felt when you found out the truth?*

Yes. She sat up straighter in her chair, but she held tightly to Gabe's right hand. "I may have made myself forget the details, but the darkness has haunted me for twelve years. The first time Gabe and I made love, I lost it. I was terrified. He saw the darkness and was able to control it, surrounding it with light so that it didn't frighten me, and it worked. Do you realize that was the first time I ever had an orgasm during sex? I'm Chanku, Dad. We don't have issues with sex, but I did."

Oliver sat down, but he still looked furious. Gabe tried to read him, but his thoughts were locked tight. Em glanced at Gabe and then focused on her father again. "When Annie told me what had happened, I didn't believe her. I thought she was making it up, but her story felt right, and I had no memories at all of myself during my teens. At least in the years between fourteen and about eighteen, when I left for college. But you know what the worst thing about this is, the most awful thing any parent could do to their daughter? You took away something that should have changed my life in a good way. Yes, I was kidnapped, I was raped, I would have been murdered. But you know what's important here? What you denied me all those years?"

She stood up and planted her hands on the table and faced her father. He blinked, jerked back in surprise, but he watched her. "I survived. Not because someone rescued me but because I rescued myself. I killed the bastard before he could kill me or anyone else. I waited for someone to rescue me. I didn't want to kill him and have it come down against the pack, have some reporter turn it into a story about those murderous Chanku. I called out for help for two fucking days, Dad. No one heard me. I finally figured it had something to do with his alarm system. It had an odd buzzing noise that made me dizzy, so I figured I was on my own. Then I found an album and it was filled with pictures of young girls, teens and young women, all of them dead. He'd carved pictures into their flesh, and I was looking at that and trying to figure out how I'd get away when I smelled the same gas he'd used to knock me out. Gabe said it's chloroform, but he was coming up behind me with it and I didn't think about the pack or what the news would report or anything but saving myself.

"I shifted, and I chose the leopard because of something Mom had told me, that people are so busy looking at their teeth and front claws, they ignore the threat of their hind feet. I jumped him and I gutted him and I bit down on his windpipe just enough to eventually kill him, but I wanted him to die slowly and painfully. I wanted him to know how those young girls, those women and teens, had suffered. I could do that because I was stronger than him. I could have done it a day earlier, but I was so afraid of getting the pack in trouble I held off. And for all these years, I've felt like a victim, not a survivor. I had no idea I could be that strong."

Tears were streaming down her cheeks and Gabe covered one of her hands with his. He didn't think he'd ever been as proud of anyone in his life. She was absolutely amazing.

And yet her father still hadn't said a word. If anything, he looked ready to explode, though Mei appeared on the verge of collapse. What the hell had they done?

17

Em sat back in her chair, wiped her tears with her cloth napkin, and took a sip of her wine. She'd been so afraid of telling her story, but with Gabe beside her it had been a whole lot easier than she'd imagined. She shot him a grateful look and he shared a smile with her that seemed to warm her from the inside out. She'd blamed the Montana cold, but it wasn't the Montana chill at all.

Merely nerves making her shiver.

Once again she faced her father. If anything, he looked even more pissed off. She didn't get it, but she wasn't going to let his anger stop her. "I saved myself that day, but you took that victory away from me. Why? And how did you get everyone else to forget? Gabe didn't know I'd been kidnapped; neither did Mac. Gabe's done a lot of online research, and I'm not mentioned in the story at all. Not even alluded to as a nameless victim. Nor was the fact he'd been killed by an obvious predator part of the story, but I can guess that the pack wanted that bit left out. Still, Luci and Phoenix were with me that day, but they've never said a word." She glanced at Anton and shrugged. "Sorry, but when she was little, Luci couldn't keep a secret if her life depended on it. Not without help. Did you help cover this up, Anton? Were all of you part of it?"

Without warning, her dad exploded up from his seat. "Yes, damn it! Anton was part of it. I was part of it. Our fucking goddess was part of it. We did it for you, and if you're so ungrateful, so . . . He turned away and cursed, then ripped his clothes off and shifted. A snow leopard, snarling and out of control, raced from the room.

"Oliver!" Her mom was on her feet the moment her dad leapt from his chair, but he was gone before she'd stripped out of her jeans. "Let me go after him. Please, Anton?" When he nodded, a second snow leopard left.

Gabe was on his feet, ready to chase after them, but Em clung to his hand. "No," she said, sobbing. "No, Gabe. Stay. He's furious. He could kill you when he's like this."

Anton had stood but he'd stopped unbuttoning his shirt when he heard Mei's plea. Now he turned at Em's cry. "Do you think Oliver could be that violent, Em? He's usually so calm, so organized."

She shook her head. "I don't know, but sometimes . . . There was always so much anger in him. Mom could calm him down, but he used to scare me when he'd get upset about something. It was worse after I was kidnapped, though I didn't know that until the memories came back. Something about what happened to me affected him strangely. I don't think he's acting like a man upset his daughter was abducted. It's more personal for him."

"I think, for now, we let your mom have her wish and see if she can handle things." Anton glanced at Keisha, and she nodded. "Good. If my mate agrees, it means I didn't make a stupid decision. Believe me, she has ways of letting me know."

"I tell him." She looked at Anton and shook her head, as if this was a long-standing agreement between two who had loved long and well. "As hardheaded as he can be, I've discovered the direct approach is best." She turned back to Em and said, "Emeline, I know this has got to be so unsettling for you, but whatever is going on, your father will come around. He loves you, and he knows he is much loved in return."

Em took a deep breath and thought about that for a moment, and hated the first thing that came into her mind. "Do I? Do I love him? Everything he does makes me furious. Why?"

Keisha smiled softly and reached for her hand. Squeezing Em's fingers, she said, "It's because you love him. Because his responses, his actions, fall below your standards, and as a daughter, you have very high standards. You should. Daughters are what make men better than they might otherwise have been. They will do their best to be good role models for their sons, but they want to be magical princes for their daughters. Think about it. When you were small, didn't you expect him to slay dragons for you?"

Em realized she was smiling. "Or at least get Aaron to quit picking on me."

"Me? But I was a perfect big brother."

She turned so quickly she almost fell out of her chair. "Aaron? How did you know to come?"

"Anton called me. What's going on with Dad, sis?"

Gabe interrupted. "Aaron, do you remember when Em was kidnapped by the serial rapist?"

"What? That never . . ." Stunned, he glanced from one face to the next. "When? Why don't I know anything about something so awful?"

"Something we're trying to figure out," Anton said. Then he turned to Em. "For what it's worth, Em, your father was wrong. I had no part in covering the story up. I don't remember the details either. It's like a memory written in smudged, pale pastels when everything else is sharp and clear." He glanced at Keisha. "What about you?"

She shrugged and held out her hand to Aaron. "Aaron, sit down. Have a sandwich. Gabriel? Em? Eat. As for you, my love? No, I don't remember and it infuriates me that my memories have been tampered with. I know it was not you, and I know you are as angry as I am, but I can only imagine how Emeline feels. It's a rape of the mind to have memories stolen."

Em glanced at Keisha and felt as if a huge weight had lifted. She didn't want Gabe's parents to be involved. It was bad enough that her own had done this. Smiling through her frustration, she turned to Anton. "In my case, I can accept that I buried them myself, but Gabe and I were certain that you were the only one with the strength to make others forget. I am so glad it wasn't you, but even the online records of the case are incomplete. How could that happen?"

"What the hell happened?" Aaron grabbed the untouched sandwich off his mom's plate.

Em gave him the much-abbreviated story, and Aaron kept shaking his head in total denial. "Wow, Em. I had no idea. None." And then he turned to Anton as if he held all the secrets.

Anton laughed and raised his hands. "For once, I'm innocent. I didn't do it."

"No, Anton. I did."

They all turned at the same time as Eve walked across the room and took Oliver's empty chair. "Anton, I could really use a drink."

Even the pack alpha had a bemused expression. Eve was entirely corporeal, as real as any of them at the table, and she never, ever ate or drank on this earthly plane. "Cognac or wine?"

"Bring the Hennessy. I think I'm going to need it." She looked directly at Em. "To you, my dear, I owe my deepest apologies. You were a child when I deferred to your father's wishes, but he had long been my friend, and, for a brief time, my lover. I knew his history. His childhood was stolen from him. You know his story, and it was awful. A toddler sold into slavery, castrated to become a safe"—and she practically snarled the word—"*plaything* for the daughter of a wealthy man. If Adam, my mate at the time, had not figured out a way to give Oliver what had been taken from him, you and Aaron would not exist."

Anton set a glass of cognac down in front of Eve. She took a sip and closed her eyes with a look of utter bliss. "Thank you. We have wonderful wine on the astral, but no one has figured out yet how to make cognac appear at the flip of a wrist. We need to work on that."

"Obviously, I would not do well there." Anton sat down and sipped at his own glass.

"Don't worry, Anton. You and Keisha have long lives ahead and many things yet to do. It will be a long, long time before you pass through the veil." She held her glass up and stared sadly into the depths. "I cannot stay long, but Em, I am the one who dampened the memories of those involved. They were not removed entirely and I have set in motion the process that will allow them to return slowly, so as not to frighten anyone. For that we have the Mother to thank. She rarely interferes, but in this case her assistance was more than welcome. Your memories were so deeply buried that I honestly didn't think they would ever surface, not even during mating." She dipped her head in Gabe's direction. "But then I did not take into consideration the power of the one who would love you, or the strength of his love."

She finished her drink and stood. "I must go. By taking this form, I've exhausted my time here, but I needed to see you, needed to tell you how sorry I am. I hope your father will come to see that hiding the truth is never good for anyone. I've learned my lesson, but I am so sorry it was done at your expense. I ask you to forgive me. I know it will be a long, long time before I forgive myself, or make such a terrible mistake again. Be happy, love well, and love long."

Em wasn't sure how quickly Eve faded from sight. Her eyes had filled with tears as she thought of the agony her abduction must have meant for her father. He had his own horrible past to think of when she'd been taken. She grabbed Gabe's hand. "We need to find Dad. I want to tell him that I understand. Will you . . . ?"

"Of course I will." He leaned close and kissed her, and then smiled at his parents. "Mom, Dad, I think we need to go make peace with the man who's going to be my father-in-law before too long. That is, if my mate will agree to marry me at the winter solstice?"

She laughed at the question in his voice. As if there was ever any doubt what her answer would be.

• • •

They shifted on the deck beneath a gloomy sky after leaving their clothes inside, and damn but it was cold in the few seconds before he managed to cover his bare skin with thick fur and a wooly undercoat. They'd decided to go as wolves, though Em figured she'd shift to her leopard form once they found her dad, since wolves and leopards could not communicate well. She leapt from the deck first, following the clear prints her father's leopard had made across the snowy meadow.

Gabe followed her lead. Watery sunlight shivered off the ice, but clouds moving in from the west spread shades of gray across the monochromatic landscape. Their broad paws crunched over the surface, breaking through scant inches in some of the softer places but finding firm footing most of the way.

Oliver's tracks were easy to follow, and it appeared he might be heading toward a rocky outcropping that overlooked the valley where most of the houses had been built over the years. The afternoon was bitter cold. As they followed Oliver's trail across the frigid landscape, what little sunlight there'd been disappeared behind the clouds, and then behind the mountains as they drew closer to the shortest day of the year. Their breath left vapor trails as they ran, but the only sounds were the crackling of ice underfoot and their harsh breathing as they raced through the gloomy afternoon.

Emeline ran with complete confidence. Gabe proudly followed her, his respect for her growing with each step they took across the icy ground. She was willing to face her father and settle their differences now. Too often he'd watched humans and Chanku alike put their problems aside, avoiding them rather than dealing with them. That wasn't his way, and he was pleased to see that it wasn't Em's, either.

It was amazing that he knew so much about her, and yet so very little. Their minds were filled with one another's memories and knowledge, but they'd not had time to sift through those memories enough to make sense of them. He'd found the knowledge of Em's language skills, though, and he fully intended to put those to use. He'd already had fantasies of wooing his mate using an obscure Mandarin dialect. Anything to surprise her.

There were so many things they still had to learn about each other, but they had the rest of their lives to find out. And they'd only been back together now for a little over a week.

I'm picking up my mother's and father's mindspeech. They're not very far ahead, but they're leopards and I can't understand what they're saying. I'm going to shift. If we stay within sight of one another, will you stay wolf? Your senses will be more attuned to any danger. My cat senses aren't as strong.

She shifted as she ran, something Gabe had never seen her do. It was absolutely beautiful, almost as if one creature flowed into the other. Her wolven coat was snow leopard–marked, and it was almost as if the wolf ran ahead of the leopard as the leopard crawled in beneath the skin of the wolf to emerge fully cat when the shift was complete.

Her pace changed, from the easy ground-covering lope of the wolf to the choppier gait of a leopard genetically designed for leaping across craggy mountains in search of game. She was quiet, though, moving soundlessly across the frozen snow, her paws barely marking the icy surface.

Emeline paused and Gabe raised his nose to the air. He scented Oliver's leopard, but it was a bit farther up ahead. Mei was coming closer, and he shifted, taking his snow leopard form so that he could understand her. She slipped out of the trees, as quiet and as beautifully graceful as her daughter. Walking up to Em, she touched muzzles with her and then sat back on her haunches. She turned and gazed at Gabe, where he waited a few feet away to give the two women privacy.

Come closer, Gabriel. You need to know what has happened. She waited until he took his place next to Em.

Emeline, your father is very ashamed. He doesn't want to face you. He admitted to me that he lied about Anton, that his anger wasn't with you, it's with him. I told him he's a coward. He agrees. I've been against his actions and his lies since the day you came home so terribly emotionally wounded, but he wouldn't hear it. He made me promise not to say anything to you, and it's put a terrible strain on our mating bond. I'm angry and disappointed with him, but I told him I will no longer lie. It wasn't fair to you that he put his fears and his inability to deal with those fears on you, his only daughter. I hope that someday you will be able to forgive me. I'm not sure I have it in me right now to forgive myself or your father.

She stood and walked a few paces before looking back at them over her shoulder. *I'm going back. It's time to apologize to Anton and Keisha. Our pack alpha must be absolutely disgusted with us. But I am so glad you have found love, Emeline. And so happy it's with a man both your father and I admire. Blessings to both of you, and Gabe, welcome to our family. We're not always this odd. I must admit, while I still love Oliver more than life itself, I don't like him very much right now. Emeline, I hope you can get your thickheaded father to accept he was wrong.*

Em head-butted her mother's side. *Do whatever you need to do. I just want my parents back. I've missed you. Where's Dad? It's getting late and we need to get him home.*

He's at Adam's tree. Just sitting there, staring at the clouds and the mountains.

Em stopped in her tracks, tilted her head to one side. *He doesn't have a rope, does he?*

No. No rope. He's hardheaded, but he's not stupid. I love you, Em. I've always been so proud of you, but never more than I am today. Before Em could answer, Mei turned and trotted back along the way they'd come.

Em led the way up the narrow trail that led to the huge oak leaning out over a small, snow-covered meadow that was always covered in pretty blue flowers in the spring. Gabe's parents called it Eve's meadow, but the tree had a dark history. They all knew it was the tree where, burdened by overwhelming grief when his mate died, Adam Wolf had hanged himself.

Jace had talked about it one time, about his father's horrible agony when Eve died. How he'd attempted suicide, only to be rescued by the Goddess Liana and the mate he'd loved who had died before her time. Eve and Liana had saved his life and then Eve had taken over as goddess and Liana had been unceremoniously booted out of the only life she'd known for eons. Adam had hated the ex-goddess at first, but then he'd slowly fallen in love with her and she'd become his mate and mother to their daughters, Eve and Phoenix, and Gabe's best friend, Jace.

So odd how that had worked out, but Gabe hadn't been up here for years. It always made him feel as if he were trespassing on a private place. Jace disagreed. He said it felt like a church, as if he could come here with his problems and find peace.

Maybe that's what drew Oliver. The same peace that Jace felt. They followed the trail through the woods until they broke out onto a rocky outcropping. The tree was at the western edge, leaning out over the small meadow below. A snow leopard sat beside the tree, staring off into the distance.

Will you wait here for me?

Of course. He watched as she walked along the rocky crest to sit beside her father. The air was still and the clouds heavy with snow and growing darker by the minute, but Em sat beside Oliver and stared off into the same distance as her father.

Gabe found a slab of granite that was bare of snow and lay down on it. It was cold and uncomfortable, but he'd wait as long as he had to. This was his mate's journey, not his, but he fully intended to make sure she didn't travel it alone.

• • •

Em sat beside her dad for what felt like a very long time before she spoke to him. And then it wasn't what she'd planned to say. *Eve came, right after you left.*

Eve?

Yes. She wanted to apologize for her part in hiding the truth.

The snow leopard hung his head and refused to look her way. *I was wrong, but I fear that if it happened again, I would beg for the same thing. I didn't want you to suffer. You were just a little girl, and he was such an evil, horrible man. You didn't deserve what he did to you.*

She thought about that. Tried to see it from his point of view, with his past experience, but she still couldn't agree. *Bad things happen to good people, Dad. You didn't deserve what happened to you, either. But you survived and you were stronger because of it. Taking away the memories of the horrible things that happened to me also took away my memory of beating the sonofabitch who kidnapped me. I killed him. Fourteen years old and I tore a killer to shreds. I wish I'd known that for all these years. Wish I'd known I was strong enough to save myself.*

It took what felt like a very long time before he raised his head, slowly turned and looked at her, eyes dark amber to her green. Still, Em knew she was very much her father's daughter when she saw the moment that he'd finally heard and understood what she'd been trying to tell him.

Why couldn't I see that? When you couldn't recall what had happened over the days you'd been missing, I thought it a blessing of the Mother that allowed you to forget, to go on and have your own life. That's when I begged Eve to erase the memories of everyone who knew. I was beside myself with grief, with anger that I hadn't been there to protect you, that we hadn't been able to find you. That was the worst of it, knowing you were out there with a madman, a killer, and we couldn't find you.

It was all due to his alarm system. Gabe told me that Igmutaka, Star, Sunny and Fen had the same problem when they were captured a few months ago. A cheesy little alarm system that put out some kind of current that stops our mindspeech from going anywhere. That's why you couldn't hear me. I'm sorry you were afraid, Dad. I was terrified, but I was more angry than afraid, if that makes sense, only I didn't realize that. I've had twelve years of feeling like a victim. It's time I get to celebrate being a survivor, one who not only lived but managed to take out the bastard who hurt me. I did it by myself. It was wrong to take that away from me.

I didn't take it away. You said you buried those memories.

You're right, but because you buried everyone else's, there was no one there to ask me how I was, what it was like to kill a killer, how I'd managed to survive. Answering those questions would have forced me to remember, and yes, it might have been painful, but I wouldn't have spent the next half of my life afraid of living.

Oliver snarled and bared his teeth at Em. She didn't even flinch.

Why did you come here? he asked. *To remind me what a failure I've been as a father? How I destroyed your life by loving you too much?*

Em stood and gazed at Gabe. *Is this what Alex meant when he said you made things all about you?*

Yep. Pretty much.. Gabe walked across the windswept rock and stood beside Em. He hadn't realized what a big leopard he made, but he was almost a foot taller than Em at the shoulder and a good eight inches taller than her father. Oliver glared at him, his muscles bunched as if to spring, his fangs bared.

Bad idea, Oliver. Especially when you're doing what I'm often guilty of. You're taking an issue important to your daughter and making it all about you. Yes, we know you suffered as a child and we know your life wasn't easy. Your only failure as a father is in not trusting your daughter to be intelligent enough and strong enough to deal with what happened to her. Treat her like the strong, intelligent and powerful alpha bitch she is, not like an incompetent child. And what's really sad is that Emeline is here because she loves you and she's worried about you, and she wants her father back. The one who used to love her and think she could do anything she set her mind to.

Em leaned against Gabe, but her gaze stayed on her father. *There was another reason I chased him down, Gabe. I wanted to ask my father if he'd walk me down the aisle when we marry at the winter solstice. Guess that's not gonna happen.*

With that she turned away, shifted and became the wolf. But she was in Gabe's thoughts when he stared at Oliver, at the shocked and very human expression in her father's eyes, and then he shifted as well and joined his mate. It was growing dark by the time they headed back along the trail to Anton's house. Neither of them looked back, though Em couldn't help but hope the snow leopard would follow them.

• • •

At the point where the forest ended and the meadow began, where the lights of the small community twinkled brighter than any stars, Gabe scented another wolf. He nudged Em and they paused, just two more shadows among many in the early winter night. A large black wolf trotted slowly toward them. He stopped about ten feet away and lowered his head. His tail was down, tucked tightly between his legs, and he wouldn't meet their eyes.

Gabe walked toward him, sniffed and growled. He wasn't going to allow this man to hurt Em any more than he already had. Emeline joined them. She stopped beside her mate, showing both men where her loyalties lay, but she stared at the black wolf for a moment and whined softly.

The wolf raised his head but he looked at Emeline, not at Gabe. *Will you forgive me? I promise to do my best to be the father I should have been. I love you, Emeline, and I am so sorry for the hurt I've caused you.*

I love you, too, Dad. It's over. We need to put it behind us and move forward. Let's go back. It's been a long day and it's cold out here.

It's been a long twelve years, and that was my fault. And there is nothing I would love more than walking my daughter down the aisle at her wedding. He paused and glanced at Gabe, then back at Em, and he sighed. *Giving you to another man is not going to be easy.*

He looked directly at Gabe then, and some of the old humor was back in his eyes. Gabe couldn't help but wonder what it would be like if he and Em had daughters. How far would he go to protect them?

Probably every bit as far as Oliver.

Nothing good is ever easy, Gabe said. Then he turned toward his father's house and led them out of the forest.

18

One week later . . .

Gabe stood beside the large wood-burning stove in Jace Wolf and Romy Sarika's cottage near the edge of the forest. It had been much smaller when Jace had been single. Finding a mate tended to change a man's priorities, and when he'd told the pack he needed more room, they'd come through.

Gabe had been one of those working on the addition to the cottage. Romy now lived in a home worthy of the strong, brave woman she was, a woman who wanted space to raise the family she and Jace hoped to have one day.

Tonight, Jace and Romy had invited all the newly mated couples to join them for a chance to discuss their upcoming wedding. The winter solstice was three days away. "Wouldn't you know it," Jace said, "there's a blizzard predicted to hit on Tuesday and last through Friday."

"Then we hold the celebration indoors." Romy was always the voice of calm. "The airplane hangar is huge. I'm sure we could make it look nice."

Igmutaka, once an immortal spirit guide who had only recently—as time among immortals is measured—taken corporeal form and was now fully Chanku, sat on one of the couches in front of the fire with Mikaela Star Fuentes in his lap. Beside them were Sunny Daye and Fenris Ahlberg. All of them were bonded mates in the only four-way mating among the entire pack. The fact both Ig and Fen were Berserkers, that warrior branch of the Chanku family tree, meant that their upcoming induction into the pack would be breaking new ground.

So many changes in such a brief span of months.

Gabe glanced at Ig and the two exchanged brief smiles. Then his gaze swept everyone in the room, all of them preparing to take the legal step beyond their Chanku mating and do the very human wedding ceremony. Even Lily had admitted that, while mating was an indescribable joy and the one thing that would bind them together forever, there was something almost mystical about pledging their love in front of their packmates with the pack's alpha leading their vows.

Lily and Sebastian weren't here tonight. They'd wed shortly after meeting, not long after mating, and even the most cynical among them would have to admit that Lily was a changed woman after her marriage to Sebastian Xenakis.

There was a light knock on the door. Alex stepped in, holding it open for Annie. She shook snow out of her hair in the entryway, laughing at something Alex must have said. "Sorry we're late. No excuse."

Alex laughed and kissed her. "Yes, there is. She wanted to make Tinker sweat. He knew we were all supposed to meet here tonight. We were there for dinner, and he kept checking his wristwatch and suggesting it was time for us to go. Annie kept shrugging him off. I swear, if the man has a stroke, it's her fault."

"He's driving me crazy." Annie rolled her eyes as she took off her coat. "All he can talk about is the wedding and what he should wear and what are Alex and I going to say."

Alex leaned close and kissed her. "He used to drive me nuts, and then your mom said something that made me think."

"Something made you think?" Annie slammed her hand over her heart. "What was it?"

"Something I'm sure bridegrooms have heard for centuries. She said, 'How do you think you're going to act when you have a daughter and some man comes along and wants to take her away from you?'" He shook his head. "I realized that Tinker wasn't crazy at all, because it will be a cold day in hell before some horny jerk comes along and marries our daughter."

"You don't have a daughter, sweetie." Annie kissed his chin.

"We could. Someday. And I'm already sympathetic to your father."

Gabe handed Alex a cold beer while Annie took the glass of wine Romy had poured for her. "Are any of the girls coming? They're going to be part of the celebration too."

"They backed out." Alex took a swallow of his beer. "Not of the celebration, the planning part. Said they'd show up and do what they're told."

Gabe glanced at Em. "How come you never say that?"

She frowned at him. "What?"

"That you'll show up and do what you're told."

"You are in so much trouble . . ."

He ducked and covered his head with his arms. "I don't know what made me say that. Honest. I really don't."

"Wishful thinking," Ig said, and ducked when Star took a mock swing at his head.

Romy moved to the center of the room and clapped her hands. "Okay. Now that the boys have that out of their collective testosterone-driven systems, where are we going to hold this celebration? The meadow is out unless we want to risk freezing to death. I suggested the hangar. Any other ideas?"

Em glanced at Gabe and showed him an image. He nodded. "Yeah," he said. "That would work. Probably needs to be cleaned out."

"We can do that."

He grinned at everyone here, all longtime friends except for Romy, but their few weeks together had cemented their friendship for all time, and Fen, who had slipped into the pack as if he'd been born here. Em's idea was perfect.

"Twenty-six years ago," he said, "the entire pack took refuge in the caverns beneath my mom and dad's house. When we came outside, I remember the blackened ground and the burned remnants of the house I'd grown up in, and I thought then that we'd never be whole again, because our entire world had been destroyed."

He glanced at Em and thought of all the changes in their lives. She'd been about nine months old then, too young to understand the magnitude of the damage the fire had caused, but he remembered. They'd had other forest fires since then, but none as close or as destructive as the one that hit them the month before he and Mac turned four. That was the same year when the world learned they existed, when the Chanku finally came out of the closet in a very big way.

"Mating is a huge change for each of us, but marriage is something we choose beyond the mating bond. Not only does it make us more human-like to the outside world, but it somehow seems to cement a bond that we've already created. Makes it stronger. I think it's got to be like a rebirth, which is how I felt walking up the stairs and out into what was left of my parents' house. Mom made a point of telling me it was a chance to start fresh, to shape our lives the way we wanted them. Em suggested we hold the celebration in the big cavern, the one beneath Mom and Dad's house. It's huge—we'll all fit inside with room to spare—and we might even get Eve to stay a little longer than her usual quick visit."

Romy glanced at Jace, and then focused on Gabe. "I've never seen the caves, though I recall some wonderful times in a cavern somewhere in Idaho . . . or was it Washington?"

Gabe laughed. "I think it was both."

"Tell me more," Em said.

"Later, sweetie." Gabe kissed her.

"I was asking Romy."

"Oh."

Gabe was pleased when they agreed on the cavern, and when Lily and Seb stopped in unexpectedly, she suggested opening the doorway to the astral and leaving it open, so that Eve might attend without having to leave her *when* and *where*.

The party broke up after midnight. Alex and Annie went off with Lily and Sebastian, while Sunny, Fen, Star and Ig headed over to Sunny's little cottage to spend the night. Ig and Star had their own home, but it was higher on the mountain and no one wanted a long run through the heavy snow.

Romy and Em had hit it off even better than Gabe had hoped. Both of them had led totally different lives, yet they seemed to find common ground with their strange histories. He admitted to Jace that he'd never figure out the feminine mind, even though the mating had given him access unlike anything he'd imagined.

"That was difficult for Romy and me, as the days went by and those memories became more accessible to me. Things began coming together and I found myself feeling afraid so much of the time, knowing how horrible her life had been, how cruel her father was."

"Was he really her father?" Gabe had often wondered if her father had instead been the reverend, the one who had shot her mother.

Jace shook his head. "They did DNA tests. Reverend Ezekiel, otherwise known as Franklin Ambrose Smith, was her biological father. In a way, I think it was easier for her to know that the man raping her all those years wasn't really her father. Her life was hell, but she's so damned strong, so loving. I don't think I would have the ability to forgive the way she has. Or to love." He sort of shook himself and then grinned at Gabe. "So, are you going to tell me about you and Em?"

Gabe thought about the question for a moment. Thought about how his life had changed, how Jace's had changed. "I don't know what to say. I went to San Francisco expecting to find funny little EmyIzzy and instead I found my mate. I didn't know that at first, but within a couple of days I was thinking of her that way, trying to figure out how to convince her we might have something important." He laughed. It all seemed so convoluted, but it was really very simple.

"She had a darkness in her that I knew had to go, and for some weird reason I decided I was the one to take care of it." He focused on Jace, remembering. "The fact I was able to help her was due to something you said, that so often healing isn't all that complicated, that it's about common sense, and following your gut instinct. That's what I did, and it worked. I took light to the darkness in her memories, but it ended up being so much more than just being able to help a little bit." He had to fight the stupid grin that spread across his face, but this was Jace, and he already knew exactly what Gabe was feeling. He had the same thing with Romy. "It sounds so corny, but she completes me. She makes me better than I really am. It's like finding your other half and feeling whole for the first time." He glance at Jace. "What? No wiseass comment?"

Jace merely shook his head. "Not from me. You just said exactly what I feel for Romy. But you know, we can't let on that we think about them that way. We'll never hear the end of it."

Too late, boys.

"I should have known Em would be listening." Gabe chuckled and grabbed Jace's arm. "We've got two women in the bedroom, and I don't think they're talking about the wedding. I think they're naked and finding other ways to entertain themselves."

"What say we join them?" Jace bowed and waved Gabe forward. "After you."

• • •

Night of the Winter Solstice

Gabe glanced at Em beside him and thought of how quickly they had come to this point, how very much had happened over the past three weeks. The six young women they'd rescued were beside them—four of them Chanku, two human. The first two humans ever welcomed into the pack, but Nina and Lindy were a perfect fit, loved by everyone who met them.

Sissy, Mbali, Janine and Mary stood patiently in their wolven forms. Nina and Lindy carried silk sarongs, similar to the ones they wore in brilliant jewel tones, one for each of the women to put on once they were officially welcomed into the pack.

Anton waited beside an ancient stone altar on the far side of the pond in the depths of the cavern. Lily had opened the doorway into the astral so that Eve was able to attend, watching the proceedings from her own world. She sat on brilliant green grass beneath a cerulean sky, her white robe glimmering against the green, her long blonde hair flowing about her body, spread across her knees and covering her bare toes. To those standing in the cavern, it appeared as if they watched their goddess on a flat screen against the cavern wall.

It was a magical doorway that even Anton couldn't explain. As he'd tried to tell his children, there are some things you have to accept on faith.

Gabe glanced again at Em. It was impossible not to look at her, smiling and so relaxed standing within the curve of his arm. Impossible not to look and give thanks that she was his. Her father was on her left and Mei, Em's mom, was next to Oliver with their arms linked. Anton called the new members of the pack forward. Gabe, Em, Alex and Annie walked with them as their sponsors, circling around the end of the pond until they stood in front of Anton with Eve watching from just over his shoulder. Tinker McClintock, Annie's father, stepped out of the crowd and joined them.

Anton named each new member, and then he raised his voice to the crowd filling the cavern. "Do you accept these new members to the pack? Mbali Jefferson, Mary Elizabeth Ryder, Janine Cross, and Sissy Long, and our first human members, Nina Marquez and Lindy Marlette?"

A cheer went up and Em glanced at Gabe with tears in her eyes. He bent to kiss her. He couldn't help himself—she was much too beautiful to ignore. He held her close, paying attention as Anton went to each of the wolves and asked them, individually, if they accepted the responsibility of membership, to live an honorable life and always be true to their packmates.

As he repeated the vow to each wolf, she shifted and agreed, and either Nina or Lindy stepped forward to hand her a shimmering silk sarong to cover her nudity. He asked Nina and then Lindy, and they each voiced acceptance, until only the wolf Mbali remained.

Finally, Anton turned to Mbali and paused.

Em clutched Gabe's free hand, and he heard her sniffing back tears. Annie stood beside Em and wept openly.

"Mbali, I told you the news earlier and asked you to hold the secret until tonight. You have proved beyond a doubt that you can keep secrets." He chuckled and ran his hand over the fur between her pointed ears. "Your cousin Annie and your Uncle Tinker . . ." He paused at the hushed gasp from the pack. "Yes," he said, "It's true. Mbali's mother was Tinker McClintock's sister, a woman he'd only suspected might exist. DNA confirms the family link, and we are so thankful she, and her sisters of the heart, have been found and brought into the pack.

"Do you, Mbali Jefferson, accept the responsibility inherent with life as part of our pack?"

She shifted. Standing tall and very proud, she softly answered Anton, "I do." And then she took the ice-blue sarong that Lindy handed to her and wrapped it carefully around her body. She'd barely covered herself before Tinker threw his arms around her and hauled her high for a hug and a big kiss. He tugged Annie into the hug, and when he set Mbali back on her feet, all three of them were crying.

Mbali quickly pulled herself together and wiped her tears with a handkerchief Alex handed to her. She was laughing when she handed it to Alex. Then she and the other five young women turned and faced their packmates. Gabe thought of a bouquet of exotic flowers as their shimmering silk dresses reflected the candle and lantern light illuminating the huge cavern. A deep garnet red for Mary, Mbali's ice blue, dark purple for Janine and teal blue for Sissy. Nina was in bright yellow, and Lindy's deep forest green set off her bright red hair.

Mbali left the altar with Tinker on one side and Annie on the other. Alex, Gabe and Em escorted the rest of the women back to the other side of the pond, where they quickly moved into the crowd. Gabe noticed that Mac had Sissy beside him with an arm looped casually over her shoulders, while Aaron had taken Janine's hand. When he noticed Mary standing next to Jack Temple, Gabe made sure that Em saw them, too. Jack had his father's good looks and his mother's sense of humor, and so far none of the women in the pack had been able to nail him down. Would shy, quiet Mary be the one to finally catch him?

He was sorry that Mary's father had decided not to come, though he'd finally spoken with his daughter. He'd admitted that, in spite of much prayer, he'd not been able to accept her new reality. She'd told him very simply that she loved him but she couldn't accept his inability to break free of a religion that taught only hatred. They'd agreed to disagree, and nothing had been solved, except that Mary had, for the first time, fully taken charge of her life. She'd begun to open up, to show a side that none of them had expected, including a sense of humor and a powerful sense of honor that nothing could shake. Even her father.

Gabe glanced up as Anton tapped a bell beside the altar. He'd not dressed any differently for the celebration, but in his usual black slacks and a black silk shirt, he looked like the man he was—a powerful wizard, a strong leader, and Gabe's dad. He was always proud of his father, but at times like this . . .

Anton called Alex and Annie first. Tinker let out a loud cheer and grabbed his daughter's arm. Laughing and hanging on to her dad, Annie walked around the pond to meet Alex at the altar. Alex's father stood beside him, and the pride and love in his expression had Gabe's eyes welling with tears. Alex had come so close to losing Annie, and this moment might never have happened.

Anton let his gaze rest on Annie and then Alex. He sighed dramatically and gave Alex's dad a lopsided smile. "Stef, how could you and I have been so wrong? Annie is the perfect mate for your son."

Everyone laughed—it had become a running joke over the years that Lily and Alex would mate if their fathers had anything to do with it, but Lily had, as always, gone her own way and defied expectations when she'd mated Sebastian Xenakis, the son of their enemy. Alex had fallen for Annie the moment he saw her after many years apart, much to her father's chagrin. But as they said their vows, Tinker stood to one side, wiping his eyes with a big white handkerchief—tears of joy, not sadness. Both moms stood with their men, obviously thrilled with the match.

This was the way it should be, the pack coming together, celebrating love in spite of the dangers they often faced. Gabe held Emy even closer.

Igmutaka, Star, Sunny, and Fen were next. They walked around the pond as a group with Star's parents Mik, AJ and Tala Fuentes-Temple following behind. Before the wedding, Anton introduced the two new members to the pack first.

"Igmutaka has been among us for many years, a part of our pack as spirit guide to Miguel Fuentes, then as puma, and finally as a man. But despite his various forms, he has always been a spirit guide with duties outside the pack. Now Igmutaka has chosen the pack over the spirit world, and in so doing has given up that part of him tied to the spirit realm. He has chosen life among us as Chanku, and as Mikaela Star's mate and husband. I also introduce Fenris Ahlberg to the pack. Fen, like Igmutaka, is Berserker by birth. He has chosen life with us and will live as Chanku, and as a member of our pack."

He quietly asked each man if they accepted the responsibility of membership to the pack. When they agreed, he turned to the crowd and asked, "Do you accept Fenris Ahlberg and Igmutaka as members of this pack?"

The cheers echoed off the cavern walls. Em turned to Gabe, grinning broadly. *I heard that Star stayed away from Montana even longer than I did, so it's cool that she and Ig are finally together, but part of those cheers are because everyone loves Sunny. Fen is perfect for her, and she still gets to keep Ig, and he finally got Star. Doesn't get much better than that.*

Gabe leaned over and whispered in her ear. "Is that a hint that there's another man you'd like to add to your harem?"

She whispered back, "Romy and I have already discussed it. I'm adding Jace, she gets you."

"Good of you to let me know." He tugged her close against his side and she giggled. And he realized he couldn't stop grinning. Ig and Star said their vows, Sunny and Fen said theirs, and then the four of them made a promise among them that had many in the cavern wiping away tears.

Romy and Jace were next. Adam stood with Jace and Liana, his mom, with Romy. Romy had admitted to Em that with Jace she'd also gotten the family she'd never had, that Liana reminded her of the mother she'd loved but lost so long ago. Adam was merely an older version of his son. Most of the time, though more often than not it was Jace who was the adult. As she'd confided to Gabe and Em, "What's not to love?"

Their promises were made and they walked back to join the crowd. Gabe took Em's hand while her father held his arm for her. Mei stood beside her husband, and already tears were streaming from her eyes. Em shot her a teasing glance. "Mom! You promised me you wouldn't cry."

"I lied. Now let's get moving."

Gabe saluted—even Mei had to laugh at that—and they walked around the pond to stand in front of Gabe's dad.

Anton looked at them and then shook his head. "If you'll recall, Gabriel, I wept through the entire ceremony for your sister. I thought it wouldn't happen with yours. You are my son, after all. Father's don't cry over their sons' weddings. Well, I was wrong. I thought I should warn you." He whipped out a handkerchief and wiped his eyes and then glanced at Keisha standing beside him, smiling. "Your mother always has been the tough one."

Keisha kissed his cheek and said, "While he's composing himself, who gives this woman in marriage?"

Oliver leaned over and kissed Em's cheek. "Her mother and I do." Then he stepped back and took hold of Mei's hand. She handed him an extra tissue.

Anton made little shooing motions at Keisha. "I can handle this now." He smiled at Gabe, and his eyes still sparkled with tears. "Gabriel Fane Cheval. You and Emeline Isobelle Cheval have already mated. Why do you choose to wed?"

Gabe took Em's hands in his and looked into eyes as green as new growth on spring willows and knew he would love her forever. "Because I finally know what love is, because of Em. Because I have found a woman who is brave and resourceful, strong, compassionate and honorable. A woman who makes me a better man. I could not ask for more in a mate, but I realized I wanted even more of her, and so I asked her to be my wife, to stand before our pack, our family, our goddess, so I could swear my undying love in front of the people who mean the most to me. Will you marry me, Emy? Will you take care of me when I'm ill, be with me when I do stupid things that make you crazy, will you love me even if I sometimes screw up and you're ready to murder me in my sleep?" He chuckled softly at the grin spreading across her face. "Will you love me as much as I love you?"

"I will, Gabe. And I promise not to murder you in your sleep."

He turned to his father and said, "You notice she left open the option of when I'm awake?"

"I did. Smart woman. Emeline Isobelle Cheval, you and Gabriel Fane Cheval have already mated. Why do you choose to wed?"

She glanced at their clasped hands, and her smile spread across her face. "Because I love him. Because my life was filled with darkness and he found a way to bring me light. He offered me a refuge when I thought I didn't deserve love, and when he finally found my demons, he fought them, every single one of them, until they were gone." She glanced at her parents and her tears were running as freely as theirs. Gabe wanted to hand her a tissue, but he wasn't about to let go of her hands.

She trembled, and he felt the emotion welling up inside her. "I was estranged from my parents for many years and I didn't know how to close the gap between us. Gabe found a way, and once again I have my mom and dad back in my life. For that alone, I would love you forever, Gabe, but there is so much more. You're funny and sweet and serious and smart. You make me laugh and you make me better than I ever thought I could be. I love you so much."

She was sobbing now, but she smiled through her tears, and then she laughed. "And it's been almost three weeks and you haven't called me EmyIzzy once. For that alone I could love you. I do love you, Gabe. I really do love you."

It felt as if they were the only two in the cavern. Gabe wrapped his arms around Em and lifted her off her feet and then lost himself in the most beautiful kiss he'd ever known. Then his dad was pronouncing them man and wife and Em's mom and dad were there, hugging them, and then his mom. His dad hugged and kissed Emy, and then grabbed Gabe as if he didn't want to let him go, and he was crying every bit as much as Em was. As hard as Gabe was crying. But Gabe's heart was so damned full, and Em was his. Forever.

He lifted his head, and Eve smiled at him. Then she waved and the doorway into the astral faded. But Em was still in his arms, and his mom and dad were beside them, laughing and crying, and the pack was all around.

As he watched, his dad broke away from his mom and went to Oliver. They'd also been estranged for far too many years. Friendships can't endure with lies between them, but Anton pulled Oliver into his arms and their embrace was heartfelt and filled with meaning. Gabe glanced at his mom, and she was watching her mate with an arm looped through Mei's.

It was all so damned good. It made him think of something his father had said to him once, how a stone thrown into a pond sends out ripples to roll up against the shore. He and Em had been the stone, and the ripples continued to spread. He picked Em up and she wrapped her arms around his neck. He carried her away from their parents, away from the pack, beyond the pond, toward the tunnel that led out of the cavern. The party would go on far into the night, and he doubted anyone would miss them, but there was something even more important waiting.

A cottage, set aside for the two of them. He'd seen to the fire himself, the refrigerator was stocked, and he figured they wouldn't have to come up for air at least until Christmas.

"I love you, Em. I never dreamed anything like this. My dreams were never this good."

"Forever, Gabe. I will love you forever."

He paused long enough to kiss her. "We're Chanku, sweetheart. Thank the Goddess, forever really can last forever."

About the Author

Kate Douglas is the author of the popular erotic paranormal romance series Wolf Tales and Demon Lovers, the erotic SF series Dream Catchers and StarQuest, as well as the DemonSlayers series. She is currently writing the next book in the Spirit Wild series. The first three books in the series are *Dark Wolf*, *Dark Spirit*, and *Dark Moon*.

Kate and her husband of over forty years have two adult children and six grandchildren. They live in the beautiful wine country of Sonoma County, California, in the little town of Healdsburg.

Write to Kate at kate@katedouglas.com. She answers all her email. Connect with her on Facebook at www.facebook.com/katedouglas.authorpage or on Twitter @wolftales.

29977669R00105

Made in the USA
Charleston, SC
31 May 2014